THE EARL'S DAUGHTER: A REGENCY ROMANCE

LAURA BEERS

The Earl's Daughter: A Regency Romance
By: Laura Beers

Text copyright © 2020 by Laura Beers
Cover art copyright © 2020 by Laura Beers
Cover art by Blue Water Books

❀ Created with Vellum

MORE ROMANCE FROM LAURA BEERS

The Beckett Files
Regency Spy Romances

Saving Shadow
A Peculiar Courtship
To Love a Spy
A Tangled Ruse
A Deceptive Bargain
The Baron's Daughter
The Unfortunate Debutante

❧ 1 ❧

"MY FATHER IS DEAD."

Lady Isabella Beauchamp gasped as she looked up from her writing desk. "Oh no! That is horrible news!" she exclaimed. "How did he die?"

Glancing down at the black trimmed stationery, Lady Charlotte Taylour replied, "Consumption." She lowered the note to her lap. "Apparently, he had been suffering for some time."

"When is the funeral?"

"It was last week," she revealed. "My stepmother and half-sister also did not attend. Grieving publicly is discouraged amongst the *ton*, you know."

Isabella rose from her chair and moved to sit next to her on the bed. "I'm truly sorry, Lottie."

"Don't be," she replied, her voice surprisingly calm. "I hardly knew the man."

"True, but he was still your father."

"He was a terrible father."

Isabella nodded. "I must agree with you there."

Charlotte shifted her gaze towards the window of their bedchamber, feeling slightly guilty that she felt no emotion at this horrific news.

"I can count on my hand how many times I've seen my father since I was sent to Miss Bell's Finishing School," she reasoned.

"What are you going to do now?" Isabella asked.

"I don't know," she said honestly. "My grandparents are dead, and I doubt that I would be welcomed at my ancestral home."

Isabella shifted on the bed to face her. "Come to London with me," she invited eagerly. "You can stay with my family for the Season."

Charlotte shook her head. "I couldn't possibly intrude," she insisted. "Besides, my father's solicitor is requesting my presence for a meeting at his London office in three days. He's even sending a coach to transport me to Town."

"What is the meeting for?"

"Mr. Stanton stated that my father requested his entire family to be present for the reading of his will," Charlotte shared.

"Perhaps your father has left you a ridiculous amount of money, and you will be an heiress," Isabella declared.

"I doubt it since he has neglected me for so many years."

Isabella gave her an understanding smile. "I can only imagine how hard that has been on you."

"I was pleasantly surprised when my father informed me that I was to have a Season in London, but now my life has taken a dramatic twist. I might even be forced to seek employment."

"That is rubbish," Isabella replied. "Your father was the Earl of Huntley. Surely, he made provisions for you."

"I doubt it. He practically banished me the moment I was born."

Isabella's gaze turned knowing. "Which was for the best. Your grandparents were kind and gracious people."

"True," she murmured. "I did have a happy upbringing."

"And your father had the insight to enroll you in Miss Bell's Finishing School," Isabella said, "where we met and became the best of friends."

"That is true, as well."

Isabella smiled. "You must dwell on the bright side. Now you won't be forced to endure the dreaded marriage mart this Season."

"Unlike you, I had been looking forward to the balls, soirées, and attending the theatre, even if it was alongside my father," she admitted.

"My mother is forcing me to have a Season this year," Isabella shared. "She even informed me that she is sending my older brother, Hudson, to escort me back to London."

"That is to be expected since you are eighteen years old."

"As are you."

Charlotte smiled. "I am well aware of my age."

Isabella blew out a puff of air. "Most likely, my mother is worried that I will refuse to leave Miss Bell's Finishing School, so she sent along my brother to ensure that didn't happen."

"Are you and your brother close?"

Isabella shrugged one shoulder. "We aren't enemies."

"That was rather vague," Charlotte remarked, laughing.

"Hudson is my older, annoying brother," Isabella shared. "I hardly see him when I'm on holiday because he's busy working as a judge."

"I thought he was a barrister?"

"Last year, he was hired on as a district judge."

"That sounds impressive."

"I suppose so," Isabella replied. "It might come in handy if I ever get arrested."

"And why would you ever get arrested?" Charlotte asked, amused.

Isabella shrugged. "It could happen."

"No one would dare arrest the sister of the Marquess of Northampton," Charlotte said knowingly.

"Perhaps you are right."

"I know I am right."

Smoothing out her pale pink, silk gown, Isabella asked, "If not with me, then where do you intend to stay while you are in London?"

"I don't know, and Mr. Stanton didn't specify in the note," she replied. "However, I know I can't stay at my father's town-house, because that is where my stepmother and my half-sister will be staying. I have the foresight to know that I won't be welcome."

"Is your stepmother truly that awful to you?"

"No, but I hardly know the woman."

"Then, it is decided," Isabella declared. "You will stay with me."

Charlotte shook her head. "I couldn't possibly intrude, especially since your brother—"

Isabella cut her off. "You won't be intruding," she insisted. "Our townhouse is enormous, and I doubt that my brother, Everett, or his wife, Madalene, would complain."

"I would love to see Madalene again," Charlotte mused. "Does she still climb trees?"

"She does," Isabella replied. "It drives Everett mad now that she is expecting."

"What wonderful news!"

"That it drives Everett mad or that Madalene is expecting?" Isabella joked.

Charlotte laughed. "No one is as good as Madalene at climbing trees."

"I don't know," Isabella replied. "You have a knack for it, as well."

"True, but I doubt that Miss Bell is impressed by our tree climbing skills."

Isabella nodded. "You are right about that, but just think of all the trees that you can climb at our townhouse."

"Are you sure your mother won't mind?"

Isabella gave her a knowing look. "You have spent enough holidays at our country home to know that my mother loves you. I daresay she dotes on you more than me."

"I suppose it would be better than staying at an inn."

"An inn is hardly an appropriate place for a lady to stay," Isabella stated. "After all, you must think of your reputation."

Charlotte lifted her eyebrow. "Are you truly lecturing me about my reputation?"

Isabella laughed. "I am."

"Weren't you the one riding astride this morning wearing trousers?"

"Trousers are much more comfortable to wear when riding astride," Isabella defended.

"Have you considered riding side saddle like the rest of us?"

Isabella smirked. "Where is the fun in that?"

"London is not ready for the likes of you."

"Perhaps not, but I have no intention of marrying anytime soon, so London can take me as I am."

Charlotte shook her head at her friend's tone. Isabella was a beauty with her blonde curls, fair skin, and bright, expressive eyes.

"I have no doubt that men will be lined up to court you," she said.

"As will you."

"I doubt that. Remember, my father just passed away, and I'll be in mourning."

Isabella cocked her head. "Will you be mourning your father for six months?"

"I suppose I must, assuming my father left me some provisions to purchase some mourning gowns. However, I won't know for certain until I speak to Mr. Stanton."

"If not, we could dye a few of your dresses black," Isabella suggested.

Glancing over at her two large trunks positioned near the window, Charlotte said, "It might be best if I start packing for my trip to London. Mr. Stanton informed me that my coach will be arriving tomorrow afternoon."

Isabella fell back onto the bed, groaning. "I hate packing. I can't wait until I have a lady's maid again."

"What a rough life you lead," Charlotte teased.

"Isn't it though?" Isabella asked, sitting up. "Why don't we forget the packing and go riding through the woods?"

Charlotte smiled. "Didn't you want to ignore our needlework class this morning to go riding?"

"I did," Isabella replied, unabashed.

"I'm afraid I can't," she said with a shake of her head. "I need to pack, and then I wanted to finish my embroidery."

"Please tell me that you are joking."

"I'm not," Charlotte responded. "I want to show Miss Bell my completed project before I leave."

"Why do you love needlework so much?"

"I don't rightly know," she answered, "but I find the repetitiousness of it enjoyable."

Isabella frowned. "I find it boring."

"I know you do," Charlotte said. "In fact, I think everyone at Miss Bell's Finishing School knows your thoughts about needlework."

Isabella rose from the bed. "Well, if you will excuse me, I believe I will go riding before it gets too dark."

"Enjoy," she said, then chuckled. "If possible, try to stay out of trouble."

Walking backwards towards the door, Isabella replied, "I never seek out trouble. It just happens to find me."

Charlotte laughed as she watched her dear friend exit the room. She felt immense gratitude that Isabella had become her friend, nearly on the first day she had arrived. Together, they had grown closer than she ever thought imaginable. Now when she thought of her family, she thought of Isabella.

She glanced down at the note still in her hand. Her father was dead. Unwelcome tears came to her eyes, and she quickly blinked them away. Her father hadn't cared about her, so why should she care that he was gone?

She didn't.

She wouldn't.

These tears were not for him, she reasoned, but for what could have been. He could have been a doting father, but he wasn't. He had sent her away to live with her maternal grandparents after she was born. He only sent for her on occasional holidays, and she was hardly able to spend time with her younger sister.

She crumbled the note in her hand. Why had her father been so cruel? It didn't make any sense. She was his daughter, his flesh and blood. Yet, he cast her out as if she meant nothing to him.

No, she would not mourn his death. She had been doing just fine without him.

Charlotte watched as her trunks were loaded onto the back of the coach. It was almost time for her to leave Miss Bell's

Finishing School and start a new adventure; an adventure that was filled with uncertainty. Did her father leave provisions for her or would she be expected to live off the good graces of the new Earl of Huntley? Or worse, her stepmother, the Countess of Huntley?

She placed a hand on her fluttering stomach and took a deep breath. She could do this. Frankly, she had no choice. It was time for her to start a new chapter in her life, ready or not. She couldn't very well continue residing at school forever.

Could she? Charlotte closed her eyes, considering the possibility.

"Are you nervous, my dear?" Miss Bell asked from behind her.

Nodding, she replied, "I am. There is so much uncertainty in my life right now."

The tall, brown-haired headmistress came to stand next to her. "You have grown into a remarkable young woman, Lottie," she said. "I have taught you everything you need to know to dazzle the *ton*."

"But what if I decide not to enter Society?" she asked. "What if I would rather be a companion or a governess?"

With a smile, Miss Bell responded, "Whatever you decide to do, you will do so brilliantly."

"You are much too kind."

"I am merely being honest," Miss Bell said. "A strong woman can accomplish many great things in this world. But, first, you must believe in yourself."

"Thank you, Miss Bell," Charlotte responded, her voice hitching, "for everything."

Miss Bell pulled her into a warm embrace. "You have been a delight to have at my school. Go forth and greet life with joy. Be happy."

"I don't think it is that simple."

Leaning back, Miss Bell said, "It is. You are the only one

who can decide if you are happy or not. It is all about perspective. So, I beg of you, choose to be happy, Lottie."

"I want to be happy, but I'm scared."

"Being a little bit scared is a good thing."

"Is it?"

Miss Bell bobbed her head. "It is. Trust me."

"I will."

"If you find yourself ever in need of a job," Miss Bell began, "I would be happy to hire you to teach needlework to the younger students."

Charlotte let out a sigh of relief. "You have no idea how relieved I am to hear you say that, Miss Bell."

"It doesn't pay much, but I can offer you room and board. Furthermore, you can have full use of our stables, and all the trees that you can climb."

"I must admit that working here would be a better option than being a governess," Charlotte observed.

An aging woman with puffy silver hair exited the school and approached. She stopped in front of them, and her lips stretched into a thin smile, giving her a surly appearance. "Are you ready to leave, Lady Charlotte?"

Charlotte nibbled her bottom lip. "I suppose so, Mrs. Jordan, but I had been hoping to say goodbye to my dear friend, Isabella."

Miss Bell pressed her lips into a disapproving tight line. "I take it that Lady Isabella is not back from her afternoon ride?"

"No, she is not, but you know how Isabella gets."

"I most assuredly do," Miss Bell confirmed. "Have you had a chance to say your goodbyes to the rest of the girls?"

"I have," Charlotte replied.

"Come," Mrs. Jordan said, placing a hand on her sleeve. "We must hurry if we want to arrive at the inn before it grows too dark."

As Mrs. Jordan led her to the coach, Charlotte heard the

rapid four-beat gait of a horse galloping in the distance. She turned her head and saw Isabella racing her white gelding towards the cobblestone entrance of the school. In a swift motion, Isabella reined in her horse and dismounted.

"Welcome back, Lady Isabella," Miss Bell said with an uplifted brow. "You took a rather long afternoon ride, did you not?"

Isabella had the decency to look ashamed. "My apologies, Miss Bell. I'm afraid I lost track of time as I raced through the woods."

"You are going to break your neck if you keep galloping through the trees like that," Miss Bell chided. "Furthermore, it is not proper for a lady of your station to be riding astride."

"Yes, Miss Bell," Isabella said, lowering her gaze to the floor.

Miss Bell sighed as she held out her hands for the reins. "Say your goodbyes to Lady Charlotte while I hold your horse."

A smile came to Isabella's face as she placed the reins into Miss Bell's hand. "Thank you, Miss Bell." Then, she turned towards Charlotte. "I'm hoping you still intend to stay with me during the Season."

"I have every intention to, but I won't know for certain until I speak to my father's solicitor."

Mrs. Jordan interjected, "It is time for you to say your final goodbyes, Lady Charlotte."

Charlotte watched as a footman assisted Mrs. Jordan into the coach before saying, "I suppose it is time for me to leave."

Isabella pulled her into a tight embrace. "I wish you luck with your new companion," she murmured into her hair. "She seems like a killjoy."

Leaning back, Charlotte shared, "Mr. Stanton sent along a companion, a footman, and a driver."

"I told you," Isabella said, lowering her voice. "Your father left you an enormous amount of money in his will, and you are going to be an heiress."

"Or just properly chaperoned as I travel to London," Charlotte contended as she started walking backwards towards the coach.

"You're no fun," Isabella teased, smiling.

Charlotte returned her smile and waved. "I will see you in London," she said as she stepped into the coach. Once she was situated across from Mrs. Jordan, she smoothed out her blue traveling gown.

"Lady Isabella is quite a character, is she not?" Mrs. Jordan asked in a disapproving voice as the coach started rolling down the road.

"Oh, she definitely is," she replied. "There is no one quite like Lady Isabella."

Mrs. Jordan frowned. "She will need to learn to handle herself with more decorum when she is amongst polite Society."

"I have no doubt that Lady Isabella will behave appropriately when she is mingling with the *ton*."

"I should surely hope so," Mrs. Jordan huffed. "I have never met a woman who rides astride before. It was quite scandalizing to witness."

"Was it?" she questioned. "I found it to be quite tame."

Mrs. Jordan pressed her lips together. "It is only proper for a woman to ride side saddle."

Finding herself already tired of her companion's pompous attitude, Charlotte turned her head to gaze out the window, and it wasn't long before she was staring out at the rolling countryside. The trees and meadows were a fresh, vivid green. Everywhere she looked, there were purple lilac blossoms, swaying in the wind.

"The English countryside is beautiful," Mrs. Jordan murmured.

"It is," she agreed.

Turning her attention towards her chaperone, Charlotte said, "Thank you for escorting me to London."

"You are most kindly welcome."

"I'm afraid I know very little about you," she remarked. "Have you always been a companion?"

"Heavens, no. I was a governess for many years for the Harris family in London," Mrs. Jordan replied. "After their youngest son went to Eton, I was able to secure employment as a companion for Lady Worthlin."

"Did you enjoy working for Lady Worthlin?"

Mrs. Jordan nodded. "I did, until the day she died."

"Oh, I am sorry to hear that."

"Don't be," Mrs. Jordan replied, waving her hand in front of her. "She was nearly ninety-years old when she passed away."

"Oh, my."

"Lady Worthlin was a feisty woman, and she refused to be sedentary," Mrs. Jordan said, smiling. "She declined to use the Bath wheelchair that her son had purchased for her. She called it an 'invalid chair'."

"Is that so?"

Mrs. Jordan's smile grew. "Oh, yes. She and her son would get into quite the heated arguments over it."

Charlotte had opened her mouth to respond when she noticed that the coach had started to pick up speed. Unexpectedly, the coach jerked, causing her nearly to slide off the bench.

"Good heavens," Mrs. Jordan cried as she righted herself in her seat. "What on earth is going on out there?"

Glancing out the window, Charlotte saw two riders coming up fast on the right side of the coach. Both were dressed in black clothing, with scarves covering the lower half of their faces, cocked hats low on their forehead, and they held pistols in their right hands.

"Highwaymen!" Charlotte exclaimed with dread in her voice.

Mrs. Jordan let out a cry. "We are going to die in this coach!"

"No, we aren't," Charlotte declared, her voice calmer than she felt. "We just need to fight back."

"But how can we do that?"

"Look under your seat and see if there is a box," Charlotte ordered as she felt under her own bench. Her heart dropped as her hand brushed up against a spare blanket. She was quite certain that a blanket would not help in this situation.

Relief flooded over her as Mrs. Jordan said, "There is a box under my seat." She slid the iron box out.

Charlotte reached down and opened the lid, revealing an overcoat pistol. She grabbed the pistol and held it up proudly. "We can win this fight."

Mrs. Jordan stared at her in disbelief. "Do you even know how to use that?"

She nodded decisively. "My grandfather taught me."

The first highwayman rode past her window, with the other highwayman remaining close behind, and she watched as he aimed his pistol towards the driver.

Knowing that she had to act, she kicked open the door, hitting the rear highwayman's horse in the side. In response, the horse reared, and upended its rider onto the dusty road.

The remaining highwayman turned his attention back towards her, and she could see the narrow slit of his eyes. For a brief moment, she feared that he was going to shoot her, but instead he turned back towards the driver and fired his pistol.

The coach jerked again, and Charlotte grabbed the sides of the doorway to avoid being thrown out. She felt the coach sway back and forth, losing speed, making it evident that the driver had been shot. She had to get rid of this other highwayman and help the driver before it was too late. Either they would succumb to this highwayman or to some horrifying carriage accident.

Bringing up her pistol, she took aim at the highwayman and fired, hitting him squarely in the left shoulder. He howled in pain as he reined in his horse and immediately fell back. She dropped the pistol onto the ground and reached for the coach door, grateful that it was now going slow enough for her to do so. Once she grabbed the handle, she used all her strength to close the door and latch it.

She stuck her head out of the window and was pleased to see that the highwaymen were nowhere to be seen. They must have scurried off into a section of trees that sat back from the road, but she had no doubt that they were not far off. To add to the direness of the situation, the coach was now moving at a leisurely pace along the road. If the highwaymen regrouped and attacked, they wouldn't be able to fight them off.

It only took her a moment before Charlotte knew what she needed to do. She turned and sat in the window opening.

"What on earth do you think you are doing, child?" Mrs. Jordan cried.

"Isn't it obvious?" she asked. "I'm going to help drive the coach."

"You can't just climb out of the window!"

Charlotte gave her a mischievous smile. "It is just like climbing a tree."

"No, it is not!" Mrs. Jordan exclaimed. "You are going to get yourself killed. Get back in this coach this instant."

"If I do nothing, then the highwaymen might come back and kill us."

Without waiting for Mrs. Jordan's response, Charlotte reached up and grabbed the thin metal bar running the length of the carriage top. She pulled herself onto the roof and steadied herself before she dropped down onto the elevated bench next to the driver.

"Give me the reins," she ordered.

The thin man with black, bushy eyebrows just stared at her in amazement. "Can you even drive a coach?"

"No, but you can teach me," she said, placing her hand out.

The driver let out a low groan as he placed his hand on his shoulder, refusing to relinquish the reins.

"You are being quite ridiculous," she chided. "You have been shot, and I need to drive this coach, or we will all die."

Wincing in pain, the driver reluctantly extended her the reins. "We should be coming up on a coaching inn in a few miles."

Adjusting the reins in her gloved hands, Charlotte replied, "Now kindly tell me everything you know about driving a coach."

2

LORD HUDSON BEAUCHAMP SAT AT A CRAMPED TABLE INSIDE THE Rusty Bucket coaching inn with a drink in his hand. A piece of stale bread lay forgotten on the table as the sun dipped below the horizon. He was biding his time until he could retire for the evening. He had ridden all day in the saddle, alongside the coach, and he was only a few hours away from retrieving Isabella.

How his mother had talked him into picking up his sister from her boarding school was beyond him. Earlier in the month, he had complained to his mother about his caseload, and in the next breath, he was agreeing to pick her up from Miss Bell's Finishing School.

His mother was good. He had to give her that. Besides, the family was taking bets whether Isabella would even leave school. They all knew that she was dreading the upcoming Season. She had been quite vocal about it.

Not that he blamed her.

He completely understood her hesitation. He had no intention of participating in the marriage mart himself. He was much too busy to even contemplate taking a wife. A wife would just complicate his life, and he didn't need any more distractions. Besides, he had already learned his lesson when it came to love.

No.

He would never be foolish enough to fall in love again.

A dark-haired older woman sashayed over to him. "Can I get yer anything else, love?" she asked, leaning over to show him her ample bosom.

He averted his eyes. "No, thank you."

"Pity," she purred, running her hand along his arm. "Are you sure I can't keep you company tonight?"

Reaching into his jacket pocket, he pulled out two shillings and placed them on the table. He slid them towards her and said, "I'm sure."

The woman gave him a slight pout. "It won't cost much more."

"I am not interested in what you are offering," he replied, his tone brooking no argument.

As Hudson watched the woman walk away, he felt only pity for what that woman must have to endure to survive. The room was filled with rowdy, dirty looking men who were becoming increasingly inebriated. A few of them gave the woman a lewd look as she passed by their table.

He had just taken a sip of his watered-down ale when the inn door was thrown open, causing the room to grow silent. The most beautiful creature he had ever seen stormed into the room. The young woman had high cheekbones, a slim face, with a narrow jawline and chin. Even though her brown hair was disheveled, and her traveling habit was ripped on her right sleeve, it didn't diminish her beauty in the least.

Her wide, panicked eyes scanned the room as she shouted, "I need help!"

The heavy-set innkeeper spoke up from the far side of the room. "What is it, lass?"

"Highwaymen attacked my coach, and my driver was shot," she announced. "Is there a doctor in town?"

"There is not," the innkeeper said as he crossed the room, "but my wife can help him. She can fix him up in no time."

"Thank you," she sighed. "That is most kind of you."

The innkeeper stopped in front of her. "Where is your driver?"

"He is still on the driver box," she shared. "He was shot in his shoulder and needs help getting down."

Turning towards the men in the room, the innkeeper asked, "Anyone willing to help?"

When none of the other men in the room moved to assist her, the young woman turned her pleading eyes towards him. "Can you help, mister?"

He didn't dare refuse a lady's plea for help, especially one as beautiful as she. He rose and tugged down on his riding jacket. "I would be honored to."

"Thank you," she said. "I need to check on my companion."

Hudson crossed the room in a few strides and stepped outside to see four beautiful horses harnessed to a black coach. He saw the innkeeper was assisting the driver off the driver's box, so he went over to help him.

After the driver was on the ground, the innkeeper placed an arm over his shoulder and escorted him inside. Hudson was about to follow them when he heard the young woman speak from inside of the coach.

"Mrs. Jordan. You need to wake up," she said in an exasperated voice.

He walked over to the open door and saw the young woman was sitting next to an elderly woman, who appeared to be unconscious.

"Can I be of any further assistance?"

The young woman turned to face him, and the fatigue was

evident in her eyes. "Yes, please. It would appear that my companion has fainted."

"Are you quite sure, miss?" he asked. "Perhaps she hit her head?"

"I don't believe that to be the case."

"And why is that?"

"Because I drove this coach most proficiently," she answered with a hint of a smile playing at her lips.

Fearing he misheard her, he asked, "You drove this coach?"

"But, of course," she replied, squaring her shoulders. "How else do you think we arrived here?"

"I had assumed the driver had driven you here."

"But he was injured," she pointed out.

Hudson didn't know what to make of this fascinating young woman. "I must admit that you have piqued my interest, but it might be best if we continued this conversation *after* we arrange for accommodations for your companion," he suggested.

"I agree." The young woman exited the coach and came to stand next to him. "Would you be so kind as to carry Mrs. Jordan into the coaching inn?"

"I would be happy to," he replied. "Then, I shall ensure that your horses will be properly tended to tonight."

"That is not necessary," she assured him. "The footman hired to escort me escaped with no injuries. He can see to the horses after he unloads our trunks."

"As you wish."

As he reached into the coach to pick up the elderly woman, her eyes fluttered open, and she swatted at his hands.

"Unhand me!" she exclaimed.

Hudson withdrew his arms. "Pardon me, ma'am, but I was assisting you into the coaching inn."

"I have two perfectly good legs, and I am more than capable of walking on my own," Mrs. Jordan declared, bringing her hand up to her head. "What happened?"

"You fainted," the young woman said from behind him.

"That is utter nonsense," Mrs. Jordan replied. "I have never fainted before."

"Perhaps you fell asleep then?" he suggested.

Mrs. Jordan shot him an annoyed look. "Young man, if you cannot think of anything clever to say, I would suggest that you remain silent."

Hudson's brow shot up, and he heard the young woman giggle behind him. "My apologies, ma'am," he muttered.

Mrs. Jordan frowned. "The last thing I remember was my charge exiting the moving carriage through an open window so she could help drive the coach."

Taking a step back, Hudson turned towards the young woman with disbelief on his features. "Did you truly accomplish that feat?"

"I did," she answered.

Mrs. Jordan moved to step out of the coach and held her hand out for him to assist her. "That was only after she shot the highwayman in the shoulder and caused the other highwayman's horse to rear up by slamming our coach door into its side."

After Mrs. Jordan slipped her hand out of his, Hudson turned his attention back towards the young woman. "You shot a highwayman?"

"I only shot him *after* he shot our driver," she defended. "He really left me no choice in the matter."

Hudson ran his hand through his hair. "I would like to hear more of your daring adventures, but perhaps it might be best to let you two rest."

"I really don't feel tired," the young woman remarked. "I am more famished than anything."

"Speak for yourself," Mrs. Jordan stated. "I would prefer to lie down. After all, this escapade was rather taxing for an old woman."

"Of course," the young woman graciously replied. "I will need to secure accommodations for the evening."

"Allow me to escort you inside," Hudson offered, holding out his arm.

He saw the young woman's shoulders relax slightly as she placed her hand on his sleeve. "I would appreciate that very much."

Hudson escorted the ladies inside, and he watched as all the men halted their conversations and turned their gazes towards the young woman. They stared at her, their smiles twisted in grimaces of lust and desire. He could feel her shrink back, and he had a sudden surge of protectiveness come over him.

"It will be all right," he assured her. "I won't let any harm befall you. You have my word as a gentleman."

"Thank you," she murmured as she visibly relaxed.

The heavy-set innkeeper exited a back room and approached them with a solemn look on his face. "My wife just removed the bullet, and she is stitching up the wound," he informed them. "Sadly, he won't be able to drive the coach for at least a few days."

"That is most unfortunate news," the young woman replied.

"On a more pleasant note, I do have two rooms available for the evening," the innkeeper said. "Would you ladies care to lie down, and I will send up a tray of food to your room?"

"That would be most satisfactory," Mrs. Jordan answered.

The young woman spoke up. "Actually, I am not ready to retire for the evening. Do you have a private room where I can eat supper?"

The innkeeper tipped his head. "We do," he replied.

Hudson met her eye. "Would you object if I join you?"

A smile came to her lips. "I have no objection."

"But, I do," Mrs. Jordan huffed. "I will have no choice but to chaperone you while you eat dinner with a strange man."

The young woman's smile faded. "That is not necessary. I am more than—"

Mrs. Jordan cut her off. "Nonsense. I shall join you for supper."

"If you insist."

"I do."

Hudson attempted to hide his disappointment at the thought of spending additional time with the young woman's ill-tempered chaperone. He found the mysterious young woman intriguing, and he couldn't wait to spend more time with her.

First, and foremost, he had to learn her identity.

"I think she is asleep," Charlotte said as she watched her companion's head slowly rise and fall as she sat on the chair by the fireplace.

In response, Mrs. Jordan let out a slight snore.

"I would agree with you," the blond-haired man said. "That didn't take long."

"The good news is that I am being properly chaperoned," she joked, smiling.

"That you are."

Charlotte picked up a piece of cheese off the tray and plopped it into her mouth. She savored it for a long moment as she snuck a peak at the handsome man sitting across the table from her. He was tall, broad-shouldered, and his clothing clearly marked him as a gentleman. The faint stubble along his square jawline only enhanced its masculine shape.

He met her gaze, and she realized that she had been caught staring.

"I truly thank you for your assistance earlier," she rushed to say.

"It is always a pleasure to help a damsel in distress." He smiled. "Although, after hearing how you saved your traveling party from the highwaymen, I believe that you can protect yourself."

She returned his smile. "My grandfather taught me that I can't wait around for someone else to save me. I must use my wits to save myself."

"Is that so?" he asked. "What an interesting lesson that must have been."

"When I was younger, I was determined to be a jockey," she shared.

The man's brow lifted. "You wanted to race horses?"

She nodded. "With all my heart," she said, "but I had the misfortune of being born a girl."

"Which is a curse and a blessing," he teased.

"It is, and everyone knows that a woman can't be a jockey," she replied. "However, that didn't stop me from spending count-less hours racing my horse through our fields. There is no greater feeling than the air blowing through my hair."

"You are beginning to sound like my sister," he said, picking up a piece of cheese.

"She sounds wise."

The man chuckled. "She is a hellion."

"It sounds like we would be friends then."

"I have no doubt." He reached forward and broke off a piece of bread. "I am still curious about when you received your lesson from your grandfather."

"One morning, I fell off my horse as he jumped over a ledge, and I twisted my ankle," she said. "I kept waiting for someone to find me, but it was hours before my grandfather discovered me curled up next to the ledge. That is when he taught me that I am in control of my own destiny. He told me that the world is a cruel place, and I need to rely on my inner strength to survive."

"Did your grandfather expect you to walk back to your home on a twisted ankle?"

"Not that time. He carried me back home," she replied. "But the next time I hurt myself, I always found my own way home."

"Did you hurt yourself often?"

She grinned. "Of course. Pretending to be a jockey is a dangerous pastime."

"Do you still dream of being a jockey?"

Charlotte shook her head. "No, my dreams have changed over time."

"That is wise, considering England will never employ women as jockeys."

"I assumed as much."

The man brushed his hands together and small breadcrumbs fell to the table. "Did your grandfather encourage you to give up your dream?"

"No, he would never do that," she said.

Holding up his hands, he asked, "So what is your new dream?"

"I haven't decided yet."

He smiled. "You could be a pirate. There have been female pirates before."

"I would prefer something that won't get me hanged."

"So, highwaywoman is out, then."

"I would imagine so."

The man rubbed his chin thoughtfully. "You could be a smuggler."

She laughed. "Can you think of anything that won't get me arrested and hanged?"

"I'm attempting to," he replied, "but it is rather difficult to come up with another person's dream. Perhaps if you offer up some ideas."

Charlotte turned her gaze over to Mrs. Jordan when she started mumbling something in her sleep.

"You can't force yourself to become someone you are not meant to be. Every experience, every trial, prepares you for becoming the best version of yourself."

The man eyed her with curiosity. "I'm afraid I know very little about you, other than you come from privilege."

Charlotte arched an eyebrow. "And how did you determine that?"

With an amused expression, the man said, "Not only do you have a companion, but you are traveling with a driver and footman in a private coach. Your traveling habit is made from the finest cloth, you have a coral necklace around your neck, and you are wearing kid boots. Furthermore, except for the hole in your glove from where you were holding the reins, your gloves are a pristine white, leading me to believe that you are not accustomed to labor of any kind." He smirked. "Do I need to go on?"

"Your powers of observation are astounding," she remarked.

He leaned back in his chair. "I have always been one who has paid attention to the most minute details. It is fascinating to me to see what I can discover about others."

"I agree," she replied. "Everyone is battling their own trials, their own heartaches, and we should never be quick to judge another."

The man studied her for a moment before saying, "You are exceptionally wise for your young age."

"I am eighteen years old, sir," she announced.

"My apologies, I misspoke earlier," he teased, "you are exceptionally wise for your *old* age."

She laughed. "Thank you for correcting your most grievous error."

"I believe you were at the part that you were going to tell me your name," he said slowly.

Charlotte sat back in her chair. "Now where is the fun in that?" she asked. "I propose we play a game first."

"I do like games."

"As do I," she asserted. "I propose we each divulge one thing about ourselves that we haven't told another person."

"That is easy," he said. "I have always wanted to be a captain of my own ship."

"You have?"

He bobbed his head. "My younger brother joined the Royal Navy when he was fourteen, and I was always envious of him."

"Why didn't you sign up as well?"

"My mother wouldn't let me," he answered. "Apparently, one son in the Royal Navy was enough for her. So instead I became a barrister."

"That is an admirable profession."

"I agree," he replied. "I have worked exceptionally hard and now I am a district judge in London."

She gasped. "You must know Lord Hudson Beauchamp then."

"How do you know that name?" he asked, eyeing her suspiciously.

"My dear friend, Lady Isabella Beauchamp, has a brother who is a district judge in London," she shared.

The man wiped his chin with his hand, thoughtfully. "You know Isabella?"

"I do." She gave him a baffled look. "Do *you* know Isabella?"

"I should say so," he replied. "I am her brother."

"You are Lord Hudson?"

He nodded.

A bright smile came to her face. "You are different than I imagined."

"How did you imagine me?"

She took a moment to collect her thoughts before saying, "I thought you would be much more pretentious and stuffy."

"Why is that?"

"Because I have spent many holidays at Isabella's country

home, and I have never met you," she shared. "You have always been busy working."

"I am exceptionally busy with my caseload."

"I can only imagine, you being a fancy judge and all," she teased.

He leaned forward in his chair and rested his forearm on the table. "Have you truly been to our country house?"

"I have."

"Interesting," he replied. "Then I must assume that you are Lady Charlotte Taylour."

Her lips parted in surprise. "How did you guess that?"

Lord Hudson smiled, drawing her attention to his lips. "My mother does keep me informed of what is going on with the family, sometimes to a fault."

"I see," she replied. "Well, I thank you for your assistance, Lord Hudson."

Reaching for his tin cup, he said, "I assume that you are heading to London."

"You are correct," she answered. "My father recently passed away, and his solicitor has summoned me to his office for the reading of his will."

Lord Hudson took a sip of his drink. As he placed his cup back onto the table, he remarked, "I am sorry for your loss." He glanced down at her traveling habit. "May I ask why you aren't wearing mourning clothes?"

Charlotte smoothed out her blue traveling habit, carefully choosing her next words. She didn't want to confess that she was still debating about whether she would grieve for her father. "I had no mourning gowns available to me at school." There. That part was true.

"That does make logical sense," he replied. "What is your father's solicitor's name?"

"Mr. Henry Stanton."

Lord Hudson bobbed his head approvingly. "I have worked with him before, and he is a good man."

"That pleases me." A yawn slipped past her lips, and her hand shot up to cover her mouth. "My apologies," she said, "I must be more tired than I thought."

"I am not surprised. After all, you've had a taxing day," he acknowledged, rising. "Would you like me to escort you to your room?"

She rose from her chair. "That won't be necessary."

"Before you go," he started, "you forgot to tell me one thing about yourself that no one else knows."

Charlotte took a moment to consider her response. "I love to go to fairs and watch pig running," she announced.

"Pig running?"

She nodded. "Yes, a pig is soaped and greased after having its tail cut short. Then the pig is let out in a pen to be caught. Whoever catches it and holds it overhead, wins the pig."

"That is an interesting pastime for a lady," he said in an amused tone.

"I also like tup running."

"What is tup running?"

"It is similar to pig running but with a ram."

Lord Hudson furrowed his brow. "Please tell me that the winner does not have to hold the ram above their head."

Charlotte giggled. "No, the winner just has to take him by the tail and hold him fast."

"Ah, silly me," Lord Hudson said. "I am not familiar with rural sports practiced at fairs."

"You are missing out, my lord," she teased.

Lord Hudson stared at her for a long moment before saying, "I suppose I am."

"Well, goodnight," she murmured, dropping her gaze.

She had just taken a step towards her companion when Lord Hudson said, "Perhaps it might be best if I escort you to London.

After all, my sister would never forgive me if something happened to you."

Fearing she misheard him, she asked, "Pardon?"

"If you are not opposed, then you can ride with Isabella in the coach," he suggested, his words sounding rushed. "You would be doing me the favor since I intended to ride alongside the coach, and I know that my sister will be exceptionally bored."

Charlotte's gaze shifted towards her companion. "My driver is injured, and I do need to get to London," she rationalized.

"Then it is settled," Hudson declared. "I will escort you and your companion to London."

"Are you sure we won't be intruding?"

He shook his head. "Not at all. In fact, I have no doubt that Isabella will be thrilled by this unexpected news."

She dipped into a curtsy. "Thank you, Lord Hudson. I appreciate this gesture greatly."

He bowed. "You are welcome, Lady Charlotte."

"Now I just need to get Mrs. Jordan to bed." She walked over to her companion and shook her gently. "Are you ready for bed?"

Mrs. Jordan let out a snort as her eyes flew open. "Did I fall asleep?"

"Only for a few moments," she lied.

"Good," Mrs. Jordan murmured, rising slowly from her chair. "I can't very well leave you alone with a strange gentleman, now can I?"

With a side glance at Lord Hudson, she revealed, "Actually, we discovered he is the brother of my dear friend, Lady Isabella."

"The young lady who was riding astride?" Mrs. Jordan asked.

She nodded.

"That does not surprise me in the least," Mrs. Jordan huffed. "Them being siblings and all."

Charlotte brought her hand up to cover the growing smile on her lips, amused that Mrs. Jordan had taken an immediate dislike for Lord Hudson.

The gentleman in question stepped to the door and opened it, letting in the rowdiness from the main hall. "I insist that you allow me to escort you to your room. This coaching inn is full of ruffians."

"Thank you, Lord Hudson," Charlotte responded, feeling grateful for his show of kindness.

3

HUDSON STOOD NEXT TO LADY CHARLOTTE AS THEY WATCHED the mail coach ride away from the Rusty Bucket coaching inn, taking Mrs. Jordan along with it.

"I am sorry your companion decided to travel on to London without you," he said, glancing over at her.

"Don't be," she replied. "Mrs. Jordan was rather a crabby soul."

He chuckled. "Yes, she was."

"I do understand her hesitancy about traveling back to the school," she stated. "After all, we were attacked by highwaymen on that very same road only yesterday."

"But you successfully thwarted their attack," he pointed out.

"That is true, as well," she agreed. "I daresay that Mrs. Jordan was relieved to discover that you were related to Lady Isabella."

"You believe so?"

She nodded. "I do. I think she felt justified in knowing that it is appropriate for a gentleman to escort a lady if he is a close friend of the family, thus relinquishing her commitment to me."

He turned to face her. "You will be under my protection until we arrive in London. Which means this time I will be the one to fight off the highwaymen," he said, puffing out his chest playfully.

"I suppose it would only be fair to let you have a turn," she remarked, smiling.

"That is most kind of you, my lady." Hudson extended his arm towards her. "Allow me to escort you to the coach."

"Thank you," she said, placing her hand on his arm.

They walked the short distance to the black traveling coach emblazoned with his family crest, and he assisted her in. Once she was situated, he asked, "Are you sure you don't mind if I ride alongside the coach?"

"Not at all. It is a nice day for a ride," she replied. "I brought along some embroidery to occupy my time."

"If all goes according to plan, we should arrive at Miss Bell's Finishing School in three hours."

Lady Charlotte's eyes lit up with amusement. "I can't wait to see the look on Isabella's face when she sees me in the coach."

"No doubt she will be surprised."

"The trip to London will be much more enjoyable with Isabella than Mrs. Jordan."

"I would agree with you there."

Hudson felt a twinge of guilt as he closed the door and walked over to his black gelding. He placed his foot into the stirrup and paused. As much as he wanted to ride, he realized that he would rather spend time conversing with Lady Charlotte.

Hudson tossed the reins back towards an awaiting footman. "Tie my horse to the back of the coach," he ordered. "I am going to ride inside today."

"Yes, milord," the footman said with a tip of his head.

He opened the door to the coach. "Do you mind if I sit inside with you?"

"Not at all," she replied. "But I thought you wanted to ride?"

"I changed my mind." He ducked into the coach and sat

across from Lady Charlotte. "I thought you might prefer some company."

She smiled at him. "I would, very much."

For a moment, they stared at each other. "I'm afraid I know very little about you," he said as the silence threatened to stretch awkwardly.

The coach lurched forward as she replied, "What would you wish to know?"

"Besides saving yourself from highwaymen," he started, "what else occupies your time?"

Glancing out the window, she said, "The usual pursuits, I suppose. I enjoy playing the pianoforte and the harp. Furthermore, I am accomplished in singing, dancing, and drawing."

"But not needlework," he teased.

She brought her gaze back to meet his. "I am more than proficient at needlework. I find the repetitiveness to be quite rhythmic."

"I daresay I wish that Isabella felt the same way," he admitted. "All she cares about is riding horses."

"She is quite good at riding."

"I have no doubt, but very few gentlemen of the *ton* are interested in a wife who is only accomplished in riding."

"Perhaps the gentlemen of the *ton* are looking for the wrong attributes in a wife," she challenged.

"I won't argue with you there," he replied. "Sadly, we live in a society that cares more about appearances than anything else."

"That is a shame."

"It is."

Lady Charlotte smoothed out her traveling habit. "And what occupies your time?"

"I work."

"But what do you do for fun?"

"Work."

She arched an eyebrow. "Surely you hunt."

"Rarely."

A line appeared in between Lady Charlotte's brows. "You must have some pastime that is enjoyable."

He nodded. "I do. Work."

"You can't possibly work all the time."

"I can, and I do," he said.

"That sounds rather exhausting."

With a shake of his head, he replied, "I disagree. I love being a district judge. It gives a sense of purpose to my life."

She gave him a weak smile. "What a wonderful feeling that must be."

"Do you not have a sense of purpose?"

Hudson saw a wistful expression in her eyes, and she grew silent. For a moment, he feared that he must have offended her with his question. He started to apologize, but she spoke first.

"Frankly, I am still trying to discover where I belong."

"You don't know?"

She shook her head. "My own father didn't want me," she revealed, her voice soft. "He sent me to live with my maternal grandparents right after I was born, and I rarely saw him."

"What of your mother?"

Lowering her gaze to her lap, she replied, "She died during childbirth with me."

Hudson felt like a fool for asking such personal questions, especially since he could hear the heartache in her voice. "I am sorry for asking…"

She spoke over him. "Don't be, please," she said. "It is I who should apologize for my display of emotions—"

"Don't ever apologize for your emotions," he asserted, cutting her off. "It is nothing to be embarrassed or ashamed of."

Lady Charlotte's green eyes searched his while saying, "That is not what we were taught at school."

"Then whatever your teacher taught you is wrong."

A small laugh escaped her lips. "Miss Bell would be furious to hear you say so."

"Then so be it," he replied. "I am not afraid of Miss Bell."

She arched an eyebrow. "Now you are just being arrogant, my lord."

"That was not my intention," he responded, chuckling.

"Then what was?"

He paused, only for a moment. "I suppose I just wanted to see you smile again."

"It worked brilliantly," she replied as a genuine smile lit up her face.

"I'm glad," he said. "We are similar, you and I."

"In what way?"

"I rarely saw my father, either," he responded. "Later, I discovered that he had a whole other family that we knew nothing about."

Charlotte pressed her lips together. "My father remarried shortly after my mother died, and I suspect that he spent all his time with his other daughter. He never sent for me," she said, her voice trailing off, "even though I kept waiting to be invited back home."

"Were your grandparents unkind to you?"

"Oh heavens, no!" she declared. "They were always loving and kind. I thrived at their estate, but they were older. Slower. They had a hard time keeping up with me."

"I can only imagine, if you were racing horses on their property."

"My father did send my mother's horse to me for my eighth birthday," she revealed. "I thought that was a rather touching gift."

Hudson worked hard to keep the irritation out of his voice. "It was, but I'm not sure if that makes up for years of neglect."

"No, but at least I had something else that belonged to my

mother," she said as she started fingering the coral necklace around her neck.

"I take it that the necklace belonged to your mother, as well."

She nodded. "My father gave it to her on their wedding day."

Finding himself curious about one thing, he asked, "How long did your father wait to remarry after your mother passed away?"

"One month," she murmured.

Hudson's brow shot up. "He got married one month later?"

"Yes."

"How long were your parents married?"

"A little over a year," she replied.

Shifting his gaze away from her, Hudson couldn't believe that her father would be so callous as to remarry after only a month. Didn't the man mourn for his wife at all?

"I know what you are thinking," she said, breaking him out of his musings, "and I agree. My father didn't love my mother enough to even mourn her death properly."

"Well, it sounds like your father was a nincompoop," he declared. "He was a fool to treat you in such a horrendous fashion."

Lady Charlotte smiled as he hoped she would. "Thank you for that."

"You are welcome." He smiled. "Now perhaps we could speak of things that are more pleasant."

"Such as?"

He adjusted his blue riding jacket as he leaned forward in his seat. "Tell me more of your adventures as an amateur jockey."

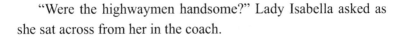

"Were the highwaymen handsome?" Lady Isabella asked as she sat across from her in the coach.

Charlotte shrugged. "I don't know. They had cloth covering the bottom half of their faces and were wearing cocked hats low on their forehead."

"I bet they were handsome," her friend said decisively.

"I don't think their looks matter when it comes to highwaymen."

"It does," Isabella defended. "They probably were like Robin Hood, and they were robbing you so they could feed people in need."

"I highly doubt that to be the case, especially since they shot the driver."

"How else were they going to stop the coach?" Isabella questioned.

"They could have asked nicely."

"Would you have stopped?"

Charlotte smiled. "No, but that would have been the polite thing to do."

Isabella pouted playfully. "I had no idea that highwaymen were so inconsiderate."

"Sadly, it is true."

"Perhaps they just wanted to dance with you?"

Charlotte let out an amused huff. "I think you have been reading too many books about highwaymen. Except for Claude Duval, no other highwayman has asked a lady to dance with him after he robbed them."

"That is a pity."

"It is," she replied. "I have no doubt they had nefarious intentions towards us."

With a shake of her head, Isabella said, "I can't believe you fought off two highwaymen. I hadn't even realized you could shoot a pistol."

"Every woman should know how to shoot a pistol," she contended.

"I don't."

"Then I will need to teach you."

Isabella tucked a lock of her blonde hair behind her ear. "Where did you even learn how to shoot?"

"From my grandfather," she replied. "He would take me hunting with him."

"Your grandfather would let you go hunting with him?"

She nodded. "We would mainly hunt grouse."

Isabella frowned. "My brothers refuse to let me go hunting with them, even though I am sure I could outride most of them."

"Do they ever have hunting parties?"

"Everett does at our country estate," she replied. "But the grooms are under strict orders not to let my horse leave the stable that day, for any reason."

"I can't believe you haven't found a way around that yet," she remarked knowingly.

Isabella grinned. "It gets even worse. On the days of the hunt, my mother is adamant that I remain inside with her and help entertain the other guests."

"Oh no, that sounds horrifying," Charlotte joked.

"Trust me," Isabella said, shuddering. "It is."

Shifting her gaze towards the green countryside, Charlotte commented, "We are almost to the coaching inn, and I have seen no signs of highwaymen."

"That is a shame," Isabella replied, crossing her arms over her chest. "Our coach has never *once* been robbed by highwaymen, and we have traveled this road many times."

"It might be best if you stop idolizing highwaymen," she attempted. "They are criminals."

"But handsome criminals."

Charlotte laughed. "You are past hope, my dear friend."

"Speaking of handsome gentlemen—"

She spoke over her friend. "I believe *you* were the one who was speaking of handsome highwaymen. Not me."

Uncrossing her arms, Isabella continued. "As I was

saying, before you so rudely interrupted me," she said, hesitating, "I was surprised to see you and Hudson sharing a coach earlier."

"Why was that?"

"Because Hudson never sits in the coach with me."

"Never?"

Isabella shook her head. "Not once."

Not liking where this conversation was going, Charlotte responded vaguely, "I wonder why that is."

"I have a pretty good idea."

"Which is?" she asked, dreading her friend's answer.

Isabella smirked. "I'm not prepared to tell you."

"You aren't?" she questioned. "But we tell each other everything."

"Clearly not, since I only just discovered you go hunting."

"That is just a trivial detail."

"Is it?" Isabella asked. "Or are you withholding secrets from me?"

Charlotte shifted her gaze to look out the window, where she took a moment to admire Hudson as he rode alongside the coach. She couldn't help but acknowledge what a dashing figure he made in his blue riding jacket, chestnut hued trousers, and polished black Hessian boots.

"Did you know my brother was engaged once?" Isabella asked.

"I did not," Charlotte responded as she turned away from the window.

"It is not something that we discuss freely, mind you, but he was engaged while studying at Oxford."

"What happened?"

"His fiancée, Hannah, broke the engagement and went on to marry a rake, who was the heir to a dukedom."

She gasped. "How awful."

"I'm just relieved that my brother didn't marry that insipid girl," Isabella replied. "She clearly was only chasing after a title."

"How did your brother react to the news?"

Isabella glanced out the window towards her brother. "He has never spoken about it."

"Never?"

"At least not to me."

"You are his little sister," she pointed out.

"True, but I daresay that he has kept his feelings to himself," Isabella said.

"Perhaps he has discussed it with a friend."

Isabella exhaled loudly. "He has no friends. All he does is work."

"I am sure he has friends."

"I haven't met any."

Charlotte shook her head, amused. "That doesn't mean he lacks friends."

Isabella had just opened her mouth to respond when the coach lurched to a stop. A moment later, the door was opened, and Hudson announced, "We have arrived at the coaching inn for the evening."

"It is about time," Isabella muttered under her breath.

Hudson chuckled. "You are the most impatient person that I know." He held his hand up. "May I assist you ladies inside?"

Charlotte slipped her gloved hand into his and exited the coach. "How was your ride?" she asked as she withdrew her hand.

"Uneventful." He reached back in the coach to assist his sister. "I kept waiting for the highwaymen to make an appearance."

"As was I," Isabella said, coming to stand next to her. "I was hoping to witness Charlotte thwarting their attack again."

"We decided that it was my turn to fight the highwaymen," Hudson remarked.

Isabella arched an eyebrow. "And how would you do that? Bore them to death with your legal ramblings about being a judge?"

"I would have you know that some people find my work fascinating."

"I won't disagree with you there," Isabella started, "but I doubt studying at Lincoln's Inn prepared you for defending yourself against highwaymen."

Hudson extended his arm towards her. "My dear, misguided sister, you don't know what I am capable of when my loved ones' lives are at risk."

Placing her hand on his sleeve, Isabella said, "Apparently not."

"Lady Charlotte?" he asked, extending his other arm. "May I escort you inside?"

"You may," she replied.

As they stepped into the coaching inn, Charlotte noticed that it wasn't nearly as crowded as it had been the night before. A few men glanced their way, but mostly they all appeared to be into their cups.

The familiar innkeeper approached them with a smile on his weathered face. "Welcome back to my humble establishment, milord," he greeted. "May I get you some rooms? Supper?"

Hudson spoke up in an authoritative voice. "We would like two rooms, and we would like to eat supper in a private room."

"As you wish," the innkeeper said with a tip of his head. "Follow me."

They wove between the rectangular tables and approached the back room that they had eaten in the night before. The innkeeper took out a key, unlocked the door, and pushed it open. "I will have our serving girl bring in a tray of food shortly," he informed them, standing to the side.

Charlotte had just stepped into the room when Isabella turned towards the innkeeper and asked, "Would you mind showing me to my room?"

"I would be delighted."

Hudson took a step closer to his sister. "I will escort you."

"That is not necessary," Isabella insisted. "You stay here and entertain Charlotte. I will be down shortly for supper."

"I don't know. It isn't safe for you to be alone," Hudson said, the indecision on his face.

Isabella placed a hand on her hip. "I am eighteen years old. I am not a child anymore."

"I never said you were," he replied. "However, we are at a coaching inn, and you are young and naïve."

The innkeeper interjected, "If I may, milord, the rooms are only accessible by a set of narrow stairs by the kitchen. No one from the main hall is allowed up the stairs unless they have rented a room for the evening."

"All right," he conceded, turning his attention back towards his sister, "but if you are not back in this room by the time that our supper arrives, I will come looking for you."

Isabella flashed him a smile. "Thank you, brother."

Once the door to the room was closed, Hudson turned back to face her. "My sister gave me strict instructions to entertain you," he said with a little lopsided grin. "What would you wish to discuss?"

"Do you know any jokes?" she asked as she sat down at a chair near the table.

"I'm afraid not."

"What about any anecdotes?"

Hudson came to sit down across from her. "None that I can think of at this very moment."

"That is a shame."

"I can regale you with stories from my youth," he said.

She leaned forward in her chair. "That sounds promising."

As he adjusted his riding jacket, he shared, "I have two

brothers, and we were all quite rambunctious in our youth. We used to run our mother ragged with our antics."

"Such as?"

"We would go swimming in the pond, build boats, torment our tutors with reptiles, and even managed to convince Isabella that she was a year younger than she actually was."

Charlotte laughed. "When was that?"

"On her sixth birthday, my older brother, Everett, informed her that she was actually only five years old, and that our parents had gotten the date wrong."

"And she believed you?"

Hudson smirked. "We were all in on the ruse, and it went on for months. Finally, my mother stepped in and insisted that we tell her the truth."

With a smile tugging at her lips, she replied, "That is awful of you to tease Isabella at such a young age."

"I can assure you that she deserved it," he said. "She used to follow us around and beg us to play shuttlecock and battledore with her."

"At least she wasn't asking you to play dolls with her," she pointed out.

"That is a good point," he replied. "I should consider myself lucky then."

"Do you play shuttlecock?"

He nodded. "I do, and I play it exceptionally well."

"As do I."

"We shall have to play a game then."

The crackling of the fire drew her attention briefly as she said, "I will only agree if you go into the game with a mindset that you shall lose."

His eyes flickered with amusement. "Is that so?"

She bobbed her head animatedly. "Miss Bell ensured we excelled at all lawn sports. She felt that girls should not be afraid of being well tired when they play battledore and shuttlecock, but we were to avoid excessive fatigue, whenever possible."

A knock came at the door before it was pushed open, and a young serving maid walked into the room with a tray of food. "I brought you some supper, milord," she said in a soft voice.

"Place it on the table," Hudson ordered.

The serving maid lowered her gaze as she went to do his bidding. "Would you care for anything else?" she asked, taking a step back from the table.

"No, thank you," he replied.

The serving maid quickly departed from the room without saying another word.

Hudson's eyes darted towards the door as he asked, "Do you suppose I should go look for Isabella?"

"If it would ease your mind, then you should do so."

He rose from his chair. "I shall return shortly. Please start eating without me."

Charlotte watched Hudson leave the room, closing the door behind him. She relaxed back in her seat as she took a moment to reflect on the last few days. So much uncertainty still filled her life. Her father was dead. Her London Season was over before it even started. And now she needed to prepare herself to see her stepmother, a woman that she hardly knew.

She was grateful that she had run into Hudson at the coaching inn. The trip back to London was much more enjoyable with Hudson and Isabella by her side.

❦ 4 ❧

"Your townhouse is magnificent," Charlotte said as the coach rolled to a stop in front of a three-level structure with a black iron fence surrounding the property.

"It is rather grand, isn't it?" Isabella agreed as she stared out the window. "What is your father's townhouse like?"

She shrugged. "I have no idea. I never spent time with him when he was in Town for the Season."

Isabella lifted her brow. "Never?"

"I have only been to his country estate in Blackpool."

"So, you have never been to London?"

She shook her head.

Isabella let out a shrill scream of excitement. "We are going to have such fun this Season! We are going to attend the theatre, go riding through Hyde Park, visit Vauxhall Gardens, and tour the Royal Menagerie."

"That does sound exciting, but you seem to forget that I will be in mourning."

Before Isabella could respond, a footman opened the door and let down the steps of the coach, extending his hand towards her, offering his assistance.

Once Charlotte stepped down onto the pavement, she released the footman's hand and watched as Hudson handed off his reins to an awaiting footman.

"Mother will be immensely pleased that you have come to visit. I'm sure of it," Isabella declared, looping her arm through hers.

Hudson approached her. "You will be our honored guest this Season, Lady Charlotte."

"That is most kind of you, but I'm afraid I won't know for certain what my plans will be until after the will is read tomorrow," she explained.

He grew solemn. "If you are not opposed, I would be more than willing to attend the meeting with you."

"You would?" she asked, surprised.

He nodded, his blue eyes unreadable.

"I would love that."

A brief smile came to his lips. "I will plan on it then."

"Are you sure that you have time? After all, I know your duties as a judge must keep you quite busy."

Isabella leaned closer and whispered, "Don't try to talk him out of it, Lottie."

Hudson chuckled. "I will have to shift some things around, but it would be my honor to escort you to the meeting tomorrow. I want to ensure that you are treated fairly."

"Thank you," she said in a relieved voice. "I would appreciate that very much."

As Isabella started leading her towards the ebony door of the townhouse, it opened and a tall, balding man stood to the side and greeted them.

"Welcome home, Lady Isabella." He tipped his head towards Lord Hudson. "Lord Hudson."

"Good evening, Howe. Is my mother home?" Hudson asked as he removed his top hat and extended it towards the butler.

"Yes, milord," he replied. "She is in the drawing room."

Hudson nodded approvingly. "Will you ready a guest bedchamber for Lady Charlotte Taylour?"

"I will arrange it," Howe stated with a slight bow.

"Come, I can't wait for you to see Mother," Isabella said, tugging her across the entry hall.

Charlotte barely had time to admire the ornate woodwork running the length of the ivory-colored walls, the richly painted ceiling, or the numerous works of art hanging throughout the hall.

Stepping into the drawing room with its green-papered walls, Charlotte saw the dowager marchioness sitting on the settee embroidering a white handkerchief. Her shoulders were slumped, and her skin was pale, making her appear frail.

"Mother!" Isabella exclaimed as she dropped her arms.

Lady Northampton placed the handkerchief onto the table next to her and rose from her chair. "Isabella, my child. You are finally home," she greeted, holding out her arms.

Charlotte felt like an interloper as she watched Isabella and her mother embrace affectionately. She felt a twinge of sadness deep within her heart knowing that she would never share a moment like this with her mother.

Lady Northampton leaned back and smiled lovingly at her daughter. "I have missed you these past few months."

"I have missed you, as well," Isabella replied.

"And I see that you brought a friend," Lady Northampton said, glancing her way. "It is good to see you again, Charlotte."

She stepped forward and curtsied. "Thank you, Lady Northampton."

The tall, thin dowager lifted her brow. "I believe I have asked you to call me 'Mary' on multiple occasions."

"Yes, you did… uh… Mary," she stumbled out.

Hudson chuckled from behind her. "You might want to work

on saying my mother's given name. That was rather awkward to witness."

"Leave poor Charlotte alone," Mary chided lightly. "We wouldn't want her to feel anything less than welcomed in our home."

Hudson stepped past her to embrace his mother. "You are looking well, Mother."

"I believe that you are attempting to flatter me, my son," she said in a loving tone. "Although, I must admit that I am surprised to see you here."

"You are?" he asked, taking a step back.

Mary nodded. "I had assumed you would return immediately back to your office to start working, especially after being on the road for nearly three days."

With a side glance at her, Hudson replied, "I just wanted to ensure that Isabella and Lady Charlotte arrived home safely."

"That was most thoughtful of you," his mother remarked. "Would you care to stay for dinner?"

Hudson adjusted his cravat. "I'm afraid not. I have no doubt that my caseload is piling up as we speak."

"That is the brother that I know and love," Isabella said, smirking.

Mary gave him a sad smile. "That is a shame. I had hoped to spend some time with you."

He pressed his lips together, appearing to choose his next words carefully. "I suppose I could return for dinner, but I would have to leave shortly thereafter. I would have no time for card games."

Clasping her hands together, Mary replied, "That is wonderful news. You haven't dined with us in months."

"I apologize for neglecting you," he started in a genuine tone, "but I have been exceptionally busy."

"And I am not contesting that, my dear. I am just grateful to spend any time I can with you," Mary said.

Isabella walked over to the window and looked out. "Where are Madalene and Everett? I would have thought they would have been here to receive us."

"They went on a carriage ride through Hyde Park," Mary informed them, "but they will be joining us for dinner tonight."

"How delightful," Isabella said.

Mary pointed towards the settee. "Please have a seat, Charlotte. Can I offer you some refreshment?" she asked as she reached for the teapot.

"Yes, please," she replied as she went and sat down on the velvet settee. "The tea at the inn was rather disappointing."

Hudson grimaced. "Was that supposed to be tea?"

Laughing, Isabella said, "That is why I didn't drink it."

Charlotte watched as Mary poured her a cup of tea and placed the teapot onto the tray. As she extended a cup towards her, she asked, "What brings you to London?"

"My father died recently, and his solicitor has summoned me for the reading of his will," she revealed plainly as she accepted the cup.

Mary stared at her blankly. "Dear heavens, child. What awful news."

"I suppose," she replied, taking a long sip of her tea.

"I know you and your father weren't close..."

She huffed. "You could say that."

"But it still must be hard to lose your father," Mary attempted.

Charlotte brought the cup down to her lap and said, "I didn't know my father well enough even to mourn him."

The dowager pressed her lips together in a disapproving fashion. "Is that why you are not in mourning attire, my dear?"

She shook her head. "I haven't the funds to procure mourning gowns. I won't know if my father left me any provisions until I meet with his solicitor."

"Then I shall take you shopping tomorrow, and have you fitted for new gowns," Mary said.

Reaching forward, she placed her cup and saucer on the table in front of her. "That is most generous of you, but, unfortunately, tomorrow I will be attending the meeting with my father's solicitor."

"Just you?"

"No, my stepmother and half-sister will be in attendance, as well," she answered.

Hudson spoke up. "And I will be escorting Lady Charlotte to the meeting to ensure she is properly represented."

Mary's lips parted in surprise as she shifted towards him. "That is most kind of you, Hudson."

"It is the least I can do." He turned towards Charlotte. "I will also send word to Mr. Stanton that you have arrived safely and are residing with my mother."

"Thank you, Lord Hudson."

He bowed. "Now if you will excuse me, I'm afraid I must depart. I shall return for dinner."

They all watched him as he exited the room, and Mary was the first one to speak. "Well, that was rather telling."

Isabella bobbed her head. "I agree."

Unsure of what they were speaking of, Charlotte remained silent.

Mary turned towards her with a knowing smile on her face. "Would you care to lie down before dinner?"

"No, that is not necessary," she replied. "I would be much more interested in a tour of this magnificent townhouse."

Mary rose and said, "That would be my pleasure."

With a book in her hand, Charlotte was laying on the chaise lounge in her bedchamber when a knock came at the door.

"Enter," she ordered.

The door opened, revealing a dark-haired young woman, no older than she, dressed in a maid's uniform. She kept her hand on the door handle as she said, "The housekeeper, Mrs. Davies, sent me up to assist you in changing for dinner."

Charlotte placed the book down onto the chaise lounge and asked, "Is it already time to dress for dinner?"

"It is, milady," she replied, closing the door behind her. "The dinner bell will be ringing soon."

"I must have lost track of time while I was reading."

The maid walked further into the room. "It is easy to get lost in a good book."

"That it is," she agreed. "Do you enjoy reading, as well?"

Nodding, the maid replied, "Lady Northampton allows us to read certain books in the library, assuming we return them when we are finished."

"That is most gracious of her."

"It is." The maid walked over to the armoire and opened the door. "I came in earlier and unpacked your trunks," she informed her. "And, if you are in agreement, I selected a gown for you to wear this evening."

"Whatever you think is best," Charlotte said, rising.

The maid pulled out a white gown with a square-cut neckline and short puffy sleeves. She walked it over to the bed and laid it down.

"First, we need to style your hair," the maid instructed.

Charlotte walked over to the dressing table and sat down. "I'm afraid I didn't catch your name."

"It is Ellen," she replied, picking up a brush from the dressing table.

Shifting in the chair, Charlotte met her gaze and said, "It is nice to meet you, Ellen."

Ellen smiled at her. "Likewise, milady. I must admit that I was pleased when Mrs. Davies specified that I should act as your lady's maid during your stay."

Turning back in her chair, she asked, "Is that so?"

"My dream has always been to one day become a lady's maid," Ellen remarked in a wistful tone as she began to run the brush down the length of her hair. "I know that may sound silly to someone like you…" Her voice trailing off.

"Not at all," she replied. "Everyone is entitled to have their own dreams, and I think it is wonderful that you know what you want out of life."

"That is kind of you to say. It means the world to me," Ellen breathed, placing the brush down onto the dressing table. "For your hair, I intend to pile it high on your head and create small ringlets with the hot curling tongs."

"That sounds perfect."

A short time later, Ellen stepped back to admire her handiwork and asked, "Are you pleased with your hairstyle?"

Charlotte turned her head to one side and then the other, admiring the ringlets framing her face. "Well done, Ellen."

"Now, we shall dress you for dinner," Ellen said as she walked over to pick up the dress.

After Ellen fastened the last button on her dress, a knock came at the door, only moments before it was opened, and Isabella entered. She was dressed in a pale blue gown that accentuated her creamy white skin.

"I came to escort you down to dinner," Isabella announced.

Charlotte let out a sigh of relief as Ellen handed her a pair of white gloves. "Thank heavens for that," she said. "I was unsure of which drawing room we were assembling in this evening."

"I assumed as much," Isabella remarked, smiling.

As they stepped out into the hallway, Charlotte asked, "Did you enjoy your rest before dinner?"

Isabella nodded. "I did, immensely. I read a book on physics."

"Dear heavens," she gasped, feigning outrage. "A lady must never read a book on physics or logic. It is just simply not done. After all, what is next? Coming up with your own ideas or thinking too hard?"

Isabella laughed as she hoped she would. "It is true, but I freely admit that I am a bluestocking. I embrace my peculiar personality."

"That is why we are friends," she replied. "We both are a little odd."

They had just stepped into the drawing room when she heard Madalene, the Marchioness of Northampton, shout, "Lottie!"

In the next moment, she was wrapped up in her friend's loving embrace.

Madalene stepped back and said, "It is so good to see you again."

"I believe congratulations are in order."

Placing a hand to her increasing stomach, Madalene replied, "We are thrilled beyond words."

Everett, the Marquess of Northampton, came to stand next to his wife. "It is good to see you again, Lady Charlotte."

She curtsied. "Thank you for allowing me to be a guest in your home."

"Nonsense," Everett said with a dismissive wave of his hand. "You are always welcome."

Mary approached her and kissed her on the cheek. "You are looking lovely this evening, Charlotte."

"Thank you, Mary."

A clearing of a throat came from the door, and Charlotte turned her head to see Hudson standing there, looking deucedly handsome. He was dressed in a black jacket, black trousers, white waistcoat, and white cravat. His hair was brushed forward, and she had a strange desire to run her hand through it.

Where had that thought come from, she wondered, as she quickly banished it.

"Doth my eyes deceive me?" Everett asked in a mocking tone. "Is that my elusive brother, Hudson?"

Hudson gave his brother an exasperated look as he walked into the room. "Good evening, brother." He walked over and kissed Madalene on the cheek. "How are you this evening?"

"I am well," Madalene replied.

"I am sorry that you have to deal with my intolerable brother," Hudson joked.

Madalene laughed lightly. "I find him charming," she replied, sharing a private look with Everett that was filled with love.

Hudson huffed. "Love has blinded you, Madalene."

"Then so be it," she replied.

Turning his attention towards her, Hudson's eyes briefly perused the length of her. "You are looking lovely this evening, Lady Charlotte."

"Thank you, Lord Hudson," she responded with a slight curtsey.

"Can I get you something to drink?" Everett asked his brother as he walked over to the drink cart.

Hudson shook his head. "Nothing for me. I need a clear head this evening. I have some more work that I need to finish up before I will be able to go to bed."

"I worry that you work too much," Mary said, placing her hand on his sleeve. "You need to take a holiday."

"I don't have time for a holiday, especially not with my caseload overfilling at the moment."

"Would you care to join us at the theatre tomorrow?" Everett asked, pouring himself a drink. "If I am not mistaken, I believe that Mother is forcing Isabella to come along."

Isabella placed a hand on her hip. "Do I have to go to the theatre?"

Mary nodded. "You do."

"Botheration," Isabella mumbled under her breath, drawing a laugh from Madalene.

"I appreciate the offer, but I am much too busy," Hudson replied.

Everett took a sip of his drink. "You are always too busy," he commented as he lowered his glass. "How will you ever find a girl to wed if you don't put forth an effort."

"I have no desire to marry at this time," Hudson said, looking displeased. "I am content with the way things are."

"Are you?" Everett questioned. "All you do is work."

"I enjoy working," Hudson contended. "It gives me a sense of purpose."

"Or perhaps you are running away from your past?" Everett asked with a knowing look.

Hudson grew visibly rigid. "That is none of your concern."

"You need to confront your past sometime, Hudson," Everett pressed.

With annoyance on his features, Hudson asked, "And why is that?"

Mary spoke up. "Boys, this might not be the best time to discuss such things." She tipped her head towards Charlotte. "After all, we have a guest with us."

"My apologies," Everett said, taking a sip of his drink. "I should have never brought it up."

"No, you shouldn't have," Hudson replied in a steely tone.

Mary forced a smile to her lips. "I asked our cook to prepare a special dessert for Hudson," she shared, attempting to lighten the mood. "It is baked apple pudding."

"Oh, I do love baked apple pudding," Isabella acknowledged.

Hudson smiled, but it didn't reach his eyes. "Thank you, Mother."

Charlotte could see the depth of pain lingering in his eyes, and it surprised her. What had caused him to experience such pain? And why was he hiding it behind a smile?

Hudson shifted his gaze towards her, and their eyes met for a moment. The glance that flickered between them had been a wordless message of understanding. He wasn't ready to talk about his pain.

Howe stepped into the room and announced dinner was ready, breaking the spell that had come over them.

"Shall we?" Isabella asked, looping arms with her.

5

THE COACH ROLLED TO A CREAKING STOP OUTSIDE OF HIS ancestral townhouse. Reaching out of the small, opened window, Hudson turned the latch and exited the coach, not bothering to wait for his footman to come around.

What was he doing here, he wondered, and not for the first time. He didn't have time to escort Lady Charlotte to her meeting with the solicitor. He was immensely busy at work, and he hardly had any time to even sleep last night. So why had he offered in the first place?

Unfortunately, he knew the reason. Something about Lady Charlotte intrigued him, but he didn't know what it was. When he looked deep into her eyes, he felt a familiarity, as if only she could comprehend his pains and sorrow.

"Which is ridiculous," he muttered under his breath as he walked up the stairs. "I hardly know the girl."

The main door opened, and Howe stepped to the side to allow him to enter.

"Good morning, milord," the butler said with a slight bow.

Hudson removed his top hat and gloves, extending them towards him. "Good morning, Howe. Is Lady Charlotte awake?"

Howe nodded. "Yes, she is in the dining room with Lord Northampton and Lady Isabella."

"Very good," he murmured before he crossed the entry hall and headed towards the family's private dining room.

As he stepped into the dining room, Everett greeted him from the head of the table. "Good morning, brother," he said, lowering the newspaper down to the table. "Would you care to join us for breakfast?"

"I believe I will," he replied, heading towards the buffet table.

A footman handed him a plate, and he filled it with eggs and plum cake. He sat down next to Lady Charlotte, who was dressed in a white gown with a pink ribbon tied around her waist.

"Good morning, Lady Charlotte," he said as he placed his white linen napkin across his lap.

She glanced over at him with a hint of a smile on her lips. "How are you faring this morning, Lord Hudson?"

"I am well. And you?"

The smile grew. "I slept spectacularly," she shared.

"You did?"

She nodded. "The feather mattress was so comfortable. It put my mattress at school to shame."

He chuckled as a footman poured tea into his cup. "That is good to hear."

Isabella spoke up from the other side of the table. "After Charlotte's meeting today, we were hoping to go on a carriage ride through Hyde Park," she revealed. "Would you like to join us?"

Reaching for his teacup, he replied, "I'm afraid I am unable to. I have to…"

"Work," Isabella said, finishing his thought. "I assumed as much, but I thought I would ask."

Everett folded the paper and placed it next to him on the

table. "It is nice of you to escort Lady Charlotte to meet with her solicitor."

"It is the least I can do," he remarked, before taking a sip of his drink. "After all, I want to ensure that she is dealt with fairly."

Everett bobbed his head. "I agree."

Charlotte placed her hands in her lap, and her shoulder slumped slightly.

"What is it?" he asked.

Her eyes held vulnerability as she admitted, "I have no doubt that whatever is in my father's will, will change my life forever."

"You could be an heiress," Isabella said after taking a sip of her chocolate.

"Or," Charlotte paused, "I could be left nothing and no prospects."

Everett placed his fork and knife onto his plate and pushed it away. "Won't you be able to live with your stepmother, the Countess of Huntley?"

She shook her head. "I believe that she hates me."

"And why is that?"

Charlotte sighed. "My father only sent for me on occasional holidays, and I spent minimal time around my stepmother. It almost seemed that my father spent time with me out of obligation and not because he wanted to. I can't help but wonder if my stepmother was involved in that decision."

Everett leaned to the side as a footman reached down to collect his plate. "You are always welcome in our home. I hope you know that."

"I don't wish to become a burden," Charlotte said.

Isabella gasped. "You could never become a burden, Lottie."

"That is true," Everett agreed. "Furthermore, my mother was just saying yesterday that she is in need of a companion."

Charlotte didn't appear convinced. "I don't believe that to be the case."

"Then, I will hire you as Isabella's companion," Everett said. "You might even be able to keep my sister out of trouble."

Charlotte laughed. "I truly doubt that. I don't think anyone can keep Isabella out of trouble."

Isabella crossed her arms over her chest. "I can hear both of you."

"I am well aware of that, sister dearest," Everett teased with a wink.

Hudson finished his last bite and placed his fork onto his plate. He shifted towards Lady Charlotte. "Are you ready to attend your meeting?"

He watched as she straightened herself up to her full height.

"I am," she answered confidently.

"That is good."

He rose and extended his hand towards her. She slipped her ungloved hand in his and allowed him to assist her in rising. As she withdrew her hand, Charlotte met his gaze and a faint blush crept up her cheeks.

"Thank you," she murmured, averting her gaze. "I will go inform my lady's maid that we are ready to depart."

Hudson watched as Charlotte departed from the room before he turned his gaze back towards Everett, who had an infuriating grin on his face.

"Where is Madalene this morning?" he asked.

Everett's grin faded. "She was not feeling well, so I requested a tray be sent to her room."

"That is unfortunate to hear."

"It is, but she still intends to attend the theatre this evening," Everett said. "Are you sure you wouldn't like to join us?"

He shook his head. "I am afraid that is an impossibility."

"You need to stop working so hard and start enjoying life," Everett pressed.

"I enjoy working."

Everett frowned. "You used to attend the theatre with our

family, attend balls, and were even known to place some bets at Whites."

"That was a long time ago," he said. "I am a vastly different person now. I have different goals and ambitions."

"I am proud of you for all that you have accomplished, but I still contend that you are the same person, deep down. You have just forgotten who you are."

Hudson stared at his brother for a long moment before saying, "I am tired of this interrogation. I am going to wait for Lady Charlotte in the entry hall."

"This is not an interrogation," Everett insisted.

"No? It feels like one," he stated as he spun on his heel and headed towards the door.

Once he was alone in the entry hall, Hudson ran a hand through his hair as he started pacing on the black and white tiles.

How dare Everett speak to him like that? He knew nothing about his life. He had worked hard to become a district judge, and he refused to let his brother make him feel guilty for that.

Lady Charlotte's calming voice broke through his musings. "Lord Hudson," she started, "are you all right?"

He stopped pacing and gave her a weak smile. "I am now."

She came to stop in front of him, and he could hear the compassion in her voice. "What has you so irritated?"

"It is of little consequence."

"Why do I not believe you?" she asked, her eyes searching his.

He averted his gaze, afraid of what she might discover in his eyes. "It matters not."

Charlotte placed a straw bonnet on her head. As she tied the ribbons under her chin, she replied, "I would contend that it does matter."

"Unfortunately, we do not have time to discuss it." Hudson offered his arm to her, and he was pleased when she accepted it. "We need to hurry if we want to arrive to your meeting on time."

Howe met them at the main door and extended his gloves and hat towards him.

As they stepped outside, the footman hopped down from the back of the coach and opened the door. Hudson assisted Lady Charlotte and her lady's maid into the coach before he stepped inside, choosing to sit across from Charlotte.

"Mr. Stanton's office is across town," Hudson informed them.

With a rigid back, Lady Charlotte said, "I want to thank you again for coming with me, Lord Hudson. I am rather anxious to get this meeting over with."

He held up his hand. "It is nothing, Lady Charlotte. Friends look out for one another."

"I'm glad you are my friend," she said, her voice full of gratitude.

"I feel the same way."

Hudson turned his head towards the window, and his eyes scanned the bustling pavement as men and women walked around street vendors attempting to hawk their goods.

His eyes strayed back towards Lady Charlotte, who was conversing politely with her lady's maid. He took a moment to admire the elegant curve of her neck and her olive skin. He cleared his throat and turned his attention back towards the window.

He needed to be mindful not to be distracted by a pretty face. He was attending the meeting to represent Lady Charlotte, not to flirt with her.

Charlotte started wringing her hands in her lap as the coach came to a stop in front of a brick, two-level building on the edge of the fashionable part of town.

The coach door opened, and a footman re-extended the step. Lord Hudson exited first, then stretched his hand to her, assisting her as she stepped out of the coach onto the awaiting ground.

Charlotte stared up at the building and felt the trepidation growing inside of her.

"There is no need to be nervous," Hudson said as he stood next to her. "I will be with you every step of the way."

She had to admit that just having Lord Hudson near her provided her with much needed reassurance, but she didn't dare admit that. At least not to him.

"Thank you," she murmured, adjusting her white gloves in an attempt to delay the inevitable.

Lord Hudson extended his arm towards her. "Shall we?"

She reluctantly accepted his arm and said, "I suppose we must."

"It will all work out; you shall see," Hudson encouraged as he led her into the building.

Charlotte glanced over her shoulder to ensure her lady's maid was trailing behind them before asking, "Is that what you would tell your clients?"

Hudson chuckled. "No. I would be much more direct with them."

"And if I was your client, what would you say to me?"

With a side glance at her, he said, "I would tell you to keep your head up, face expressionless, and to handle the reading of the will with decorum, regardless of what is written."

"Is that so?"

He nodded, his expression solemn. "You are the daughter of an earl, and you need to conduct yourself with the grace befitting your station."

"So, no yelling?" she joked. "Cursing, perhaps?"

"None." Hudson stopped them in front of a closed door. "Do you have any additional questions for me?"

She shook her head, causing the curls framing her face to swish back and forth.

He placed his hand on the handle and said, "Smile, Lady Charlotte. You are not facing the executioner today."

A small laugh escaped her lips, and her gloved hand came up to cover her mouth. "That was not the least bit funny, Lord Hudson."

"Wasn't it?" he asked, opening the door and stepping to the side to allow her to enter first.

As she stepped inside the small room, she noticed another door leading to an adjoining office. The door opened, and a short, red-headed man stepped into the room. He closed the door behind him and said, "You must be Lady Charlotte."

She tipped her head graciously. "I am."

"Enchanted," he remarked. "My name is Mr. Henry Stanton, and I was the solicitor for your father, the late Lord Huntley."

"It is a pleasure to meet you, Mr. Stanton."

A slight frown marred his features as he said, "I was horrified when Mrs. Jordan informed me about highwaymen attacking your coach, and I was immensely relieved to hear that you came out unscathed."

Charlotte found herself relaxing in the solicitor's presence. "It was a taxing experience."

"I have no doubt," Mr. Stanton replied. "What good fortune that Lord Hudson was at the coaching inn and was able to escort you the rest of the way to London."

"I agree."

Mr. Stanton's eyes shifted towards Lord Hudson. "It is a pleasure to see you again, Lord Hudson. Do you intend to join us for the meeting?"

"I do. Lady Charlotte is a dear friend of my family, and I have come to ensure that she is properly represented," Hudson explained.

"You are more than welcome," Mr. Stanton encouraged,

placing his hand on the door handle. "Everyone else has assembled in the room. Would you care to join them?"

"I would," she replied, keeping her head held high.

Mr. Stanton opened the door and held out his hand. "After you, Lady Charlotte."

Charlotte walked into the room, and she saw her stepmother, the Countess of Huntley, already seated next to the window, with her twelve-year-old daughter, Lady Rebecca, sitting in the chair next to her. Both were dressed in black silk gowns, and a black hat sat slightly askew on her stepmother's head.

A rather handsome gentleman stood across from her stepmother. He had a wide forehead, straight nose, and strong jaw lines. He wore a black armband around his right sleeve, black gloves, and a black cravat.

Her beautiful, petite, blonde stepmother acknowledged her with a forced smile. "Charlotte. It is good to see you looking so well."

"Thank you, stepmother," she replied, her voice clipped.

She watched as Lady Huntley's eyes perused the length of her gown, the disapproval evident on her features.

"May I ask why you are not mourning your father?" Lady Huntley asked.

Smoothing out her white gown, Charlotte replied, "I'm afraid I don't have any black gowns at my disposal."

Lady Huntley's face softened, and the frown lines lessened around her eyes and mouth. "Then we must procure you some, and quickly."

"I would appreciate that," she said.

To her delight, Rebecca kept her hand low to her side as she waved at her.

Charlotte genuinely smiled at her sister. "Good morning, Lady Rebecca."

Rather than respond right away, Rebecca glanced over at her

mother, as if seeking permission to speak. Her mother nodded her head, granting permission.

Rebecca spoke up in a soft voice. "Good morning, Lady Charlotte."

Mr. Stanton walked into the room, closing the door behind him, and headed towards his desk. "Why doesn't everyone take a seat? We have much to discuss."

Charlotte sat in a chair next to the back wall and was pleased when Lord Hudson claimed the one next to her.

Mr. Stanton gestured towards them. "Allow me to introduce you to Lord Hudson. He is a district judge and was gracious enough to escort Lady Charlotte this morning."

"Should I have brought my solicitor?" Lady Huntley asked.

Mr. Stanton shook his head as he sat down in his chair. "That is not necessary," he replied. "The purpose of the meeting is to read the late Lord Huntley's will and to honor his last wishes."

The handsome gentleman spoke up. "I have already read it since his will was on file at the local parish."

"Do you disagree with anything in it?" Mr. Stanton asked.

A slight frown marred the gentleman's features. "I do, but I do not contest its validity."

"That is good," Mr. Stanton acknowledged. "Because it would benefit no party if the will were to be contested."

Mr. Stanton reached for a file on his desk and brought it in front of him before turning his attention towards her. "I did fail to introduce you to Mr. Duncan Puttock, the Earl of Huntley. He is a distant cousin of yours."

Lord Huntley shifted in his chair to face her. "It is a pleasure to meet you, Lady Charlotte."

"Likewise, Lord Huntley."

A slow grin came to his face. "I'm afraid being called by my new title still seems a little surreal to me."

Mr. Stanton opened the file and removed a piece of paper. "The late Lord Huntley was insistent that you all be present when the will was read," he said as he reached into his pocket and pulled out a pair of rounded spectacles.

After placing the spectacles on his face, Mr. Stanton asked, "Are there any questions before I begin?"

No one spoke up, and Mr. Stanton nodded in approval.

He cleared his throat before he started reading, "I, Charles Taylour, the eleventh Earl of Huntley, being of sound and disposing mind, and free from fraud, duress, menace or undue influence, do hereby make, declare, and publish this, my Last Will and Testament."

Mr. Stanton glanced up from the paper and turned his attention towards Lady Huntley. "To my wife, Lydian Taylour, the Countess of Huntley, I leave £30,000, and Duxford House, the dowager house that sits on the grounds of our country estate, Braysdown Hall, in Blackpool, for the duration of her life. Furthermore, she is entitled to a monthly allowance of £30 from my estate."

Her stepmother let out a sigh of relief as she relaxed back in her chair. "Thank heavens," she breathed.

Mr. Stanton shifted his gaze towards Charlotte. "To my eldest daughter, Lady Charlotte Taylour," he paused, "I leave £100,000, Chatsmoor Hall, and the hunting lodge in Aboyne, Scotland."

Charlotte gasped, and her hand flew up to cover her mouth. Was this truly happening? Not only had her father left provisions for her, but she was now an heiress. A very wealthy heiress.

Mr. Stanton placed the will on the table and reached for an envelope in the file. "Your father was adamant that I give you this letter," he said, rising. "He wrote it himself right after he took ill."

Lady Huntley straightened in her chair and looked curiously at the solicitor. "Did my husband write me or Lady Rebecca a letter, as well?"

Mr. Stanton winced uncomfortably. "I regret to inform you that he did not."

"I see," Lady Huntley murmured, her eyes turning downcast.

Extending the letter over his desk, Mr. Stanton said, "I believe this letter will answer the questions you most likely have."

Charlotte leaned forward in her chair and collected the letter. Rather than read it, she tucked it into her reticule.

Mr. Stanton sat back down and picked up the will. He continued reading. "To my youngest daughter, Lady Rebecca Taylour, I have set aside an account with the amount of £20,000 to be accessed only as her dowry."

Lady Huntley leaned over and patted her daughter on the knee.

Mr. Stanton continued. "Lastly, all the rest, residue, and remainder of my estate, real, personal, or mixed, I give, devise, and bequeath to my heir, Mr. Duncan Puttock, the twelfth Earl of Huntley."

Once Mr. Stanton finished speaking, he placed the paper back down on the file. A long, uncomfortable silence filled the room with unanswered questions hanging between them.

"Does anyone have any questions for me?" the solicitor asked, breaking the silence.

Everyone remained quiet, retreating into their own thoughts.

The solicitor closed the file, intertwined his fingers, and rested them on the desk. "I know this is a difficult time for all of you, and I would like to help you in any way that I can."

No one spoke up, so Mr. Stanton said, "Lord Huntley's dying wish was for his family to become united. He expressed a desire for his daughters to reside in the same house."

Lady Huntley glanced over at her before she averted her gaze. "I am not opposed to Lady Charlotte living with us," she remarked in an unconvincing, uninviting tone. "After all, we are family."

"Thank you for the offer," Charlotte remarked, "but I am

currently residing with my dear friend, Lady Isabella, and her family."

Lord Huntley cleared his throat, drawing everyone's attention. "If I may," he started, "I suggest we all reside together at our London townhouse, at least for the time being. If we don't, it might create a scandal amongst the *ton*."

Charlotte reluctantly admitted to herself that he had a point, but she wasn't ready to concede her position yet.

As she opened her mouth to decline, Hudson spoke up. "May I converse with Lady Charlotte for a moment, privately?"

Mr. Stanton nodded his approval.

Hudson rose and went to open the door. As she gracefully rose from her chair, she felt all eyes on her. After she stepped into the adjoining room, Hudson closed the door behind him. He stepped closer to her and kept his voice low.

"Lord Huntley is right," he said. "You need to go live with your stepmother."

Her lips parted in surprise. She hadn't expected that. "I shall do no such thing," she asserted in a hushed tone.

"If you don't, it could cause a scandal."

"Then so be it," she said, jutting out her chin.

His face was expressionless, but his tone softened. "I am unsure of what caused the rift between you and your stepmother, but she is your family. That must mean something to you."

"I hardly know her," she admitted.

"More reason to spend time with her," he pressed.

Charlotte's eyes darted towards the closed door. "She doesn't want me to live with her. It would be awful."

"But what of Lady Rebecca? Wouldn't you like to spend quality time with your half-sister?"

"I would."

Hudson took another step closer, and she tilted her head to look up at him.

"Then go live with Lady Huntley, at least for the time being.

If you find yourself miserable, then you can return to our town-house with no regrets."

"Perhaps you are right."

A boyish grin came to his face. "You will find that I am right the majority of the time."

"My, you are rather arrogant," she teased.

"It isn't being arrogant when it is the truth," he countered.

Charlotte found herself enjoying their closeness, and she wondered if Hudson felt the same way. They stared at each other for a long moment, and neither one of them said a word.

The door to the adjoining office opened, and Mr. Stanton stuck his head into the room. "Is everything all right?"

In a quick motion, Hudson immediately created more distance between them. "We are almost done," he said in a gruff tone.

Mr. Stanton nodded his understanding and closed the door, leaving them alone once more.

"So, we are in agreement, then?" he asked. "You will go live with your stepmother?"

She drew her lips into a thin line. "I still contend that this is a horrible idea."

"You must trust me."

The fight drained out of her, and she found herself admitting, "I do trust you."

A strange look came to his face, and she could only describe it as relief. "I am pleased to hear you say so."

"All right," she said. "Let me go inform my stepmother of my decision."

Without saying another word, Hudson opened the door. Charlotte stepped into the room and met her stepmother's gaze.

"After discussing it with Lord Hudson, I have decided it would be for the best if I came to live with you."

Lady Huntley stared blankly back at her. "How delightful," came her dry response.

"That is wonderful news," Lord Huntley said, clasping his hands together.

Charlotte turned back towards Hudson, and he gave her an encouraging smile. She couldn't help but wonder what she had just gotten herself into.

❧ 6 ❧

"I AM NOT ENTIRELY SURE WHY YOU WERE INSISTENT ON bringing your own lady's maid with you," her stepmother chided as they rode in the coach.

Charlotte kept her chin up and back straight as she replied, "Ellen was gracious enough to stay on as my lady's maid."

"But we have plenty of servants who could have acted as your lady's maid."

"I have no doubt, but I feel more comfortable having Ellen with me," she pressed.

Lady Huntley huffed. "You are stubborn, just like your father was."

Unsure of how to respond to that snide remark, Charlotte chose to remain silent, and turned her attention towards the window.

Rebecca spoke up, drawing back her attention. "Do you like to read, Charlotte?"

"I do, very much so," she replied. "Do you like to read?"

With an enthusiastic nod, Rebecca shared, "My mother says I can read any book in our library."

"Is that so?" she asked, surprised.

"But I am not allowed to discuss poetry, logic, physics, or mathematics, not even to my governess."

Charlotte smiled. "Basically, you are supposed to avoid any topic that is even the least bit interesting."

Her sister giggled. "Yes, that is correct."

"If your mother is not opposed," Charlotte said, leaning forward in her seat, "perhaps we can discuss those books together."

Rebecca's mouth dropped open, and she rushed to ask, "May we, Mother?"

Lady Huntley waved her hand dismissively while saying, "You may, as long as you are in the privacy of our own home. It isn't appropriate for a lady to be discussing such things."

"Oh, thank you!" Rebecca gushed.

"But only after your lessons and practicing the pianoforte," Lady Huntley added.

"Yes, Mother."

Lady Huntley's lips were set in disapproval. "I will never understand the infatuation with reading such subjects. It is more important for a lady to be accomplished at the art of polite conversation."

"I must contend that being well-read enhances our ability for intelligent conversation," Charlotte argued.

"And I maintain that it causes unnecessary thinking," Lady Huntley insisted.

The coach came to a stop outside of an enormous three-level townhouse. The red-brick exterior had a large pedimented portico above the main door.

"Father lived here?" Charlotte asked in awe.

"He did," Lady Huntley replied, scanning the townhouse with pride. "He spent years renovating Wellesley House, but he was never quite happy with it." Her voice grew reflective. "I just wish that he had been happy with what he had."

The door to the coach was opened, and Lord Huntley greeted them.

"Ladies, may I assist you out of the coach?" he asked with a smile on his face.

"You may," Lady Huntley replied, accepting his proffered hand.

After she stepped onto the ground, Lord Huntley withdrew his hand and reached back into the coach to assist Rebecca.

Before he had a chance to assist her, Charlotte stepped out of the coach and paused on the step, staring up at Wellesley House.

"It is magnificent, isn't it?" Lord Huntley asked, extending his hand towards her.

She slipped her hand into his. "It truly is."

"It seems like a dream that this is all mine," Lord Huntley acknowledged. "I keep waiting to wake up and have this all taken from me."

"I assure you that you are awake," she said, stepping onto the gravel courtyard.

"That is a relief." Lord Huntley took her hand and placed it in the crook of his arm. "Would you like a tour of the townhouse, Lady Charlotte?"

"I would," she replied eagerly.

The main door opened, and the butler stepped to the side, allowing them entry. The man had dark hair slicked down, combed to the side, and thick bushy eyebrows that met in the middle.

"Baxter," Lord Huntley said as he handed off his hat and gloves, "allow me to introduce you to Lady Charlotte Taylour, the eldest daughter of the late Lord Huntley."

The butler bowed. "Lady Charlotte. It is a pleasure to meet you."

She tipped her head graciously.

"Lady Charlotte will be staying with us while she is in

London," Lord Huntley informed the butler. "Please ready a bedchamber for her and send footmen over to the Marquess of Northampton's townhouse to retrieve her trunks."

"As you wish, milord," Baxter said before departing from the room.

Charlotte's eyes scanned the impressive two-story entry foyer. The domed ceiling had gold embellishments spread throughout, the papered walls were ivory, and columns were spaced evenly throughout the first floor. A deep red carpet ran down the length of the entry and up the stairs to the next level.

Lady Huntley removed the black hat from her head and placed it on a table. As she smoothed back her blonde-hair, she remarked, "I shall send word to our dressmaker that we are in dire need of a fitting. With any luck, she will be able to come tomorrow."

Turning her attention towards Rebecca, her mother ordered, "Go up to the nursery and work on your lessons."

"Yes, Mother," Rebecca murmured as she headed towards a staircase with iron railings.

Lady Huntley watched her daughter walk up the stairs before acknowledging, "That child will do practically anything to get out of doing her lessons."

"I was the same way," Lord Huntley said. "My brother and I used to go to great lengths to hide from our tutors."

Charlotte hid her smile. "I would do the same, except I had to resort to climbing out of the window of our nursery."

"What level was the nursery on?" Lord Huntley asked.

"The second level."

Lord Huntley's brow lifted. "That is quite a feat for a young lady, especially if you were wearing a dress."

"It got easier over time," she admitted. "My grandfather would get so angry with me, but I couldn't stand Mrs. Proctor. She used to hit my hands with a switch when I got an answer wrong, and she was constantly chiding me for the silliest infractions."

Lord Huntley bobbed his head. "I would have hidden from your governess, as well. She sounds awful."

"She was," Charlotte replied. "I was relieved when I was sent off to boarding school. Miss Bell did not believe in corporal punishment."

Lady Huntley interjected, "I intend to send Rebecca to Miss Bell's Finishing School next year. It is a fine institution."

"I would agree," Charlotte said. "Besides taking the required courses to become an accomplished lady, I also formed deep, long-lasting friendships with many of my classmates."

Lady Huntley appeared unimpressed by her admission. "I care more about Rebecca preparing to enter Society by receiving a proper education than making friends."

"There is no harm in doing both," Charlotte argued.

"Rebecca's only aspiration is to marry well, so her education must make her noticeable to potential suitors, setting her apart from the other young women," Lady Huntley commented.

"She is only twelve," Charlotte said. "She needs to be free to make her own choices so she can grow into a woman of worth."

Lady Huntley frowned. "I'm afraid you won't understand my reasonings until you have children of your own."

Lord Huntley clasped his hands together. "I am quite eager to show Lady Charlotte the sitting room. Shall we?"

"I'm afraid I am developing a headache, and I need to lie down for a spell," Lady Huntley said, bringing her hand up to her right temple. "Would it be a bother if you give Charlotte a tour without me?"

"Not at all," Lord Huntley replied. "It would be my honor."

As she watched her stepmother walk away, Lord Huntley muttered, "I was worried you two might resort to blows."

Charlotte laughed at the unexpected remark. "It wasn't that heated."

"Wasn't it?" Lord Huntley asked before he started walking across the entry foyer. "I'm afraid my tour will be rather boring since I have only been residing at Wellesley House for a few weeks now."

"Surely, it can't be that bad."

Lord Huntley stopped outside of an open door. "This is the drawing room. It has yellow papered walls, elegant soft furnishings, exquisitely carved furniture, and Brussel weave carpets."

Charlotte stepped inside the drawing room, and her eyes landed on a harp. "How fortunate for me that Lady Huntley has a harp."

"I assume you can play, then?"

She nodded. "I find that I prefer it to the pianoforte."

"I shall look forward to hearing you play tonight after dinner," he said, stepping back. "Now on to the sitting room."

They walked a short distance and entered a rectangular room with red papered walls, rich drapes hanging over the large bay windows, and ornate chandeliers hanging from the painted ceiling. Velvet settees were strategically placed around the room.

"This is lovely," Charlotte gushed. "There is so much natural light."

"I thought you might enjoy this room," he said. "More often than not, I find myself reading a good book down here."

Charlotte nodded approvingly. "I can see why."

"The late Lord Huntley… er… your father," Lord Huntley corrected, "had just finished renovating this room when he fell ill."

Hesitantly, she asked, "Were you with my father when he died?"

"I was," he replied. "I was summoned to Wellesley House when he had first taken ill. Your father felt it was time that he started preparing me to take his place." He grew silent for a moment. "However, neither one of us suspected how little time he had left on this earth."

"How long did you spend with him?"

"A little over two weeks," he answered. "At first, he appeared to be on the mend, but then he took a turn for the worse."

"How awful."

With compassion in his voice, he said, "You should know that he spoke fondly of you."

Charlotte tensed. "I don't believe that."

"It is true," he replied. "He had been looking forward to giving you a Season."

Lord Huntley's admission caused some tears to form in her eyes. Traitorous tears. She blinked them back furiously, refusing to let them fall. She could not cry for her father. No, she most assuredly would not. Besides, acknowledging those tears would mean that for the first time since she heard the news of her father's death, she would have to admit that she mourned his loss.

Lord Huntley's voice interrupted her musings. "Would you care to see the ballroom?"

"I would," she responded, grateful for the change of topic.

***

"I can't believe you let Charlotte leave with her stepmother... willingly!" Isabella shouted, tossing up her hands.

Hudson sighed as he gripped the back of an upholstered armchair. "As I have been trying to tell you, it was for the best—"

Isabella cut him off. "For the best?" she asked. "For all we know, Charlotte's stepmother could have stripped her of her fine gowns, forced her to wear rags, and is making her clean their townhouse."

"Why would she do that?" he questioned in disbelief.

"It could happen," she replied. "Her sister might even be calling her 'Ashfool' at this very moment."

Hudson gave her a perplexed look. "Her half-sister, Lady Rebecca, is only twelve years old. She is not a miscreant."

Isabella started pacing in the drawing room. "Poor Charlotte might be crying for help, but no one is there to help her. Not even a white bird."

"White bird?" he asked. "What would a white bird be able to do?"

"Every time Charlotte tells the bird her wishes, it will give her what she has wished for," Isabella explained.

"What nonsense are you spouting, sister?"

Isabella stopped pacing and met his gaze. "I take it that you haven't read the story of '*Cinderella*' by the Grimm Brothers."

"The fairy tale?"

She nodded, crossing her arms over her chest.

Hudson cast an impatient look at the ceiling before saying, "Rest assured that Lady Huntley is not an evil stepmother, and Lady Rebecca is not a cruel and wicked half-sister."

"How do you know?"

"I've met them."

Isabella uncrossed her arms. "You only met them briefly. They could have hidden their true nature from you."

"This is utter rubbish. I am an excellent judge of character," he declared. "Furthermore, Lady Charlotte is an heiress. Her stepmother would never force her to act the part of a maid."

"What if she locked her away in a tower?"

Hudson suppressed his annoyance. "I can assure you that there is no tower at Wellesley House."

Isabella gasped. "What if Charlotte's evil stepmother casts her out and summons a huntsman to kill her?"

"Enough!" he declared. "I am concerned that you have been reading far too many fairytales."

His mother spoke up from the sofa, directing her comments

towards Isabella. "If it would ease your mind, we could call upon Charlotte tomorrow."

"What if Lady Huntley threatened to hurt her if she reveals to us that she is in danger?" Isabella asked.

Hudson groaned, pushing off from the back of the chair. "I'm beginning to think that you have a skewed sense of reality."

Isabella sat down next to their mother. "I don't like Charlotte being with her stepmother. She was adamant that her stepmother hated her."

"I would never have advised her to leave with Lady Huntley if I thought she was in danger," he said.

"Why would you even suggest such a thing?" Isabella asked.

"You must think of the scandal that would ensue if Lady Charlotte was residing with us and not with her family during their time of mourning."

"True, but I don't like it," Isabella huffed. "Until I am sure that Lottie is all right, I am going to be worried sick about her."

Hudson came around the chair and sat down. "If you would like, I would be happy to call upon Lady Charlotte on my way to my apartment."

"Would you?" Isabella asked.

"I would be honored to."

Isabella heaved a sigh of relief. "And if she is in danger…"

Hudson spoke over her. "I will remove her at once," he assured her.

"Thank you," Isabella said, smiling. "I must admit that I would sleep a lot easier knowing Lottie was safe."

He rose, tugging down on his ivory colored waistcoat. "It would be best if you stop reading folk tales. In your case, I might even recommend books on philosophy."

"How scandalous of you, brother," she remarked, feigning outrage. "A lady should never read such topics. It might hurt our heads by causing us to think."

Lady Northampton shook her head good-naturedly. "Heavy subjects, such as philosophy or logic, might help your sense of reality."

The floor clock chimed, alerting Hudson of the time.

"I'm afraid I must depart," he said.

His mother rose from the sofa. "I had hoped that you would stay for dinner."

"That is impossible, I'm afraid," he replied. "I have files that I must review before I retire for the evening, and it could take nearly an hour to get home, depending on how many coaches are on the streets."

"Why do you insist on renting an apartment at Albany when you have a perfectly good bedchamber upstairs?" Lady Northampton asked.

Hudson stepped closer and kissed his mother's cheek. "I enjoy living on Piccadilly Street. It is closer to my work, clubs, and the shops of St. James."

"At least say goodbye to your brother before you leave," his mother requested.

He glanced over at the open door. "Is he in his study?"

"He is," she confirmed.

"All right, I will."

Isabella interjected, "Don't forget to call on Lottie."

"I won't," he replied before he exited the drawing room.

Hudson walked towards the back of the townhouse, where Everett's study was tucked into the corner. He heard male voices drifting out of the open door. Immediately, he recognized the voice of his friend, Nicholas, the Duke of Blackbourne. He glanced into the room and saw they were sitting on the sofa, their backs facing him.

He knocked at the door, and his brother and the duke turned towards the doorway.

"Hudson," Everett greeted, rising. "Do come in."

"I hope I'm not intruding," he said, walking further into the room.

The duke rose. "Nonsense. It has been far too long since I have seen you."

"I believe the last time we saw each other was during Dudley's wedding luncheon, which was only a few weeks ago," Hudson pointed out.

"Can I offer you something to drink?" Everett asked as he stepped towards the drink tray.

Hudson shook his head. "No, thank you. I need a clear head."

Everett took the stopper out of the decanter as he inquired, "More work this evening?"

"I always have work piling up."

"My wife insisted that I hire a man of business to handle the more tedious aspects of my affairs," the broad-shoulder duke said, coming to stand next to him. "It has freed up my time immensely, which has allowed me to spend more time with Penelope."

"I'm afraid I can't just hand off my work," Hudson admitted. "How is Penelope feeling?"

"She is doing well, despite being heavy with child," Nicholas replied.

Everett walked over and extended a glass to Nicholas. "Do you miss working as a barrister?"

"At times," Hudson said honestly. "But, as you both know, my dream is to one day become a High Court Judge."

Nicholas took a sip of his drink. "Would you like me to speak to Baron Eldon, the Lord Chancellor, about you?"

"Absolutely not," Hudson declared. "I will succeed on my own merit, or not at all."

Nicholas exchanged a look with Everett, then looked back at Hudson. "I understand that Isabella's friend, Lady Charlotte, thwarted a robbery by highwaymen."

"That is right."

"She sounds like a formidable woman," Nicholas commented.

"She is," he confirmed.

Nicholas swirled the drink in his hand, appearing to consider his next words carefully. "Have you considered the possibility of courting her?"

Hudson's brow shot up in surprise. "I have not. Why would you even suggest such a thing?"

"I was merely curious," Nicholas commented with a shrug of his shoulder.

"Lady Charlotte and I are friends, nothing more," he stated firmly.

Nicholas took a sip of his drink. "My apologies," he responded, lowering the glass. "I just imagine a young woman like her doesn't come along very often."

"That is a true statement," he agreed. "She is remarkable."

"But you aren't interested in courting her?" Everett pressed.

Hudson shook his head. "No. I don't have time to court anyone."

"Then make the time," Nicholas asserted.

Wanting to be finished with this ridiculous conversation, Hudson put his hands up. "I'm afraid I must depart. Isabella requested that I call on Lady Charlotte to ensure she is not being forced to clean the townhouse."

"I'm afraid I don't understand," Everett said, looking puzzled. "Why would Charlotte be forced to clean her townhouse?"

"She wouldn't," he stated. "But our dear sister has been reading too many fairy tales. She is worried that Lady Huntley is an evil stepmother who is plotting Charlotte's demise."

Everett humphed. "I have seen her reading that Grimm Brothers book on many occasions. It seems to be filling her head with nonsense."

"That it is," Hudson replied, walking towards the door. "Now if you will excuse me."

Both men raised their glasses towards him before he departed from the room. As he walked across the entry hall, he let out a slight chuckle. Court Charlotte? What a silly notion. But the more he dwelled on the idea, the less ridiculous it seemed.

7

CHARLOTTE SAT ON HER BED, HOLDING THE NOTE FROM HER father. She couldn't seem to bring herself to open it. A part of her wanted to read it, but the other part wanted to defy him. Still, she felt curious about its contents. What had been so important to him that he had spent some of his final moments writing to her?

Did she dare open it?

Perhaps he apologized for his years of neglect towards her, she thought. After all, he had left her £100,000. She was an heiress now. She could live a life of extravagance and still never want for money. Her father had left her financially secure for the rest of her days.

After an appropriate time of mourning, she would join the other members of Society. She would have her pick of suitors, but she wouldn't be required to marry for convenience. She could marry for love. What a wonderful feeling to know she wouldn't have to settle for anything less than true love.

A knock came at the door.

"Enter," she ordered.

It opened, and Ellen entered. "The mean, scary butler has informed me that Lord Hudson is here to see you, milady."

"Lord Hudson?" she asked, glancing over at the window. The sun was setting, casting orange and red rays of light across the night sky. "It is rather late to be receiving callers, is it not?"

"It is," Ellen agreed. "Would you like me to inform him you are unavailable for callers?"

She shook her head. "That is not necessary. Will you inform him that I will be down in a moment?"

"Yes, milady," Ellen said. "After you meet with Lord Hudson, shall I dress you for dinner?"

"That seems like a fine idea."

"Thank you," Ellen replied, dropping into a curtsy.

As her lady's maid turned to leave, Charlotte asked, "Out of curiosity, why did you refer to Baxter as a 'mean, scary butler'?"

Ellen took a step closer to the bed and lowered her voice. "He seems so stiff, and I can feel his brown eyes watching me."

"He does have a rather piercing stare, doesn't he?"

"That he does, milady," her lady's maid agreed.

After Ellen departed, Charlotte rose from her bed and stepped over to the dressing table. She placed the letter down and took a moment to smooth out her hair. When she was satisfied with her reflection in the mirror, Charlotte headed downstairs, stopping outside of the drawing room door. She glanced inside and saw Lord Hudson standing next to the mantle, looking handsome in his brown riding jacket, buff trousers, and black, polished Hessian boots.

"Lord Hudson," she greeted, stepping into the room. "What a pleasure to see you again today."

He bowed. "Thank you for agreeing to see me despite the late hour, Lady Charlotte. But I came on Isabella's insistence."

"Is that so?"

Lord Hudson took a step closer to her. "Isabella was worried that Lady Huntley would cast you out of the townhouse and send a huntsman after you."

Realization dawned, and a smile came to her face. "I see

Isabella has been reading '*Snow White*' again."

He nodded. "She was also worried that you would be cleaning the townhouse, and Lady Rebecca would be calling you 'Ashfool'."

"Ah," Charlotte said, amused. " '*Cinderella*' is one of her favorite fairy tales."

"Isabella may have an overactive imagination, but her concern comes from a good heart."

"I agree."

Hudson glanced towards the open door. "I was also supposed to ask if you are being held here against your will." His face was expressionless, but she detected a twinkle in his eye.

"I assure you that I am here of my own free will and choice," she replied. "Although, I would be having much more fun with Isabella."

"Is that so?"

Charlotte lowered her voice as she admitted, "Wellesley House is like a museum. It took nearly two hours for Lord Huntley just to give me a tour of the townhouse, and it is eerily quiet."

"Is that a bad thing?"

She shrugged one shoulder. "Perhaps I am just used to Miss Bell's Finishing School. Girls were always chatting away, and there was never a dull moment."

"I can only imagine." Lord Hudson pointed towards the velvet burgundy sofa. "Would you care to have a seat?"

"I would."

Charlotte walked further into the room and took a seat on the sofa.

"Has Lady Huntley been unkind to you in any way?" Lord Hudson asked, coming to sit across from her.

"No, she has not," Charlotte answered, "but she retired to her room shortly after we arrived, feigning a headache."

"I see."

Leaning forward, she admitted, "To be honest, I am dreading dinner."

"Why?"

"I imagine the conversation between Lady Huntley and myself will be awkward."

"But not with Lord Huntley?"

Charlotte shook her head. "I find him pleasant enough to be around." She paused as she thought of a brilliant idea. "Why don't you stay for dinner?"

"I'm afraid I must decline," he replied. "I have files that I need to review before I retire for the evening."

"Anything exciting?" she asked.

A line between his brow appeared. "The opposite, in fact. I have a case dealing with infanticide."

She gasped. "How awful!"

"It is," he replied. "Sadly, this is not the first case of infanticide that I have had tried in front of me. These poor women that give birth in secret, often in the privy, usually end up delivering the baby directly into the pit, where it is likely to die. If the child is not lost this way, then the filthy conditions, combined with the mother's lack of experience, leads to the almost inevitable death of the child."

"Those poor children."

"You must understand that these unmarried women are dealing with extreme difficulties just to survive. They can't possibly care for an infant, too."

"But to kill one's own baby?" she breathed.

"I agree," he said solemnly. "Fortunately, this particular young woman had asked her sister to borrow baby linens."

"What does that prove?"

Hudson gave her an understanding smile. "One of the most important factors that would lead to an acquittal is if the mother prepared normally for the birth, that is, she behaved as if expecting to care for a baby."

"That does make logical sense," she murmured.

Hudson grew silent as he shifted his gaze towards the mantle. "As a judge, I must be fair and impartial, but sometimes the cases tried in front of me cause me to question humanity." He sighed. "It can be rather taxing on one's soul."

"I can only imagine how hard that is for you."

"But I must not complain," he stated, his voice devoid of emotion. "I have been most fortunate to become a district judge at such a young age."

Charlotte felt compassion towards him. "It is all right to speak about one's emotions," she insisted. "Didn't you once tell me 'never to apologize for showing emotions'?"

"I did," he replied.

"Besides, we are friends, so we are allowed to speak openly to one another," she insisted. "Frankly, I would prefer it."

"As would I." Hudson's face eased into a relaxed smile. "Now, on to a more pressing subject," he said. "How does it feel to be an heiress?"

She returned his smile. "It feels wonderful."

"Your father must have had some affection towards you to leave you such a large inheritance," Hudson commented.

"I suppose so."

He watched her for a moment before asking, "Have you had a chance to read your father's letter?"

Charlotte lowered her gaze to her lap. "Not yet."

"May I ask why?"

"I'm afraid of what the letter might contain."

"In what way?"

She slowly brought her gaze back up. "For so many years, I have held hatred in my heart for my father, but what if the note changes everything? What if he apologizes for his ill treatment of me, and I am forced to recognize that I have been wrong about him this entire time?"

To her surprise, Hudson rose from his seat and came to sit

next to her.

"There is no good that comes from hating another," he expressed, his eyes full of kindness.

"But my father neglected me for years," she responded, her voice rising. "Am I supposed to just ignore that fact because he left me a large inheritance?"

"No, but you must learn to forgive and let go of your hatred for him," he insisted. "Don't let him have that control over you."

She pressed her lips together. "I am not ready to read the note just yet."

"Then don't," he replied. "Only read it when you are ready."

"And if I'm never ready?"

Hudson's lips curled into a crooked smile. "I have no doubt that you will be ready soon enough."

"Why would you say that?"

Leaning closer, he whispered, "Because you are the strongest woman that I know. You fought off highwaymen and saved the lives of your traveling party."

"That was easy compared to reading the note," she said, finding herself distracted by the curve of his lips and the tiny lines on the sides of his mouth.

Hudson didn't speak for a moment, remaining close.

"Now that you are an heiress," he remarked as his eyes roamed over her features, "you will need to be mindful of fortune hunters and rakes."

"I am aware of that," she replied. "I intend to marry only for love."

"Good, as well you should," he stated approvingly, "but I must caution you that some men are wolves in sheep's clothing."

Distracted by his nearness, Charlotte only managed to say, "Is that so?"

"Which is why, if you are not opposed, after you have completed your mourning period," he paused, "I would be happy to help you in your search for an appropriate suitor."

Fearing she misheard him, Charlotte leaned back and asked, "Pardon?"

"The *ton* is full of fickle people, and I want to ensure you marry a gentleman who is worthy of your affections."

Charlotte dropped her mouth open in surprise but quickly closed it. "You want to help me find a suitor?"

He nodded, looking unsure of himself. "I thought I had made myself clear."

"Why?"

"Because I care for you," he hesitated before adding, "as a friend, and I want you to be happy."

"Thank you," she muttered, furrowing her brows. "That is most thoughtful of you."

"You are welcome," he replied, rising. "Now I'm afraid I must depart."

Charlotte rose slowly. "Thank you for calling on me, Lord Hudson."

"As usual, I have thoroughly enjoyed our time together," he remarked stiffly. "If it is permissible, I would like to call on you again in a few days."

She tipped her head graciously. "I shall look forward to it."

"Excellent."

As Charlotte watched Lord Hudson leave the drawing room, she couldn't believe what had just transpired. Why would he want to help her search for a suitor? One thing was evident, though. Lord Hudson did not harbor any feelings for her, and she would be mindful not to develop any deep, lasting feelings for him. It would just end in heartache for her.

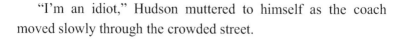

"I'm an idiot," Hudson muttered to himself as the coach moved slowly through the crowded street.

What had he been thinking, offering to find Charlotte a suitor? No. He hadn't been. Not only was she a beautiful young woman, but she was an heiress. He had no doubt that men would flock to her, begging her to accept their courtships. But he didn't want her to marry someone that was beneath her, someone who didn't deserve her.

No. Charlotte deserved a man who would love her above all else and would treat her with the kindness she deserved.

So why did the thought of her being courted by another man cause his blood to boil? It wasn't as if he could be that man. He didn't have time for a wife, especially now. His responsibilities as a judge were too great to even consider the thought of courting a woman.

It must be that he just wanted to see Charlotte happy and settled. Yes. That had to be it.

The coach jerked to a stop outside of his fashionable Albany apartment. The door to the coach was opened by a footman, and he placed his brown satchel over his shoulder before exiting.

"Good evening, Lord Hudson," a guard said as he opened the black, ornate gate that kept Albany secure.

He tipped his head towards him as he passed through the gate. The main brick building was set back from the street, and two parallel buildings framed Albany's courtyard.

Hudson crossed the cobblestones and approached the main building. He hurried up the steps and opened the dark blue door. He walked down the narrow passageway and stopped in front of his apartment. He was about to reach for the door when it opened.

"Good evening, milord," his butler said, stepping to the side. "I saw you walking through the courtyard."

He stepped into the small entry hall. "Good evening, Ford." He removed his gloves and extended them towards him. "Will you inform Mrs. Sykes that I am in need of supper this evening?"

"As you wish," Ford replied, closing the door. "Would you care for something to drink while Mrs. Sykes prepares your food?"

He shook his head. "That won't be necessary. I shall be in my office."

Hudson crossed the entry hall and headed towards a room in front of the unit. In his study, he had a mahogany desk that sat in front of a large window, yellow papered walls, and a black mantle over the fireplace.

He sat at his desk and removed the files from his satchel, placing them on the desk. He opened the first file and started reading. He became so engrossed in his reading that his mind barely registered a knock at the door.

"I recognize that look," a familiar male voice commented wryly.

Hudson glanced up from his reading and saw his dark-haired friend, Lord Ewin Colborne, leaning up against the doorframe.

"What look?" he replied.

Ewin pushed off from the doorway. "The look that informs me that you won't be joining me at White's tonight."

"I'm busy."

"You are always busy."

Hudson closed the file and leaned back in his chair. "If that is the case, then why do you keep pestering me to come along?"

Ewin walked further into the room and sat down in the chair in front of his desk. "I guess I'm an optimist," he replied, grinning. "My intent is to wear you down."

"That won't happen."

"I can be very persuasive."

Hudson gave him an impatient look. "I am exceptionally busy," he asserted. "Is there something else I can help you with?"

Ewin reached up and adjusted his white cravat. "Do you remember when we were at Oxford together?" he asked, changing the subject.

"I do."

"You used to be such fun then," Ewin said. "We would go to balls, attend the theatre, and go riding in Hyde Park nearly every day."

"I remember."

"Then you got engaged, but that still didn't diminish our fun," Ewin shared. "It only stopped after Hannah broke your engagement and married Lord Skeffington."

Hudson's jaw clenched. "Do you have a point here?"

"It is time for you to start having fun again."

"I do have fun," he contended. "I work."

"Gentlemen do not work," Ewin reminded him. "It is unbecoming of you to even say such a thing."

Hudson leaned forward in his chair. "I disagree. The mark of a gentleman is his ability to work."

A smile came to Ewin's face. "We shall have to agree to disagree, my friend."

"We always do," Hudson responded. "Pray tell, how exactly do you spend your days?"

"I am the second son of the Duke of Glossner," Ewin remarked, putting his hands up in the air. "I have the luxury of spending my days doing whatever I please, whenever I please."

"That seems like a rather sad existence."

"Again, I disagree," Ewin said. "Besides, it irks my father greatly knowing I am not under his thumb anymore. I would rather chew glass than reside with him at Stanwich House."

Hudson lifted his brow. "That seems rather extreme."

"Not extreme enough, if you ask me."

"Eventually, you will need to settle the rift between you and your father," Hudson advised.

"I daresay that is not likely to happen in this lifetime or the next," Ewin replied with a shake of his head.

"How is your mother handling the estrangement?"

Ewin grew silent. "I don't know, but I can't go back there. I won't be forced into an arranged marriage."

"I do not fault you for that."

"I know, and I am grateful. You are one of the few friends who have supported my decision." Rising, Ewin walked over to the window and peered out. "I saw her, you know."

"Who?"

"Hannah," Ewin paused, "or should I say Lady Skeffington. I ran into her at Lady Snowley's soirée."

Hudson stilled. "Why should I care?"

"Because Hannah is out of mourning," Ewin said, turning to face him. "You should know that she asked about you."

"I care not," he answered curtly.

"Don't you?"

Hudson ran a hand through his hair as he felt the familiar anger rage inside of him. "Hannah made her choice when she broke off our engagement."

"True, but I contend she made a mistake marrying Lord Skeffington."

"No, she knew exactly what she was doing," Hudson declared. "She only cared about becoming a duchess."

"Well, she failed on that account," Ewin said. "Lord Skeffington died when he was hit by a carriage outside of White's. Apparently, he was so inebriated that he started walking down the street, skirting the oncoming carriages."

"Lord Skeffington was a bloody fool," he grumbled.

"I won't disagree with you there." Ewin turned and leaned back against the windowsill. "Where have you been these past few days?"

"I went to escort my sister home from Miss Bell's Finishing School in Bath," he informed his friend. "I ended up escorting her friend back to London, as well."

Ewin eyed him suspiciously. "How did you get tricked into that?"

"I wasn't tricked into anything," he said. "I volunteered."

"What was your sister's friend's name?"

"Lady Charlotte Taylour."

Ewin's brows shot up in surprise. "The heiress?"

Hudson frowned. "I forgot how quickly news travels amongst the *ton*."

"Can I meet her?"

"No."

"No?" Ewin repeated incredulously. "Why not?"

"She is in mourning," he replied.

Ewin crossed his arms over his wide chest. "True, but there would be no harm if you went to call on her, and I came along."

"Absolutely not."

"May I ask why?"

Hudson narrowed his eyes at his friend. "Just leave it, Ewin."

A slow, knowing smile came to his friend's face. "You fancy her, don't you?"

"That is not it at all," he contended. "We are just friends."

"Then why can't I meet her?"

"Because she is too good for the likes of you."

"But not you?"

"I never said that."

"But you implied it."

Hudson turned back toward his desk and opened his file. "Enough. I need to get back to work. I assume you can see yourself out."

Ewin straightened from the windowsill. "There is no harm in moving on, Hudson. If anyone deserves to be happy, you do."

Hudson remained silent as he watched his friend cross the room.

Stopping next to the door, Ewin said, "Don't wait too long to make your move, or it could be too late."

After his friend had departed, Hudson returned straightaway to his reading. He had work to do, and he didn't have time to dwell on feelings and whatnot.

8

DRESSED IN HER DARK GREY RIDING HABIT, CHARLOTTE gracefully walked down the stairs of Wellesley House, her hand trailing along the iron banister.

Once she stepped onto the last step, the butler appeared from a side door and approached her with a stern expression. "Good morning, Lady Charlotte."

Her steps faltered. "Good morning, Baxter."

"How may I assist you today?" he asked, his piercing brown eyes watching her.

She gave him a nervous smile. "I would like to go riding this morning."

"I shall inform the head groom at once."

"That won't be necessary," she replied. "I am more than happy to walk to the stables and request that a horse be saddled."

"That is not necessary, milady," he insisted. "May I recommend that you eat breakfast while you wait for the grooms to saddle a horse for you?"

Realizing that she was fighting a losing battle, Charlotte nodded her agreement. "I think that would be for the best."

Baxter smiled at her, but it appeared forced and unnatural. "Shall I show you the dining room?"

"Yes, please."

She trailed behind the butler as they walked towards the rear of the townhouse. He stopped at the open door and gestured that she should go first.

As she stepped into the small, square room with gold colored papered walls, Lord Huntley rose from the head of the table.

"Lady Charlotte." Lord Huntley bowed. "Forgive me for starting without you, but I had wrongly assumed you would have had a tray brought up to your room."

"I have taken no offense, my lord."

"How gracious of you." Lord Huntley held out a chair for her. "Allow me to assist you."

"Thank you," she murmured as she sat down.

Lord Huntley returned to his seat, held his right hand up, and snapped his fingers. "Bring a plate for Lady Charlotte at once," he ordered.

A moment later, Baxter placed a plate of eggs and toast in front of her. "Your breakfast, milady."

Charlotte reached for her white linen napkin and placed it on her lap. "I must admit that I don't normally eat such a large breakfast."

"No?" Lord Huntley asked.

"I generally eat a piece of toast before my morning ride," she shared as a footman filled her cup with tea.

"I hadn't taken you for an early riser."

She reached for her teacup, and as she brought it to her lips, she confessed, "Mornings are my favorite time to go riding."

"Why is that?"

"It is a wonderful feeling to breathe in the fresh morning air, to hear the birds sing, and watch a new day unfold in front of me. It is a gentle reminder that I am free to choose my own destiny."

"Is that so?"

She returned the cup to its saucer. "Every day, we are faced with many choices, and we must decide who it is that we want to be."

"And who do you want to be, Lady Charlotte?"

"I'm not entirely sure right now, but I know I want to bestow kindness to all that I meet."

"That is an admirable trait to have."

Charlotte waved her hand dismissively. "My headmistress at Miss Bell's Finishing School would tell us 'a strong woman always strays on the side of kindness'."

Lord Huntley wiped the sides of his mouth with a napkin. "That is sound advice."

"I thought so, as well."

Baxter walked up to Lord Huntley and extended him a newspaper. "This just arrived, milord."

"Thank you," Lord Huntley responded, placing it on the table. "I shall read it later. I would much rather converse with Lady Charlotte." He smiled.

Charlotte found herself returning his smile. "That is kind of you to say."

"It is true," Lord Huntley remarked. "Ever since I arrived at Wellesley House, I have eaten breakfast alone. Your stepmother requests a tray to be delivered to her room, and Rebecca eats in the nursery. I'm afraid Lydian and I only come together for dinner."

"That sounds rather lonely."

"Frankly, it has been," he replied. "I have felt overwhelmed since inheriting the title of Earl of Huntley. I've spent the majority of my time in my study with my man of business. If I have to look at one more ledger, I might literally go mad. It would be nice to speak to someone else about other subjects for a change."

"What a hardship you must endure, my lord," she mocked.

He chuckled. "I see that you are not sympathetic towards my plight."

"I am not," she replied, reaching for her fork. "We each have been far too blessed to complain."

"May I ask you a personal question?" Lord Huntley asked as he reached for his teacup.

She tsked. "But we hardly know one another. It is quite unbecoming to delve into personal questions so soon."

"That is true, but I find myself curious about something."

Putting her fork down, she shifted in her chair to face him. "It sounds serious."

Lord Huntley took a sip of his drink and returned it to its saucer. "You can refuse to answer if you would prefer."

"Now you have piqued my interest."

With a glance over his shoulder at the liveried footman standing watch at the door, Lord Huntley lowered his voice and asked, "May I ask what caused your estrangement with Lydian?"

"An estrangement implies that my stepmother and I were at one point on friendly terms."

"And you were not?"

Charlotte shook her head. "I hardly know her."

"Why is that?"

"Growing up, I lived with my grandparents because my father did not want me," she confessed, glancing down at the table.

"I can't imagine that to be the case."

"It is true," she shared. "He banished me the moment I was born, and only invited me to Braysdown Hall for occasional holidays. I have only met my stepmother and half-sister a handful of times."

"That is awful," he murmured. "I can't imagine a father treating his daughter with such cavalier regard, especially since he left you a fortune in his will."

"That has been perplexing to me, as well," she admitted.

A flicker of concern briefly wrinkled his smooth brow. "I cannot seem to reconcile the difference between the man I thought I knew and the man who treated his daughter so insufferably."

"I do not wish to sully your memory of my father," she shared. "That is not fair of me."

"That is most gracious."

Deciding their conversation had turned much too serious, she intended to change the subject.

"What was your childhood like?" she asked.

"It was vastly different than yours."

"In what way?"

Lord Huntley grew reflective. "My older brother, Henry, and I were as thick as thieves," he started. "Not only were we best friends, but we were also each other's greatest rivals. We competed at everything. How quickly we could run down the stairs, how fast we could swim across the pond, or how quickly we could race up a tree. It didn't matter what it was, we always made it a competition, much to the dismay of our parents."

He smiled wistfully as he continued. "My parents doted on us something fierce, but we weren't raised in extravagance. My father owned a small country estate in Plymouth, and we employed only a handful of servants. From a young age, I was aware that Henry was Lord Huntley's heir presumptive, but it never came between us. In fact, your father paid for Henry's and my schooling at Eton, then later at Cambridge. It was only because of his kindness that I received such a rigorous education."

"I had no idea that my father could be so..." Her voice trailed off as she tried to find the right word.

"Generous," he said, finishing her thought.

She nodded.

"Not only did he educate me, but it was because of your father that I was able to obtain employment as a stockbroker," he shared. "He vouched for me when I went to apply for work at Harold & Stanch."

"That is a prestigious company."

"It is," he replied, "which is why I will forever be in your father's debt, and I intend to ensure you will never want for anything."

"That is kind of you to say."

"There is nothing kind about it," he said. "I honor my debts."

Baxter walked into the room and bowed. "Excuse me for interrupting, but I wanted to inform Lady Charlotte that a horse has been saddled and is waiting out front."

"Thank you, Baxter," she replied, rising from her chair.

Lord Huntley stood and placed his napkin on the table. "Would it be permissible for me to join you on your ride?"

"You are more than welcome, Lord Huntley."

He stepped closer to her and grinned. "Don't you think it is rather silly that we are still making use of our titles, and yet we are residing in the same townhouse?"

"Possibly."

"I would like for you to call me Duncan."

"Then, you must call me Charlotte."

Reaching down, Duncan retrieved her ungloved right hand and gently brought it up to his lips. "Thank you, Charlotte."

She could feel him smile as he kissed her skin.

When he released her hand, he turned towards Baxter and ordered, "Ensure that my horse is readied, and have it brought out front."

"Yes, milord," Baxter replied, spinning on his heel to do his bidding.

Duncan turned back towards her. "I know the perfect place to run our horses. It is on the edge of Hyde Park, near the Cumberland Gate."

"Sounds wonderful," she said. "I have never been to Hyde Park before."

"Then you are in for a treat, my lady."

As they raced their horses through Hyde Park, Charlotte had a bright smile on her face. Small tendrils had escaped her neatly coiffed hair, and they were blowing haphazardly in the wind. It felt good to be riding again, even if it was a horse that she was unfamiliar with. The way the wind brushed against her face, the feel of the powerful horse beneath her, and the rhythmic beating of the hooves on the fresh dirt below were all things that brought back wonderful memories to her.

Duncan slowed his horse's gait and shouted, "We should let the horses rest at this stream."

She followed Duncan's lead towards a charming small stream and watched as he effortlessly dismounted. After he secured his horse, he walked back over to her and reached up to place his hands on her waist. She put her own hands on his shoulders, allowing him to assist her in dismounting.

Once her feet were on solid ground, Duncan removed his hands and stepped back, wincing.

"Are you all right?" she questioned.

"I am," he said, bringing his hand up to his left shoulder. "It is an old injury that keeps flaring up. It goes back to my boxing days."

"You were a boxer?"

He smiled. "Hardly. But my brother and I would spend hours on our lawn, sparring with each other. We even received lessons by 'Gentleman' John Jackson during the Season."

"What fun."

Duncan's smile turned reflective. "I haven't boxed since my brother died, though."

"I have heard of women taking boxing lessons in the privacy

of their homes," she said. "Do you suppose I could take lessons?"

He nodded. "I believe that is a splendid idea. The practice of boxing is an excellent exercise for young women, and it will keep you nimble and healthy," he stated. "I shall inquire about a teacher for you."

"Thank you."

After she led her horse to drink, she held the reins loosely in her hands and admired the beautiful tree cover of Hyde Park.

"It is lovely here," she commented.

Duncan's eyes scanned the trees. "It is."

"Do you ride here often?"

He nodded. "Nearly every day since I inherited Wellesley House."

"I can understand why," she stated. "It feels as if we are the only two people here in Hyde Park."

"That is why I prefer riding in the morning and not during the fashionable hour." He placed a hand on his horse's neck as he continued. "I find that I do some of my best thinking when I'm riding."

"Is that so?"

He grew solemn. "When I inherited the earldom, I was given a great responsibility, and I'm humbled to know that my decisions now will effect generations to come."

"That must be a surreal realization."

"It is, I can assure you."

Charlotte gave him an encouraging smile. "You will succeed if you always choose kindness."

"I wish it was that simple."

"It can be."

He grinned. "Your naiveté is endearing, Charlotte." His smile dimmed as he shifted his gaze away from her. "I was never supposed to become the Earl of Huntley. This was all supposed to belong to my brother, but he died a little over a year ago."

"May I ask how he died?"

A pained look came to Duncan's face. "I am worried that you will perceive me differently after I tell you."

"Why would you believe that?"

"Because it was my fault that Henry died," he revealed softly.

Hearing the anguish in his voice caused Charlotte to pause. "That cannot possibly be true."

"I assure you that it is," Duncan sighed. "We had been fighting over a woman, and he had stormed out of our ancestral estate. It was pouring outside, but he still went and saddled his horse. He had galloped out to the furthest reaches of the estate when his gelding threw him. The doctor said the fall didn't kill him, but being out in the elements for hours before we found him did. The fever went to his lungs, and he died."

"How awful," she murmured. "Your poor brother."

"We had come home for the holiday and had attended a country dance the night before. We each had taken a fancy towards Miss Juliet, but Henry had been adamant that he was going to marry her," he shared. "I told him it was just a passing whim, and Henry grew angry."

Duncan hung his head. "I knew that my brother had a nasty temper. Why did I provoke him that evening?"

"You couldn't have possibly known that your brother would be thrown by his horse," she said with compassion in her voice.

"No, but I should have gone after him right away," he argued, his voice rising. "I should have, but I let my own foolish pride get in the way. I let my brother down."

Charlotte took a step closer to him. "Sometimes horrible accidents happen, Duncan, and there is nothing that we can do to prevent them."

His eyes were moist with tears. "I miss my brother," he said, his voice hitching. "I miss him every single day."

Reaching out, she placed a hand on the sleeve of his black riding jacket. "You did nothing wrong."

"Then why do I feel as if I have?"

"I believe it is normal to feel guilt when someone passes so suddenly, especially given the circumstances," she said. "But you tried to save your brother. Didn't you search for him, despite the rain?"

"I did."

"Then you did all you could have," she asserted. "Your brother wouldn't want you to harbor these feelings of guilt. He would want you to be happy."

"Do you truly believe so?" he asked.

"I know so."

He gave her a knowing look. "I must pose the same question. Wouldn't your father want you to be happy?"

She grew rigid as she removed her hand from his sleeve. "It is entirely different. My father and I were never close like you and Henry were."

"But that doesn't mean he wouldn't want you to be happy," he pressed. "After all, he did leave you £100,000."

"Money isn't the source of happiness."

"No, but it helps when you are not in need of it."

She nodded. "I agree. The greatest advantage to having my inheritance is now that I can marry for love."

Duncan laughed loudly, much to her astonishment. "I had not taken you for someone who believes in fairy tales."

"Falling in love is not just in fairy tales," she said. "I have known many people who have fallen deeply in love."

"May I ask who?"

"The Duke and Duchess of Blackbourne and the Marquess and Marchioness of Lansdowne."

"That is rare in Society," he replied. "Most people are just hopeful to find a spouse that they can tolerate for the remainder of their days."

"That is a sad way to live."

"No, that is a realistic way to live," he insisted. "It is nigh impossible to find one person to fall in love with, much less be faithful to."

Charlotte stepped back and placed a hand on her horse's neck.

"To you, it may seem unattainable, but I believe it is entirely possible, and I refuse to marry for anything less."

A silence descended over them before Duncan spoke up.

"Forgive me, Charlotte. I had no right to question what you believe. It was inconsiderate of me."

She heard the sincerity in his voice, causing her to relax her stance. "You are forgiven."

"I'm afraid I have never witnessed a happy union," he admitted. "My own parents had a marriage of convenience, and they could barely tolerate being in the same room with each other. The only thing that they could agree on was how much they loved their children."

"My grandparents loved each other very much until the day they died," she revealed. "My grandmother shared that they had eloped because her father was against the marriage. They raced towards Gretna Green, knowing her father was close behind. By the time her father caught up with them, they were married, and he was forced to acknowledge that it was legal and lawful."

"How romantic," he said.

"I thought so, as well," she replied. "My grandparents died only a few weeks apart. I was away at finishing school when I heard the news."

"I am sorry for your losses."

Charlotte turned towards her horse as she blinked back her tears. "That was the only time that I received a letter from my father. It was on black-trimmed stationery, and I was certain that I could see tear stains on the paper," she shared. "I still have the note."

"Did you keep the note because of the contents or because it was from your father?" Duncan prodded gently.

"A little of both, I suppose," she admitted.

"At least you have something from your father," Duncan professed. "I would give anything to have something written from my brother." He paused. "I am saddened by the fact that I can't even remember the sound of his voice anymore."

"I am grateful for my dreams," Charlotte said, turning back around to face Duncan. "If I am lucky, I see my grandparents there, and I wake up with a smile on my face, knowing that I saw them again, even if it was for only the briefest of moments."

"I hadn't considered that."

Charlotte adjusted the reins in her hands. "I don't pretend to understand dreams, though, because in my last dream I was being chased by a biscuit."

Duncan's brow rose. "A biscuit?"

"It was a large biscuit," she defended, smiling.

"My apologies," he replied, chuckling. "I'm afraid I have never been chased by a large biscuit in my dreams."

"Then you are missing out, my lord," she teased.

"That I am."

In the tree overhead, a dove cooed and there was a mixture of chirping voices in the morning air.

Charlotte raised her head to look at all the birds nesting in the trees. "Growing up, I had a pair of grey turtle doves that lived outside of my window. They would wake me up nearly every morning with their constant cooing."

"That sounds dreadful."

"I felt the same way, at first. But then my grandfather told me that turtle doves mate for life," she responded. "He explained that a male turtle dove courts a female by flying to her noisily, while making a distinct whistling sound with his wings. He then puffs out his chest, bobs his head, and calls to her."

"Is that how you wish to be courted, then?" Duncan joked.

"No," she replied, laughing, "but I do like what comes next."

"Which is?"

"She's smitten for life." She smiled. "After that, I didn't mind hearing the doves coo outside my window. I found it rather endearing."

"Frankly, I would have shot the turtle doves," Duncan remarked, his lips twitching.

"Most people would have, but not I," she stated. "It was a constant reminder of what I want most out of life," she hesitated only a moment before revealing, "to be loved completely."

Duncan's eyes roamed her face as he said, "You deserve to be loved in such a fashion."

"Not just me, but everyone does."

With a shake of his head, he replied, "No, that is not true."

"Why not?"

"Some of us don't deserve a happy ending."

Charlotte's heart ached at the sadness in his voice. "And why is that?"

"Because we're attempting to atone for past transgressions," he admitted softly.

Taking a step closer to him, she asserted, "You deserve to be happy, Duncan."

He swallowed slowly as he shifted his gaze away from her. "I think it might be best if we head back to Wellesley House."

"I suppose we must."

After Duncan assisted her back onto her horse, Charlotte couldn't help but notice the change in his disposition. He became aloof, clearly attempting to mask his sadness.

Poor Duncan.

She would find a way to help him feel joy again. She was sure of it.

9

CHARLOTTE REINED IN HER HORSE IN FRONT OF WELLESLEY House and slid off in a smooth motion. Then, she extended the reins to a waiting footman.

"I'm impressed that you can dismount so proficiently on your own," Duncan commented as he came to stand next to her.

"It is a habit that I picked up at Miss Bell's Finishing School," she admitted.

"I'm afraid to ask about what other habits you learned while at finishing school," Duncan said, offering his arm.

"I learned how to climb trees," she revealed.

"Why would you care to climb trees?" he asked as he led her up the steps towards the ebony main door.

She shrugged one shoulder. "Because it was fun."

"Weren't you afraid of breaking your lovely neck?"

"No," she responded with a smug smile. "My friend was a remarkable teacher."

"May I ask who your friend was?"

"The Marchioness of Lansdowne."

Duncan looked baffled. "Now I can't tell if you are serious or just toying with me."

Charlotte laughed. "I can assure you that it is all true."

"Silly me," he remarked. "I was under the impression that finishing school taught young ladies the usual subjects, French, history, needlework, music, and dancing."

"Don't forget arithmetic, mythology, and geography," she listed, "and yes, we learned all those subjects, plus a few additional ones."

The door opened, and the butler stood to the side to grant them entry.

"How was your ride, milord?"

"It went well," Duncan replied, stopping to address Baxter. "Has Mr. Weber arrived yet?"

Baxter nodded. "Yes. He is in your study."

"Very good," Duncan replied. "We shall be going over ledgers, and I do not wish to be disturbed."

The butler tipped his head. "Understood."

She had just removed her hand from his arm when she heard her name being shouted across the entry hall.

"Charlotte," her stepmother declared, her voice echoing off the domed ceiling as she crossed the hall. "Thank heavens you have finally returned. The dressmaker has been waiting in the sitting room for nearly half an hour."

Her stepmother stopped in front of her with disapproval on her features. "Did you go riding?"

Duncan spoke up. "We did, Lydian."

"That was a foolish thing to do," Lydian admonished, turning her heated gaze towards Lord Huntley. "What if someone saw Lady Charlotte? You must think of her reputation, Lord Huntley."

"I assure you that Lady Charlotte went undetected," Duncan answered firmly. "Her reputation is unscathed."

"Well, I should hope so," her stepmother asserted as she reached for her arm. "Come, we mustn't make the dressmaker wait any longer."

"I hadn't realized that she would be coming so early," Charlotte commented as she allowed her stepmother to lead her towards the sitting room.

"Neither had I, but she had a cancellation, and she was nice enough to fit us into her schedule," Lydian said. "Marie Leighton dresses only the most fashionable members of the *ton*. Not only has she created many gowns for me, but she has just come from a fitting with the Duchess of Blackbourne."

Charlotte's steps faltered. "Penelope?"

Lydian looked at her in surprise. "Are you familiar with the Duchess of Blackbourne?"

"I am," she replied proudly. "She is one of my dearest friends from school. Do you suppose I could call on her?"

Lydian shook her head. "You are in deep mourning. It is not appropriate for you to call on anyone, much less be in public."

"May I at least write Penelope a note and inform her that I am residing in London?"

"That would be acceptable, but you must not get your hopes up. The Duchess of Blackbourne is a very important woman, and I have been told that she rarely makes house calls," her stepmother replied. "Besides, you knew her before she became a duchess; before she had an air of arrogance about her."

"Arrogance?" Charlotte questioned. "Penelope is anything but arrogant."

Lydian appeared unconvinced. "It has been my experience that people change when they receive a title, and it would be my recommendation that you keep her at arm's length."

"I'm afraid I must disagree with you," Charlotte replied. "Penelope couldn't possibly have changed that much."

"Then why don't you write her a letter, and I will ensure that it is put in the post," Lydian said before she stepped into the sitting room.

"I believe I shall."

As Charlotte stepped into the room, she saw a tall, thin

woman with fading brown hair standing next to the table. She was dressed in an ornate pink gown with white lace along the neckline. In her hand was a wooden tape measure spool holder.

"I assume this is Lady Charlotte?" the dressmaker asked with a thick French accent.

Lydian nodded. "Yes, Marie."

The dressmaker waved her hand towards the door. "Close the door, if you will. We have a lot of work to do in a short period of time."

Her stepmother closed the door as she muttered, "Stop standing there like a statue. You must get closer to Marie if you wish for her to take your measurements."

Charlotte closed the distance between her and the dressmaker, stopping in front of her.

Marie pressed her lips together, as if she had just tasted something sour.

"I understand that you are in immediate need of some mourning gowns," Marie questioned.

"I am."

"Black or dark brown?"

"Pardon?"

Marie looked at her as if she was a simpleton. "Would you prefer black or dark brown gowns?" she asked slowly.

Lydian spoke up from behind her. "Black," she answered. "Lady Charlotte would prefer black. Brown would look just dreadful on her."

Nodding in approval, Marie said, "There will be no trims or decorations on the gowns, and they will be in crepe." She took a step back. "I shall also make additional gowns for the second half of the mourning period. I believe lavender, trimmed with black, would look splendid on you."

The dressmaker turned her attention towards Lydian. "It would be a rush order, but I shall have a gown for you by tomorrow evening. Unfortunately, I will not be able to create the rest of the gowns for at least a week."

"I understand," Lydian remarked. "However, we will require them before we depart for Blackpool in two weeks' time."

Charlotte frowned at that unexpected news. "Why are we leaving London?"

"Because there is nothing for us here," her stepmother began in a dismissive tone, "at least while we are in mourning. Do not fret. We will be back next Season."

Marie started walking circles around her, her critical eye perusing the length of her. "You are a beautiful young woman; one worthy of wearing my designs. After you are out of mourning, I shall design you gowns that will be the envy of the *ton*."

"Thank yo—"

The dressmaker spoke over her, clapping her hands. "Enough talk. Let us remove your riding habit, and I will begin to take your measurements."

A few moments later, Charlotte was standing only in her shift as Marie measured her.

For most of the fitting, her stepmother kept her back to her, content with staring out of the window at the lovely gardens. The scent of oleander drifted in through the opened windows, causing a wave of pleasant memories. Her grandmother had always tended to her oleander bush with loving care, and she was always rewarded with bright colorful flowers during the summer.

Lydian turned to face her with a solemn expression on her face. "Now you shall be able to mourn your father appropriately. You will be expected to be in deep mourning for at least six months and then you may start wearing your lavender gowns," she said as she sat down on a chair across from her and began fingering the round pendant hanging around her neck. "I have also commissioned a '*Momento Mori*' pendant for you, using some of your father's hair."

"That is most kind of you," Charlotte murmured.

Lydian turned her pendant over and read, " *'Remember that you will die'* ." She dropped the pendant. " *'Momento Mori'* jewelry is to remind us that life is fleeting and one day, we too must die."

Marie stopped taking measurements and nodded. "That is sound counsel."

"I agree," her stepmother replied. "Before Lord Huntley grew ill, I had always thought we would grow old together, but that was not meant to be, despite my best wishes."

"You are much too young to be a widow," Marie commented.

"I am thirty-two," Lydian revealed. "Sadly, I have known much younger widows than me."

Charlotte furrowed her brows as realization dawned on her. "You were only sixteen when you married my father?"

"I was," her stepmother replied, clasping her hands in her lap. "In fact, we married on my sixteenth birthday."

Feeling bold, Charlotte pressed, "Why did you marry at such a young age?"

Lydian gave her a weak smile. "It was an arranged marriage."

"I hadn't realized."

"Your father also felt that I was much too young to be married, so he suggested that we sleep in separate bedchambers until I turned eighteen," her stepmother revealed. "He was always patient with me, never forceful. He was a true gentleman."

Lydian's hand came back up to her pendant, and she clutched it in her hand. "I loved your father desperately," she murmured more to herself than to Charlotte.

Marie stepped back and announced, "I am finished with the measurements. Allow me to assist you in dressing."

After she was dressed and the dressmaker had departed from the sitting room, Charlotte came to sit down next to her stepmother, who was staring blankly out the window.

"I am happy to know that my father and you had a happy union."

Lydian blinked and dropped her hand from her pendant. "I never said we had a happy union," she snapped.

"But you loved my father."

Rising, her stepmother declared, "That doesn't mean that *he* loved me."

Without saying another word, Lydian walked stiffly out of the room.

Charlotte remained seated as she stared at the empty doorway. To her surprise, she felt something akin to compassion towards her stepmother.

Before she could dwell on that too deeply, Baxter appeared at the doorway and announced, "The Countess of Northampton, and her daughter, Lady Isabella, have come to call on you. I have shown them to the drawing room."

Charlotte rose gracefully. "Thank you."

As Charlotte walked through the door of the drawing room, Isabella jumped up from her seat on the sofa and exclaimed, "You are alive!"

A smile came to her face at the relief evident in her friend's voice. "I am."

Her blonde-haired friend quickly approached her. "I was so worried about you."

"I know," she replied. "Hudson informed me that you were concerned that my stepmother might have kicked me out of the townhouse and sent a huntsman after me."

"It could have happened," Isabella defended.

Charlotte embraced her friend. "I have missed you, as well."

After Isabella stepped back, she asked, "Are you ready to come back to our townhouse?"

"Not yet," Charlotte responded. "I have only been here for one day."

"It feels longer," Isabella pouted.

Charlotte laughed. "I must assume that you are bored at your townhouse."

Isabella put her hand up to her mouth and whispered, "My mother won't let me climb trees and refuses to let me ride my horse without an escort."

Mary spoke up from the sofa. "It hasn't been all dreadful," she said. "After all, I did take you shopping yesterday."

"That you did," Isabella replied, "but it would have been much more fun if Charlotte had come along."

"Charlotte shouldn't be in public when she is mourning, my dear," Mary reminded her. "Once she is out of deep mourning, she will be afforded more liberties."

Charlotte interjected, "Lord Huntley and I did go riding this morning through Hyde Park."

Mary frowned. "That was rather an unwise move on Lord Huntley's part. It is entirely appropriate for him to be out in public, but you are supposed to be grieving in private."

"Fortunately, except for your family and Penelope, no one knows me in London," Charlotte commented.

"True, but you must think of your family's reputation," Mary pressed. "If anyone did recognize you, it could cause a scandal. There is nothing more enticing to the *ton* than a scandal."

Charlotte shifted her gaze towards the window. "This is my first time in London," she said. "I had been hoping to tour the city."

"And you shall, during the next Season," Mary replied.

A knock came at the door before a thin servant girl walked into the room, holding a silver tray in her hands. She placed the tray onto the table between the sofas.

"Shall I pour, Lady Charlotte?"

"I can manage. Thank you."

The servant girl curtsied before exiting.

Charlotte came and sat down across from Mary and reached for the teapot. As she poured the tea into the three cups, she revealed, "I was fitted for mourning gowns this morning by Marie Leighton."

Mary nodded in approval. "She is a most sought-after dressmaker. In fact, Marie will be making Isabella's ball-gown, and we have had her appointment scheduled for months."

"My stepmother informed me that Marie had a cancellation in her schedule, which is why she was able to fit us in so quick-ly," Charlotte shared.

"That was most fortunate," Mary stated. "Most fortunate, indeed."

Charlotte extended a teacup to Mary and commented, "She was rather abrupt for being a dressmaker."

Mary laughed as she accepted the teacup. "Marie is not known for her charming personality, but rather for her beautiful creations."

Isabella came to sit down next to her, and Charlotte handed her a cup. "Have you had a chance to call on Penelope yet?"

With a shake of her head, Isabella replied, "Not yet, but I will soon."

"I would love to see her, but my stepmother informed me that I must not call on her."

Mary took a sip of her drink and lowered her cup and saucer to her lap. "That is true. You must be mindful that social activi-ties are curtailed, and you must not entertain beyond simple visits in your home."

"That seems rather ridiculous, considering I hardly knew my father," Charlotte muttered before she took a sip of her tea.

"Mourning, or lack thereof, is a perfect opportunity to get

back at your father by cutting down on the time of deep mourning," Isabella pointed out.

"That is a good point."

Mary shook her head. "I do not recommend that. It is disrespectful to the deceased, and the *ton* might label you as callous or cold-hearted."

Charlotte finished her tea and placed the cup back onto the tray. "How can I mourn a man who treated me so insufferably?"

"I hope you don't mind, but Hudson informed us of your inheritance," Mary said.

"Not at all," she replied. "I am glad that he told you."

"Your father must have held some affection for you since he left you £100,000 and two properties," Mary pointed out.

Charlotte smiled wistfully. "I am pleased that my father willed me Chatsmoor Hall," she stated. "I have only the fondest memories of my grandparent's estate."

Isabella placed her teacup down on the table. "What will you do now?"

"Pardon?"

"Will you retire to Chatsmoor Hall or continue residing with your stepmother?"

Charlotte shrugged one shoulder. "I haven't decided yet. My stepmother just informed me that we are departing for Blackpool in two weeks."

Isabella gasped. "You are leaving London? Why?"

"Because she said that there is nothing for us here while we are in deep mourning."

Mary bobbed her head. "It is very common for people in mourning to retire to their country homes for the Season."

"But I could choose to retire to Chatsmoor Hall instead, assuming there is a household staff," Charlotte mused.

"Or you could come stay with us," Isabella suggested.

"You have been blessed with a remarkable gift, my dear," Mary said, "and that is the gift of choices. You may choose your own path from here on out, and you have the financial freedom to do so."

A clearing of a throat came from the door, and Charlotte turned her head to see Duncan standing in the doorway.

"Please come in, Lord Huntley," she encouraged, rising. "I would like to introduce you to Lady Northampton and her daughter, my dear friend, Lady Isabella, who attended Miss Bell's Finishing School with me."

Duncan stepped further into the room and bowed. "It is a pleasure to meet you both," he said. "I was walking by, and I heard the most enchanting voices drifting out from the drawing room."

He turned his gaze towards Isabella. "Do you by chance climb trees as well, Lady Isabella?"

"Of course, my lord," she replied with a smile.

Lord Huntley chuckled. "I can only imagine the escapades that you and Lady Charlotte participated in while away at finishing school."

Isabella's smile grew playful. "I must admit that we thoroughly enjoyed ourselves."

"Splendid," Lord Huntley responded.

Charlotte spoke up. "Would you care to join us?"

"As enticing as that sounds, I'm afraid I must return to my meeting with my solicitor," he said, "but I thank you for the kind offer."

With a bow, Lord Huntley departed from the room.

Isabella's eyes lingered on the door as she commented, "You failed to mention how handsome Lord Huntley is."

"Is he?" Charlotte asked as she sat back down.

Isabella turned towards her with a knowing look. "Do you not find him attractive?"

Charlotte pressed her lips together, delaying her response. "I'm afraid I haven't noticed," she lied, uncomfortable with this topic of conversation.

"You haven't noticed?" Isabella questioned. "Do you not have eyes?"

Mary leaned forward and placed her teacup onto the tray. "Leave poor Charlotte alone. Besides, it is time for us to depart."

"Must you?" Charlotte asked.

Lady Northampton rose and announced, "We shall come around in two days' time, I promise."

"Please do," Charlotte responded, rising. "I shall be looking forward to it."

Isabella came to stand next to her and embraced her. In a serious tone, she stated, "If you find yourself hunted by a huntsman, then you may come to our townhouse, and I will protect you from your evil stepmother."

Charlotte giggled as she dropped her arms. "My stepmother may hate me, but she is not evil. I am fairly confident that she will not hire a huntsman to kill me."

"Hate is such a strong word, dear," Mary chided. "I can't imagine Lady Huntley dislikes you as much as you claim she does."

"Perhaps, but she is still rather aloof to me."

Mary placed her hand on Charlotte's shoulder. "You must remember that she just lost her husband. She might just be grieving in her own way."

"I hadn't considered that," Charlotte replied.

"Sometimes the greatest gift we can give someone is not to judge them," Mary responded with gentleness in her voice.

Charlotte nodded her understanding. Perhaps she had been in the wrong for judging her stepmother so harshly.

10

HUDSON MUST BE GOING MAD. THAT WAS THE ONLY CONCLUSION he could come to. Why else would he be in a filthy hackney coach on his way to call on Lady Charlotte.

Back at his office at the Old Bailey, he had files stacked high on his desk, enough work to last him for months, but he found that he couldn't concentrate on any of it. His thoughts kept returning to Charlotte. No matter how many times he tried banishing her from his mind, she kept creeping back in, beguiling him.

It must be because he was worried about her. That had to be it. After he confirmed that she was doing well, it would ease his mind, and he could return to his work.

The hackney coach came to a stop in front of Wellesley House, and Hudson waited for the door to be opened. After he stepped down onto the gravel courtyard, he extended a few coins towards the driver.

"Thank you, milord," the driver said, tipping his hat.

Hudson watched as the man climbed back up onto the driver's box before he went and knocked on the door.

The door opened, and the butler greeted him.

"Good afternoon, Lord Hudson," he said. "It is a pleasure to see you again."

Reaching into his green waistcoat pocket, he pulled out his calling card and extended it towards the butler. "Is Lady Charlotte available for callers?"

"She is." The butler stepped to the side, holding his calling card in his hand. "Please come in, and I shall announce you."

Hudson stepped into the entry hall and watched as the butler walked across the tiled floor towards a side room. He disappeared into the room, but quickly reemerged.

"Lady Charlotte will see you now," the butler said, standing next to the open door.

In a few strides, Hudson arrived at the drawing room and stepped inside. His eyes hungrily scanned the room until they landed on her. It shouldn't be possible, but she appeared even more beautiful than she had been the last time he had seen her.

"Lord Hudson," Charlotte said, rising from her upholstered armchair and placing her needlework onto the table next to her. She was dressed in an alluring white gown with a wide yellow ribbon tied around her waist. "What a pleasant surprise."

He bowed politely. "Thank you for agreeing to see me."

"Always," Charlotte replied with a slight curtsy. "I find your company to be most tolerable."

"Only tolerable?" he asked, walking further into the room.

A mischievous smile came to her lips. "I believe I said, 'most tolerable'."

"Ah, my mistake," he replied as he returned her smile. "How are you faring?"

"Very well." She gestured towards an upholstered chair next to her. "Would you care to have a seat?"

Hudson hesitated only for a moment. "I'm afraid I don't have long," he shared. "I have a pile of work that must be completed today."

"Then I am especially grateful that you made time to visit with me," Charlotte said, returning to her chair.

"As am I."

"I have so much to tell you."

He lifted his brow in disbelief. "How can that be? It has only been two days since I have seen you last."

She leaned closer to him and lowered her voice, which he found oddly charming. "For the past two days, Lord Huntley has been kind enough to have taken me riding through Hyde Park."

"He has?" he asked, feeling an unfamiliar feeling welling up inside of him.

Jealousy.

He couldn't possibly be jealous of Lord Huntley. Could he?

She bobbed her head. "We ride out in the early morning so as not to be detected."

"I take it that pleases you."

"It does, most assuredly," she replied. "Although, my step-mother hasn't been pleased, and she has been rather vocal about it."

He smiled at her enthusiasm. "I can only imagine."

"She fears that someone might recognize me and that my reputation will be in tatters."

"But you do not share her same concerns?"

She shook her head. "I do not, since we have not encountered another person on our rides."

"That is good," he said, his hands balled into fists.

Charlotte smiled. "Lord Huntley is also inquiring about hiring a tutor for me so that I may practice boxing."

"Boxing?" he asked, surprised. "Why would you wish to learn how to box?"

She shrugged one shoulder. "Why wouldn't I? Besides, Lord Huntley informed me that it will keep me nimble and healthy."

"I have no doubt that you will thrive in your lessons," he

stated. "However, I fear that Isabella will wish to follow your example."

"Most likely," Charlotte replied, giggling.

He hoped he managed to keep the disapproval out of his voice as he said, "You and Lord Huntley seem to be getting along quite nicely."

"We have been. He has been most kind to me."

He forced a smile to his lips. "I am glad."

Why was he so jealous of Charlotte and Lord Huntley spending time together? It was ludicrous that he was reacting this way.

"Your mother and sister came to visit me yesterday," she shared.

"Did they?"

"Yes, it was right after I was measured for mourning gowns from Marie Leighton," she shared. "I should be receiving my first gown later today."

"Is that so?"

Charlotte leaned back, and a line between her brow appeared. "Is everything all right, Lord Hudson?"

"It is," he answered. "Why do you ask?"

"Because all of your responses have been rather short."

"My apologies," he replied. "I have just been enjoying listening to you."

A faint blush came to her cheeks, but he caught it, nevertheless. "It is kind of you to say so," she murmured.

"There is nothing kind about it," he stated. "It is the truth. You have such an air of happiness about you when you speak freely."

"Is that so?"

He nodded. "Frankly, it is refreshing."

She smiled, her eyes lighting up. "Shall I continue then?"

"By all means," he encouraged, leaning back in his chair.

Charlotte took a breath before sharing, "I have found the

perfect tree to climb in the gardens, but I haven't been able to climb it yet."

"Why not?"

She glanced over at the open door when a maid stepped into the room and positioned herself in the corner. "Because my stepmother is insistent that I take along an escort whenever I step outside."

"Even in your own gardens?"

She nodded. "I fear that she doesn't trust me."

"Why do you suppose that is?"

With a shrug of her shoulder, she replied, "I am not entirely sure. But I don't dare climb a tree while a footman is standing watch."

"You disappoint me." He tsked. "I can't believe you haven't found a way around that."

She glanced over at the maid before lowering her voice. "There is a tree near my bedchamber window, and I am confident that I can climb down it."

"Then you should do it," he challenged.

She grinned. "I believe I will." Her smile dimmed before sharing, "My stepmother wants to adjourn to her dowager house in Blackpool in two weeks' time."

He straightened in his chair, displeased by this unexpected news. "Are you going with her?"

"I haven't decided yet," she replied. "Your mother said it is not uncommon for people in mourning to adjourn to their country estates during their mourning period."

"That is true," he admitted reluctantly.

"Lord Huntley has offered to let me stay here for the remainder of the Season, and then he would escort me back to his country estate in Blackpool."

His jaw clenched. "How kind of him."

"It was, but I wouldn't want to impose," she said. "I have

been debating about adjourning to Chatsmoor Hall in Scarborough, but I fear it might be rather lonely."

"Then don't go," he pressed. "You should go stay with my family."

She shook her head ever so gently. "It would be best if I remained with my stepmother, at least until I am out of mourning."

"So, you have decided to mourn your father after all?" he asked, his eyes searching hers.

"I suppose I don't have much of a choice," she replied. "If I don't, the *ton* could consider me cold and unfeeling."

"Who cares what the *ton* thinks?"

She let out a puff of air. "I believe all of us do, at least a little."

Hudson rose from his chair and walked over to the window. For some reason, the thought of Charlotte leaving London caused him great physical discomfort.

"But my stepmother has informed me that we would return for next Season," she said, her voice trailing off. "I just wish that I could have explored some parts of London before I left."

He turned back around and impulsively asked, "Who says you can't?"

She stared at him, her eyes betraying her uncertainty. "Everyone," she replied. "I can't go out in public while I am in mourning."

"You may not be able to go to the more fashionable places in London, but there are still many other sites you can go visit." He walked closer to her.

Rising, she asked, "Such as?"

"You will need to trust me," he said, his voice low.

Her lips curved into a grin. "I already do."

"Then we are off to a good start." He smiled. "Do you think you can meet me at your back gate tomorrow at two?"

"I will be there."

"Good."

She held his gaze, her expression unreadable even to him, causing him to become more intrigued. So distracted was he by staring deep into her green eyes, that he barely registered the sound of someone clearing their throat.

He glanced over and saw Lord Huntley standing in the doorway. And judging by the frown on his face, it was evident the lord was not pleased to see him.

Lord Huntley tipped his head towards him. "Lord Hudson. It is good to see you again."

"Likewise," he replied.

Lord Huntley stepped further into the room and glanced briefly over at the maid chaperoning in the corner. "What has brought you by today?"

"I came to see how Lady Charlotte was faring."

"Wonderful," Lord Huntley replied tersely, clasping his hands behind his back.

Lady Charlotte smiled, appearing oblivious to the rising tension in the room. "Isn't it though?" she asked, glancing between them.

An uncomfortable silence descended as Lord Huntley's eyes watched him. Deciding the silence had gone on long enough, he announced, "I'm afraid it is time for me to depart."

Charlotte's eyes sought him out. "Do you have to leave so soon?"

"I do," he replied. "But I shall return shortly."

"You promise?"

He smiled at her. "Always."

"Then I shall take you at your word."

"Please do, Lady Charlotte," he said. "Please do."

"You and Lord Hudson appeared rather close in the drawing room yesterday," Duncan commented as he glanced knowingly over the top of his morning newspaper.

Charlotte had just reached for her cup of chocolate when she replied, "I suppose we were. It is always a pleasure to entertain Lord Hudson when he comes to call."

Duncan folded the newspaper and placed it down on the table. "I must caution you to be discreet during this sensitive time."

"Meaning?" she asked before taking a sip of her drink.

With a solemn look, he said, "You are in mourning, and it is not an appropriate time to be carrying on a flirtation…"

She laughed, silencing him. "Is that what you think is going on?"

He nodded.

"We are friends, nothing more," she asserted, hoping she sounded somewhat convincing. She truly hoped she meant more to Hudson, but she didn't dare assume that he held her in high regard. That would most likely be wishful thinking on her part.

Duncan gave her a look that implied he didn't believe her. "Be that as it may be, I daresay that Lord Hudson does not feel the same way."

"I assure you that Lord Hudson is so preoccupied with his work as a district judge that he hardly holds me in such regard," she pressed, returning the cup to the saucer. "His protectiveness is only because I am a family friend."

With a side glance over at the liveried footman stationed near the door, Duncan admonished, "I believe you are naïve in the ways of men, and I urge you to use restraint when dealing with Lord Hudson."

"You need not worry about me." She shifted in her chair to face him and rested her arm on the table. "I am more than capable of taking care of myself."

Duncan leaned forward in his seat and placed his hand over

hers. "It is my privilege to protect you from the harshness of this world. After all, you are only a young woman, in need of a protector."

"I require no such thing."

He encompassed her ungloved hand into his and smiled. "Regardless, as the Earl of Huntley, I am honor bound to care for you. We will forever be connected, you and I."

Glancing down at their entwined hands, she said, "I do not wish to be anyone's burden."

A grin curled across his lips, drawing her attention towards his mouth. "You, my dear, could never be a burden," he remarked smoothly.

A knock came at the door just before Baxter stepped into the room and announced, "Mr. Weber has come to call, milord."

Using the distraction to her advantage, Charlotte quickly slid her hand out of Duncan's and brought it to her lap.

"Show Mr. Weber to my study," Duncan ordered.

"Yes, milord," Baxter said, spinning back on his heel and departing from the room.

Duncan gave her an apologetic smile. "I'm afraid something has come up, and I won't be able to escort you on your morning ride."

Glancing over at the window, she asked, "Would it still be possible for me to go riding, assuming I take along a groom?"

"I can agree to that, but only if you stay on our lands." He paused. "And I want you to take along two grooms."

"I have no doubt it will make my stepmother very happy knowing we didn't visit Hyde Park this morning."

Duncan chuckled. "I have no doubt." He rose and tossed down his napkin onto the table. "I hope to see you at dinner tonight."

"I should hope so," she replied. "You make dinner vastly more enjoyable, especially since my stepmother just uses the opportunity to chastise me during most of the meal."

"That is because you were eating your dessert much too fast last night," he joked. "I, too, was aghast."

Charlotte laughed. "I can't help it. I love rich pound cake."

Duncan's gaze lingered on her face for moment.

"If you need me for any reason," he said, "you shall find me in my study."

"Thank you, Duncan."

She watched as he departed from the room, wondering what had just transpired between them. It almost seemed that Duncan had been showing her favor. Which was ridiculous. Wasn't it?

Her sister appeared at the doorway, dressed in a black gown, and asked in a sheepish voice, "May I join you for breakfast?"

"Of course you may," she said, waving her in. "Please do come in."

A smile came to Rebecca's face as she walked swiftly into the room and approached the buffet table. As she picked up a plate, she shared, "My mother orders a tray to be sent up to the nursery every morning. It is always filled with eggs, rolls and toast, but it never includes bacon."

"I assume you must enjoy bacon, then."

Rebecca glanced over her shoulder as she revealed, "I adore bacon, but mother says eating bacon will make me plump."

"I see," she murmured, eyeing her half-sister's thin frame.

"The only time I get bacon is when I am able to sneak down to the kitchen before my governess catches me."

After Rebecca had filled her plate with bacon, she walked over to the chair next to her and sat down. "I wish I could eat breakfast in the dining room every morning with you and Lord Huntley."

"Why can't you?"

Rebecca placed her napkin on her lap and reached for her fork. "My mother says a young lady always eats her breakfast in the privacy of her chambers."

"Well, I don't."

"I know," Rebecca replied, smiling. "It drives my mother mad."

"That is not my intention."

Rebecca nodded. "I am aware of that, but my mother does not like change. She likes things to be predictable."

Charlotte reached for her cup of chocolate while asking, "Is that so?"

"It is true. She has a very regimented schedule for her and me every day," her half-sister remarked. "Sometimes it is rather exhausting to accomplish all the tasks on her list."

"What is on your list?"

Rebecca held up her fork while sharing, "Not only do I have to complete all my lessons with my governess, but I must practice the pianoforte, harp, dancing, singing, and my needlework. Only then am I allowed to have a riding lesson from the groom."

"That list does sound rather exhausting," she admitted.

"Oh, it is," Rebecca said as she stabbed a piece of round bacon on her plate. "Luckily, my mother hasn't been as demanding since we arrived in London."

"That is most fortunate."

Rebecca bobbed her head in agreement. "It has been," she said. "My mother must love London because she hasn't cried once in her room since we got here."

Placing her cup down, she shifted in her chair to face her half-sister. "Why would she cry in her room?"

Rebecca shrugged her slender shoulders. "I am not sure, but I know she always missed my father dreadfully when he was away on business."

"How often did he travel?"

"All the time. In fact, he was hardly around," Rebecca revealed. "It made my mother sad."

"Did she tell you that?"

Rebecca shook her head. "No, but I could tell," she stated.

"She always tried to hide the fact that she had been crying by telling me that she was just tired. But I always knew."

"Your poor Mother."

"The only time Father came for an extended period of time is when you visited for a holiday."

"It was?"

Rebecca reached for another piece of bacon. "Frankly, it was the only time I saw my father smiling."

"Why was that?"

"I assumed it was because he had missed you," Rebecca remarked innocently.

It was Charlotte's turn to shake her head. "I assure you that Father did not miss me."

"Why not?"

"I know not," she replied. "But he rarely called for me to visit."

Rebecca glanced up at her, her eyes wide with curiosity. "I always thought you didn't want to come to Braysdown Hall because you were having too much fun at Miss Bell's Finishing School."

"No, that wasn't the reason."

Rebecca grew quiet before admitting, "Father always brought me presents when he came home. He would bring me dolls and jewelry, but I didn't want any of those."

"No?"

She shook her head, sadly. "I just wanted Father to love me."

Charlotte's heart ached at the sadness in Rebecca's voice and she attempted, "Perhaps he showed you that he loved you by buying you those lovely things."

Rebecca placed her fork down. "I suppose so."

Reaching out, Charlotte placed her hand on her shoulder, hoping her next words were true. "I cannot presume to know what Father was thinking, but I choose to believe that he must have loved you very much."

"You think so?"

She nodded. "I do."

A bright smile came to the girl's face. "That makes me so happy to hear."

Her stepmother's voice came from the doorway. "There you are, Rebecca," she stated in an irritated voice. "I have been searching for you everywhere."

Rebecca jumped up from her chair. "Sorry, Mother."

"Miss Hawkins has been waiting for you up in the nursery," Lydian informed her. "You best not keep her waiting any longer."

"Yes, Mother," Rebecca muttered as she raced from the room, brushing past her mother.

Lydian stepped into the dining room and glanced down disapprovingly at the bacon left on Rebecca's plate.

"Are you going riding today with Lord Huntley?" she asked, bringing her gaze back up.

"Unfortunately, I will not be," Charlotte replied. "He is busy."

"Good," her stepmother declared. "You have been spending entirely too much time with him."

"Is that a problem?"

Lydian nodded. "It is improper for you to do so."

"Pardon?"

"You both are mourning your father, and this is not an appropriate time for a dalliance," Lydian said.

Charlotte's mouth dropped in surprise, but before she could respond, her stepmother departed from the room without saying another word.

Good heavens! She wasn't having a dalliance with Duncan. They were just friends. How could her stepmother be so cruel as to even suggest such a thing?

11

"Do you think she is coming?" Isabella asked nervously as her eyes remained fixed on the coach's window.

Hudson removed the gold pocket watch from his waistcoat and glanced down at the time. "It is not even two yet. Lady Charlotte will come."

Isabella's eyes grew wide. "What if Lottie's stepmother caught her trying to escape and locked her in the attic?"

He sighed at his sister's theatrics. "First of all, Lady Charlotte is not trying to escape. She is just slipping out undetected for a few hours," he explained. "Secondly, Lady Huntley is not an evil stepmother."

"I'm not truly convinced."

"That doesn't surprise me."

Isabella shifted her gaze towards him. "Do you suppose I should go assist Lottie?"

"Pray tell, what would you do?"

"I could create a diversion."

Hudson grinned. "Such as?"

"I could go to the main door and ask to speak to Lady Huntley," she replied, her brows knitted together in concentration.

"Once I am shown to the drawing room, I will slip out of the window and rush back to the coach. That should buy Lottie enough time to escape out of her bedchamber window."

"That is a horrible plan," he stated. "Furthermore, that might alert Lady Huntley to Lady Charlotte's attempt to leave the townhouse undetected."

She scrunched her nose. "I agree. It is not one of my finest ideas," she admitted. "I am just worried about Lottie."

"Perhaps we should just wait to see if Lady Charlotte appears," he suggested, his eyes scanning the grove of trees along the back gate.

"It was kind of you to take the afternoon off to spend time with me and Lottie," Isabella remarked.

Hudson grimaced at the thought of how much work he had left behind in his office. "It is my pleasure."

"I hope Lottie will like this surprise."

"I have no doubt she will."

Isabella arched an eyebrow. "You seem rather confident."

"I am."

Before she could reply, a lone figure, draped in a maroon colored cloak, emerged from the trees, with a voluminous hood covering the head. The figure turned towards the coach and looked up.

Hudson recognized Lady Charlotte staring back at him.

Isabella breathed a sigh of relief. "Lottie escaped."

Hudson huffed. "You really need to stop reading fairy tales. I fear you are living in a fictitious world."

"And it is a glorious world that I live in," Isabella responded with a laugh.

A footman opened the door and assisted Lady Charlotte into the coach. Once she was situated on the bench next to Isabella, she removed her hood.

"I hope you were not waiting long," Charlotte said.

Isabella shook her head. "Not at all," she replied. "We were just worried you wouldn't be able to escape."

"I engaged my lady's maid to be a part of the ruse," Charlotte shared. "As far as the household is concerned, I am resting this afternoon."

"How were you able to leave the estate undetected?" Isabella asked.

A mischievous smile came to Charlotte's face. "I climbed down a large tree outside my window."

"Ingenious," Isabella murmured as the coach lurched forward.

"I thought so, as well," Charlotte responded. "The branches were perfect for climbing, and I have no doubt that I will be able to return to my bedchamber undetected."

"Do you suppose your stepmother will lock you in the attic if she discovers you've escaped?" Isabella questioned intently.

Charlotte grinned. "No, but she might lecture me on decorum again. Her lectures are rather lengthy and exhausting to listen to."

"That sounds torturous."

"Trust me, it is," Charlotte shared. "She is constantly criticizing me on one thing or another. She finds fault, no matter what I do."

"I'm sorry," Isabella replied. "You are always welcome to reside with me."

"I know, and I thank you for that."

As Hudson listened to them converse, he found himself content just having Charlotte nearby. The thought of his growing list of demands on his time didn't seem as important as it had only moments ago.

"Where are we going?" Charlotte asked, turning her attention towards him.

Hudson smiled. "It is a surprise."

Charlotte lifted her brow. "Will I like this surprise?"

"You will," he replied, "and we are almost there. It isn't too far from your townhouse, actually."

"That is good because I can't stay away too long," Charlotte said. "Eventually, my stepmother will come looking for me. She will probably want to ensure I am practicing my embroidery again."

"I anticipated that, so I planned accordingly."

Isabella spoke up. "But you are already proficient at needlework."

"Apparently, it is not up to my stepmother's standards."

"Well, thank heavens she hasn't seen my embroidery skills," Isabella joked. "She would find me sorely lacking."

The coach stopped, and a footman came to open the door. As he put the step down, he revealed, "I'm afraid we can't go any further, milord. The crowds are too great."

"I understand," Hudson responded as he departed the coach.

Once he stepped onto the cobblestone street, he turned back to assist the ladies. His sister stepped out first, then Lady Charlotte.

His eyes scanned the busy square, and he was pleased to see many booths set up.

"It's a fair!" Charlotte breathed as she stood next to him.

He turned to face her. "It is the Portman Square Fair," he revealed. "Does this please you?"

She smiled, and her whole face lit up. "It pleases me greatly."

"I'm glad."

"I can't believe you remembered," she said.

He nodded. "I remember everything that you have told me."

Why did he just admit that?

A blush came to Charlotte's olive cheeks. "That is kind of you, my lord."

Hudson was looking into her eyes, and they seemed to be

telling him something, if only he could be sure. He thought he detected longing, but that was nearly impossible. Wasn't it?

Charlotte's gaze left his, and he felt the loss of contact immediately. Her eyes started roaming the bustling square. "I wonder how this city fair compares to one in the country."

"Let's go find out," he said, offering his arm.

He started escorting the ladies through the crowd, and they stopped at a booth with puppets entertaining small children.

As they continued walking through the hordes of people, they saw a juggler, a magician, a glass blower, a menagerie, and circus booths.

"I must admit that the exhibits are much more extravagant in the city fairs," Charlotte shared. "I have never seen glass blowing before."

"That was rather remarkable," Isabella replied. "Although, I daresay that I am not interested in walking through the freak show."

"I'd prefer not to see that either," Hudson agreed. "Displaying someone that has a deformity is not my idea of entertainment."

Charlotte tugged on his arm and said excitedly, "I think I see pig running!"

"Pig running?" Isabella questioned. "Why on earth would you care to see that?"

"Have you ever witnessed one before?" Charlotte asked.

Isabella shook her head. "I have not."

"Then you are in for a treat," Charlotte declared, leading them towards a far corner of the fair.

They approached a wooden pen. A man knelt in the center, holding a pink pig with a short tail. Five young men stood around, their bodies alert.

Charlotte stopped at the fence and released Hudson's arm. She turned towards Isabella and explained, "The pig is soaped and greased. Once the pig is let loose, the person who catches and holds it overhead, wins the pig."

"But that pig is fat," Isabella said, pointing at it. "Can anyone lift that one above their head?"

"I have no doubt."

Isabella glanced down at the muddy ground covered lightly with straw. "It is horribly filthy in there."

"That is the fun of it," Charlotte explained. "These poor people are going to get quite dirty as they chase the pig around the pen."

Isabella didn't appear convinced by the frown on her face. "If you say so."

The man in the center released the pig and stepped back. Hudson watched in amazement as these five people chased the pig, falling and slipping in the mud. As much as he enjoyed watching the competitors, it failed in comparison to Charlotte's reactions. She was laughing and cheering them along, and he found himself enamored with her.

Finally, a young man trapped the pig in the corner and was able to pick it up and hold it above his head.

Charlotte's laughter faded, and a wistful look came over her expression.

"What is it?" he asked, stepping closer so he could be heard over the crowd.

She glanced up at him, her eyes moist with tears. "Thank you for this."

The sight of her tears was his undoing.

"Did I do something to upset you?"

She shook her head. "No, quite the opposite, in fact. For a brief moment, I felt as if my grandfather was standing next to me." Her next words were spoken in a hushed tone, almost reverently. "That is the greatest gift anyone could have given me."

"You are welcome."

Charlotte continued to stare up at him, and he was distracted by the intensity in her green eyes. "I don't know what I did to deserve your friendship, but I am glad we are friends."

"As am I," he replied, enjoying her nearness.

Isabella spoke up from behind him, breaking through their private interlude. "My lady's maid is going to be furious with me. My kid boots are coated in mud," she remarked. "I should have worn my Hessian boots."

"Dear heavens," he declared, turning to face his sister. "Whatever shall we do?"

"Well," Isabella started, "it might make me feel better if you purchased a bath bun for me from one of the vendors we saw previously."

"A bath bun will make you happy?"

Isabella nodded. "It will, and Lottie would like one, too."

"Is that so?" he asked, shifting his gaze towards Charlotte.

Charlotte smiled. "I do love bath buns."

"Duly noted," he replied, extending his arms. "Let's go find you both some bath buns, and quickly."

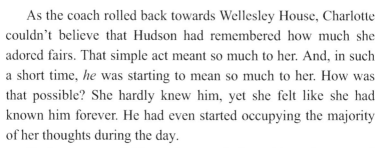

As the coach rolled back towards Wellesley House, Charlotte couldn't believe that Hudson had remembered how much she adored fairs. That simple act meant so much to her. And, in such a short time, *he* was starting to mean so much to her. How was that possible? She hardly knew him, yet she felt like she had known him forever. He had even started occupying the majority of her thoughts during the day.

Hudson removed his pocket watch from his waistcoat and announced, "We have only been gone for a little over three hours. I hope that is all right."

"That will do quite nicely," she said. "Thank you again for this fun adventure."

"You are most kindly welcome." Hudson picked up his black top hat from the bench and started fidgeting with it. "Perhaps," he hesitated, "if you are not opposed, we could go on another adventure in the near future."

She smiled. "That sounds wonderful."

Hudson exhaled a breath. "I shall call upon you tomorrow to discuss it then."

"I shall plan on it."

Isabella spoke up. "What if we took her to the Royal Menagerie?"

"No," Hudson said with a shake of his head. "That is much too crowded. We need to pick another venue."

"What if we took her to the masquerade ball that Lady Thornley is throwing tomorrow night?" Isabella asked.

Charlotte gasped. "I would love that."

Hudson winced. "That might be too risky. If anyone discovered your true identity—"

"No one shall," she said, cutting him off. "I will leave before everyone removes their masks."

"I shall have to think on it," he replied.

Isabella shifted in her seat towards her. "We are going to have such fun!"

"I haven't said yes, yet," Hudson objected, frowning.

"But you will," she replied confidently.

"Why do you say that?" he asked.

Isabella smiled. "Because I can be quite convincing."

"You seem to forget that I used to argue for a living," Hudson replied, appearing unimpressed.

Her smile grew smug. "I argue for fun, and I'm relentless."

"That you are." He chuckled.

The coach came to a stop, and the footman opened the door.

Before she could exit, Hudson stepped out and extended his hand back towards her.

As she slipped her hand into his, he gently encompassed it while he assisted her out of the coach.

When she stepped onto solid ground, she started to remove her hand, but he held firm. He slowly brought it up to his lips and kissed her gloved hand.

Charlotte let out her breath, only then realizing she had been holding it.

"Thank you for such a memorable afternoon," Hudson said with her hand still near his mouth.

She stood there for a moment, unable to formulate a response with him looking at her like that.

"I feel the same way," she finally managed to say.

A boyish grin came to his lips as he released her hand. "That makes me immensely happy, Lady Charlotte."

Isabella's voice came from the coach. "Bye, Lottie."

Charlotte dragged her eyes from Hudson and turned towards her friend. "I hope you have an enjoyable rest of your day."

"Be safe as you climb up the tree," Hudson cautioned, drawing back her gaze.

"You need not fear," she replied. "I am proficient at tree climbing."

Hudson chuckled. "You continually amaze me, Lady Charlotte."

"Thank you, Lord Hudson."

Placing the hood over her head, she departed into the grove of trees and headed towards Wellesley House. Her steps were light and quick as she approached the tree growing outside her window. With expert precision, she started climbing and didn't stop until she reached her window on the second level.

She balanced herself on the wide branch as she grabbed the side of the windowsill. Then, she stepped inside.

Charlotte had just removed her cape when she saw her step-mother sitting in an armchair in the corner.

"Where have you been?" Lydian asked, her voice calm but commanding.

"I... uh..." Her voice trailed off as she glanced back at the window. She had been caught, and she knew that it would be in her best interest if she told the truth. "I went to the Portman Square Fair," she admitted.

Lydian perused the length of her. "Dressed like that?"

She smoothed out her pale-yellow gown with a square neckline. "Yes, stepmother."

"May I ask who you went with?"

She swallowed slowly. "Lady Isabella and Lord Hudson."

"I see," Lydian said. "Thank heavens, you were at least properly chaperoned."

Charlotte remained silent, unsure of what she should say.

Her stepmother rose from the chair, her movements precise. "Did anyone recognize you?"

"I don't believe so."

"That is not good enough," Lydian declared, frowning. "Need I remind you that you are in mourning?"

"I am aware of that fact."

"If anyone recognized you, then your reputation would be in tatters. Do you not care about your reputation, your future?"

"But no one knows me in London," Charlotte protested.

"Your father was the Earl of Huntley," her stepmother stated. "He was a very important man, and unfortunately, he made some enemies during his time in the House of Lords. People who would have no qualms about ruining your future."

"I hadn't considered that."

"I know you haven't," Lydian replied, "but I have."

Charlotte lowered her gaze towards the floor. "I am sorry, stepmother."

"Please do not call me that," she said somewhat forcibly. "I would prefer it if you called me Lydian."

"Yes, Lydian."

Her stepmother walked over to the settee next to the fireplace and placed her hand on the back. "I knew you were up to something when I saw your lady's maid standing guard outside of your bedchamber door."

"Truly?"

Lydian cracked a smile on her solemn face. "Furthermore, I don't recall that you have ever taken a nap. That in and of itself was suspicious."

"Oh," Charlotte replied.

Her stepmother pointed towards the settee. "Come have a seat," she encouraged. "We have much to discuss."

Charlotte reluctantly walked over to the settee, draped her cape over the back, and sat down.

Lydian came to sit down next to her. "How was the fair?"

"It was fun," she admitted.

"I'm glad."

An awkward silence descended over them before her stepmother broke the silence. "I heard what Rebecca told you over breakfast this morning."

"You did?"

Her stepmother nodded. "I know it was rude of me to not make my presence known, but I didn't dare interrupt." She shifted her gaze towards the fireplace. "I hadn't realized Rebecca witnessed me crying in my bedchamber. I thought I had been so careful to safeguard my emotions around her."

"Was my father truly never around?"

Lydian didn't speak for a long moment, her expression unreadable. "Your father was a complex man. He was always good to me, and I dare not complain. I was indeed fortunate." She brought her gaze back to meet Charlotte's. "But your father was determined not to make the same mistakes as his father. So, he devoted his life to managing his estate. With my dowry, he was able to turn a nearly bankrupt estate into quite a profitable one, but it did require almost all of his attention."

Her stepmother's face softened. "You and your father are so much alike."

"I truly doubt that," Charlotte contended.

Lydian gave her an understanding smile. "Your father was brave and undeniably stubborn. I have no doubt that he would have snuck out by way of his window as well, given the chance."

"But you wouldn't have?"

"Heavens, no!" her stepmother declared. "That thought would have never even crossed my mind."

"Why not?"

A pensive look came to her face. "I have always strived to be the obedient daughter and the dutiful wife. I did what was expected of me."

"And now?"

Lydian looked at her in surprise. "What do you mean?"

"You are free to make your own choices now," she replied. "What do *you* wish to do with your life?"

With downcast eyes, her stepmother admitted, "I don't know." She hesitated, then added, "But I believe I'd like to become more like you."

Charlotte reared back. "Like me?"

Lydian met her gaze. "Mr. Stanton told me how you thwarted the highwayman's attack on the way to London. How did you accomplish such a feat?"

"I must admit that I just reacted," Charlotte shared. "I knew I had no choice but to fight back."

Lydian huffed. "I have never fought back. I have always accepted my fate with grace and decorum."

Hearing the resigned tone in her voice, Charlotte found herself asking, "Were you forced to marry my father?"

"I was," her stepmother sighed. "My father woke me up one morning and announced that he had purchased me a title."

Charlotte made no reply, but simply waited in silence for her stepmother to continue.

Lydian's voice grew a little stronger as she went on. "I should have been elated that I was going to be a countess, but I only felt dread," she shared. "I was married three weeks later after the banns were posted. Everything that I had ever known was taken from me, and I moved into Braysdown Hall."

Lydian started wringing her hands in her lap as she continued. "Your father's parents were awful. They constantly reminded me that my father had made his money in trade, and that I was not worthy of their notice."

"That sounds terrible," Charlotte remarked.

"It was," Lydian agreed. "Your father was hardly around, but when he was, we resided in separate bedchambers. It was a great source of contention between him and his parents. Their main concern was that I produce an heir as quickly as possible. However, it took me nearly four years before I became pregnant with Rebecca."

A twinkle lit her stepmother's eyes, defying the press of her jaw. "Rebecca is the best thing that has ever happened to me. In her, I found a new purpose. I found joy."

"I am glad," Charlotte acknowledged. "Everyone deserves to be happy."

"You should know that I didn't know about you until Albert's parents died," Lydian revealed. "I had no idea that he had been married before."

"You hadn't?"

Lydian shook her head. "That was a startling revelation when he told me, but I insisted that you come to live with us."

"But my father didn't agree?"

Lydian reached out and encompassed one of her hands. "He

told me it was for the best for you to stay away, especially since you were about to attend Miss Bell's Finishing School."

"Do you know why?"

"I do not."

Charlotte pressed her lips together in disappointment. "I should be grateful that he sent for me at all."

"Your father did love you, in his own way," Lydian said. "I believe he just didn't know how to show it."

Charlotte huffed. "I doubt that."

"It is true," Lydian replied. "Your father was not an affectionate man, and he struggled with his emotions."

A soft knock came at the door before it was opened, revealing her lady's maid.

"Pardon the intrusion, but it is time to dress you for dinner," Ellen said.

Lydian rose gracefully. "I suppose that is my cue to go change, as well." She started to turn but stopped herself. "We shall have to resume this talk later."

"I would like that very much."

"As would I," her stepmother said, smiling.

Charlotte watched Lydian leaving the room, knowing something had shifted between them. She didn't feel at odds with her anymore. Instead, she found herself believing that one day they might even become friends.

12

"I HOPE I DIDN'T GET YOU INTO TOO MUCH TROUBLE, MILADY," Ellen said as she stood behind her, styling her hair.

Charlotte met her lady's maid's gaze in the mirror. "Not at all."

"I am relieved to hear that." Ellen reached down and picked up black-dyed flowers. "When Lady Huntley demanded to see you and stormed into your room, I feared the worst."

"I must admit that my heart may have stopped for a moment when I saw my stepmother waiting for me."

"I can only imagine."

"But we ended up having the most pleasant conversation, and I am beginning to see her in a whole new light."

"In what way?"

"Lady Huntley is not the cynical person I thought her to be," she shared. "She has a good heart beneath her stern exterior."

"That is good," Ellen responded, stepping back.

Charlotte turned her head to admire her hair piled high on top of her head with two long curls framing her face.

"You are quite talented," she praised.

Ellen smiled broadly. "Thank you, milady."

"Where did you learn to style hair?"

"My sister," her lady's maid replied. "My mother was a cook in a grand house, and my sister and I were required to spend hours playing by the fireplace."

"Weren't you afraid of getting burned?"

"We learned at a young age not to get too close to the flames," Ellen said with a shake of her head.

"Where is your sister now?"

Ellen stepped over to the bed where a black silk gown was laid out. "She took over as the cook when my mother retired," she shared. "I worked for a few years as a maid before I accepted a position at Lady Northampton's townhouse."

"Why didn't you stay on and work with your sister?"

"The pay was better, and I was promised to be given the opportunity to work as a lady's maid." Ellen reached down and picked up the dress. "That was an opportunity that I could not pass up."

"Do you miss your sister?"

Ellen smiled weakly. "I do, but we see each other at least once a month. We have different days off, but we make it work. We are just both grateful for work."

"Your mother must be proud of you both."

"I'm afraid my mother is quite ill," Ellen admitted, draping the dress over her arm. "She retired as the cook because she could no longer stand for a long period of time. Sadly, I don't get to see her very often."

"That is awful," Charlotte murmured. "I insist that you take tomorrow morning off to go visit your mother."

Ellen appeared unsure. "But who would help you dress, milady? Or style your hair?"

"I will ask the housekeeper to send a maid to my room if I require assistance," Charlotte replied. "But you should know that I am not completely useless. I didn't have a lady's maid when I was at finishing school, and I managed just fine."

"I didn't mean to imply you were, milady," Ellen rushed to say.

Charlotte smiled. "I am grateful that you accompanied me to Wellesley House. I don't know what I would have done without you."

"You don't have to keep thanking me. I am just grateful for this opportunity." Ellen held up the dress on her arm. "The dressmaker sent over another dress for you."

"It is beautiful," she acknowledged.

"I agree," Ellen said. "Shall we get you dressed, milady?"

"I think that is a grand idea."

After Charlotte was dressed, she exited her bedchamber door and started walking down the hall, admiring the gold portraits lining the walls as she went. She was about to step down the stairs when she saw Duncan approaching her from the opposite direction. He was sharply dressed in a black jacket, black trousers, white waistcoat and an ornately tied black cravat.

He came to a stop in front of her with a smile on his face. "You are looking especially lovely tonight, Charlotte."

"That is most kind of you to say."

Duncan extended his arm towards her. "May I escort you to the drawing room?"

"I would appreciate that kindness," she said, placing her hand into the crook of his arm.

"Did you have a pleasant day today?" he asked as he led her down the stairs.

The image of standing next to Hudson as they watched pig running came into her mind. A smile came to her face as she replied, "I did."

"May I ask what occupied your time?"

"The usual pursuits, I suppose," she replied dismissively. "How was your day?"

Duncan glanced over at her. "It was rather dull."

"Why was that?"

"I spent the day going over ledgers," he explained. "I would have much rather spent the day with you."

"If you had, I could have taught you the finer points of needlework," she joked.

He chuckled as they stepped down from the stairs. "I would have rather gone riding through Hyde Park."

"As would I."

"Perhaps we can go tomorrow."

"I would enjoy that."

As they stepped into the drawing room, her stepmother gave her a disapproving shake of her head.

"You are late," she stated sternly. "A lady must never make other people wait unnecessarily. It is unfathomably rude."

"I am sorry," Charlotte murmured.

Lydian's lips twitched, and she detected mirth in her voice. "You are forgiven. But do try not to make this a habit. It is very unbecoming."

"Yes, stepm..." Her voice trailed off as she corrected herself. "Yes, Lydian."

Her stepmother nodded her head in approval. "You are looking remarkably put together this evening, and I must agree with the dressmaker that you do look splendid in black."

"Thank you," Charlotte replied.

Duncan leaned closer to her and whispered, "What did you do to Lydian?"

"Nothing."

He lifted his brow in disbelief, clearly not believing her.

"I promise," she said.

Lydian closed the distance between them. "I asked the cook to make the rich pound cake that you are so fond of for dessert."

"Thank you," Charlotte replied, truly touched by the gesture.

"You are welcome. I thought it was the least I could do." Lydian pointed towards the door. "Shall we adjourn for dinner?"

Duncan extended his other arm towards Lydian and led them into the dining room.

Once they were seated around the large rectangular table, Lydian asked her, "How did you enjoy growing up at your grandparent's estate in Scarborough?"

"It was lovely," she replied. "There were plenty of ruins for me to explore."

"I'm afraid I know nothing about your maternal grandparents," Lydian said. "What were they like?"

Charlotte brought her hands to her lap, taking a moment to collect her thoughts. "They were kind and loving," she shared. "My grandmother always had a smile on her face, and she only spoke words of gentleness."

"She sounds like a lovely person," Duncan commented from the head of the table.

"She was," Charlotte confirmed. "My grandfather was special to me, as well. He was constantly teaching me 'life lessons' as he called them. He also loved studying birds."

"What an unusual hobby," Lydian remarked as a footman placed a bowl of soup in front of her.

"It was. He would go on and on about the different bird species that lived around our estate," Charlotte confirmed. "But his absolute favorite bird to talk about was the ostrich."

"I am not familiar with an ostrich," Duncan responded as he reached for his spoon.

"I am not surprised, considering it only lives in Africa," Charlotte replied. "Furthermore, it is the world's largest bird and is flightless."

"A flightless bird!" Lydian declared. "Good heavens, whoever has heard of such a thing?"

Charlotte smiled. "My grandfather loved studying the ostrich. Not only is it the fastest land animal with two legs, but it can kill a lion with a kick of its long legs."

"It can kill a lion?" Duncan asked, incredulous.

She nodded. "Yes, according to the books that my grandfather read."

"That is truly fascinating," Duncan muttered before taking a sip of his soup.

Lydian smiled at her from across the table. "It warms my heart to know that you were raised by such loving people."

"I was very blessed," Charlotte acknowledged, knowing it was true.

A comfortable silence descended over them before Lydian surprised them all by saying, "Perhaps I will start studying birds."

Duncan glanced over at Lady Huntley with a confused expression. "Do you have an interest in birds?"

Lydian shook her head. "Not particularly, no."

"Then why birds?" he pressed.

"I am looking for a new hobby and researching birds seems simple enough," Lydian replied as she put her spoon down.

"May I suggest filigree?" Duncan asked. "That is an appropriate pastime for a lady."

"Filigree requires a great degree of skill. As I understand it, one must roll the narrow strips of paper into tight rolls and then apply them to the desired background," Lydian commented. "I'm afraid I am not that patient."

"Then I must assume that paper-work is out?"

Lydian nodded. "Paper-work requires a delicate hand in order to draw and cut the paper into objects."

Charlotte spoke up. "What about feather-work?" she asked. "You could sketch the birds on paper and then use feathers to complete the image. That is all the rage right now."

"Heavens, no!" Lydian declared. "Everyone knows that feather-work collects an exorbitant amount of dust."

"What about molding flowers out of wax?" Duncan attempted.

Lydian frowned. "That is only a suitable pastime for girls."

The footmen started clearing their empty bowls when Charlotte suggested, "What if we netted our reticules?"

"Mine is already netted," Lydian said proudly.

"Then, perhaps we could collect our scraps of fabric and make a patchwork quilt together," Charlotte proposed. "We made one at our finishing school as a gift for Miss Bell, and it turned out splendidly."

Lydian nodded approvingly. "Patchwork quilting does sound much more desirable than reading about birds."

Raising his glass towards Lydian, Duncan declared, "I couldn't agree with you more."

"You are welcome to join us, my lord," Charlotte joked.

Duncan chuckled. "I assure you that I would be more of a hinderance than a help."

As a footman placed a plate of food in front of her, Lydian asked, "Would it be permissible for me to join you tomorrow on your ride through Hyde Park?"

Duncan gaped at her. "I... uh..."

"Of course, you are welcome," Charlotte replied, speaking over him. "The more, the merrier."

Lydian beamed at them. "Thank you." She reached for her glass. "I promise I won't slow you down."

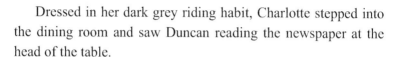

Dressed in her dark grey riding habit, Charlotte stepped into the dining room and saw Duncan reading the newspaper at the head of the table.

"Good morning," she greeted as she walked over to the buffet table.

Folding the corner of the paper, he replied, "Good morning. How did you sleep?"

"Well. And you?"

Duncan laid the paper on the table. "I also slept well."

"That is good to hear."

After she filled her plate, she walked over and sat down to the right of Duncan. A footman placed a cup of chocolate in front of her.

As she reached for her cup, Duncan leaned closer to her and asked in a hushed voice, "Why did you invite Lady Huntley to accompany us on our ride this morning through Hyde Park?"

She gave him a baffled look as she held the cup up to her lips. "Because it was the polite thing to do."

"I see."

"Do you take umbrage with her coming?" she asked, returning the cup to its saucer.

The muscles around Duncan's mouth tightened then relaxed. "Not me, per se, but I just thought it might make you feel uncomfortable."

Reaching for a piece of toast off her plate, she replied, "I can tell that my stepmother is trying to engage with us. We need to meet her halfway."

"That is true," he said. "I did notice that she was behaving oddly last night. She didn't seem as critical of you."

"Have patience with her, I beg of you."

Duncan leaned back in his chair and smiled charmingly. "I will be the epitome of patience."

Before she could reply, Baxter stepped into the room and announced, "Three horses have been saddled and are waiting out front, milord."

Duncan turned his attention towards the butler. "Thank you, Baxter. Will you send word to Lady Huntley that the horses have been saddled?"

Lydian's voice came from the doorway. "That is not necessary, Lord Huntley," she said, stepping into the room. "I am ready to go riding."

Glancing over her shoulder, Charlotte saw that her stepmother was wearing a dark brown riding habit, and a matching brown hat with netting sat on top of her neatly coiffed blonde hair.

"Would you care to eat first?" Duncan asked, rising.

Lydian shook her head. "I already ate in my room."

"You are always welcome to join us for breakfast in the dining room," Duncan encouraged.

"I prefer a tray in my room," Lydian replied.

Charlotte brushed off the crumbs from her hand and rose. "Well, I am ready to go riding."

"As am I," Lydian announced, clasping her hands in front of her. "And you are positive that we won't see anyone on this ride?"

Charlotte gave her stepmother a reassuring smile. "It is much too early for the members of the *ton* to be up and about."

"That is true," Duncan agreed. "We have hardly seen another soul on our previous rides."

Lydian breathed a sigh of relief. "That is good to hear. I don't know what I would do if someone actually recognized me. I can't even imagine the scandal that would ensue."

"You will be just fine," Charlotte encouraged. "No one will recognize you. I promise."

Lydian smiled at her. "Thank you, Charlotte."

"Come," Duncan said, "we should hurry before the sun gets too high in the sky."

A short time later, they were racing their horses through Hyde Park, and Charlotte glanced over to see a genuine smile on her stepmother's face, making her appear younger and carefree.

Lydian slowed her horse's gait, and she followed suit.

"That was exhilarating," Lydian called out to her.

"I agree."

Duncan shouted as he raced by, "I shall meet you at the stream!"

As Lydian brought her horse closer to Charlotte's, she said, "You are an excellent rider."

"As are you."

Lydian adjusted the reins in her hands as she stared straight ahead. "My father insisted that I become a proficient rider," she shared. "In fact, he was quite adamant about it."

"Was there a particular reason?"

"He was rather obsessed with me becoming a proper lady," her stepmother said with a nod. "He was sure it would raise our social standing amongst the *ton*."

"I daresay his plan worked."

Lydian grimaced slightly. "But at what cost?"

"What do you mean?" Charlotte asked.

Her stepmother pursed her lips. "My father was born with very little. He worked hard and made a fortune in trade," she explained. "He grew tired of the gentry belittling him because of how he made his money. It infuriated him, actually."

Lydian reached up and tucked an errant piece of her blonde hair behind her ear. "Alfred's father, your grandfather, was a notoriously bad gambler," she said. "It wasn't long before it was understood amongst the *ton* that he had lost nearly everything, but that hadn't stopped him frequenting the gambling halls."

"How awful," Charlotte murmured.

"My father played him at cards and beat him soundly. He could have even sent him to debtor's prison, if he had been so inclined," Lydian informed her. "Instead, they came to an agreement. I would marry Alfred, and I would bring a much-needed dowry of £20,000 to the nearly bankrupt estate."

"Your father…"

Lydian cut her off. "Bartered me off, as if I meant nothing to him."

Charlotte didn't know what to say so she muttered, "I'm sorry."

"Don't be," Lydian replied, waving her hand dismissively. "It didn't go as planned for my father."

"Why not?"

"Your grandparents never accepted my parents for who they were, and no invitations were forthcoming from the *ton*," Lydian said. "My father did manage to buy me a title, but that meant very little to me."

"What did you want?"

A wistful expression came to her stepmother's face. "I had everything that I wanted in Alfred, but I couldn't make him love me. I tried, desperately. But I could never penetrate his heart." She huffed. "Perhaps if I'd had more time with him, then I could have changed his mind."

They rode side by side in silence for a long moment before Charlotte found the courage to ask, "Did my father ever speak of my mother?"

"No," Lydian said with a shake of her head. "He never did."

"Oh."

Lydian gave her a sad smile. "After your father told me that he had been married before, I tried to ask questions about her, but he refused to answer them."

Sudden tears burned Charlotte's eyes, but she blinked them away.

"I should have assumed as much," she responded curtly.

"Eventually, my lady's maid informed me of the circumstances surrounding Catherine's death, and how quickly Alfred had remarried," Lydian said. "I was devastated and hurt. I felt betrayed by his deceit."

"I can only imagine."

Lydian stared off into the distance. "I questioned what kind of man I'd married, especially since he'd treated his first wife so callously. He hadn't even properly grieved for her."

Charlotte glanced down at her hands, knowing she had voiced the same concerns.

"That is why I insisted that you come to live with us," Lydian said. "I thought your father should atone for his wrongs."

Bringing her gaze back up, Charlotte questioned, "You claim my father loved me, but I do not believe that to be the case. He treated me just as callously as he'd treated my mother."

Lydian smiled at her. "That is what I thought at first, as well. But I was wrong."

"Why do you say that?" Charlotte asked.

"Your father didn't show emotion very often, rarely, in fact, but he did when he informed me that it was time to present you for the Season," her stepmother explained. "He was excited to host a ball for you and accompany you around Town. We were just about to send out the invitations when he grew sick."

"Then why had he neglected me for so many years?"

Lydian shrugged her shoulders. "I'm afraid I can't answer that."

Feeling bold, Charlotte asked, "May I ask why you are always so quick to criticize me?"

Her stepmother sighed. "Frankly, it is because I don't know what I am doing."

"Pardon?"

"All Alfred's mother did was find fault in me, and it eventually transformed me into the lady I am today," she replied. "I suppose I thought the same approach would work with you."

"Oh."

With a slight glance, Lydian asked, "Is it working?"

"No," Charlotte answered with a shake of her head. "It is not."

Lydian grew silent. "I'm sorry, then."

Up ahead, Duncan was sitting atop his horse as he waited next to the stream. He raised his hand in greeting.

In a low, hushed voice, Lydian admonished, "You must be careful around Lord Huntley."

"Why?" she asked.

"Because I don't fully trust him."

Charlotte lifted her brow at her stepmother's unexpected remarks. "Why do you say that?" she asked, tightening the reins in her hands.

"I don't know," she replied. "He just seems too... charming."

"Is that a bad thing?"

Lydian bobbed her head. "Sometimes. Then again, I have a natural aversion to aristocrats. I don't trust them."

"Aren't you an aristocrat?"

"Technically, yes," her stepmother replied. "Although, while I married into the aristocracy, I am still the daughter of a tradesman."

Charlotte turned her attention towards Duncan, and he smiled broadly at her, easing all her worries. Why would her stepmother caution her against Duncan? There was nothing dishonorable about him.

✣ 13 ✣

THE COACH JERKED TO A STOP IN FRONT OF WELLESLEY HOUSE, and Hudson waited only a moment until his footman came around to open the door.

As much work as he had to do today, he found himself rather excited to call on Lady Charlotte. He had to admit that he had started viewing life a bit differently since he first met her. She had brought joy back into his life, making it seem worthwhile.

The ebony door to Wellesley House opened, and the butler greeted him.

"Good morning, Lord Hudson."

He tipped his head in acknowledgement before he asked, "Is Lady Charlotte accepting callers today?" he asked.

"She is," the butler confirmed, holding the door open wide. "Please follow me."

He followed the butler across the entry hall and waited outside of the drawing room while the butler announced him.

"Lady Charlotte will see you now, milord," the butler said before walking away.

Hudson stepped into the drawing room and saw Lady Charlotte sitting on the tan sofa with a large pile of fabric scraps next to her.

"Lord Hudson," she greeted him, smiling. "What a delightful surprise to see you so early this morning. I hadn't expected you until much later."

He walked further into the room. "I just finished a trial, and I thought it was a good time for a break."

Charlotte held up two scraps of floral fabric. "Excellent. You are just in time to help us start sewing our patchwork quilt."

"Us?"

"My stepmother and I," she replied as she placed the fabric back onto the pile. Then, she began sorting through the stack. "We thought it might be a fun hobby for us to try."

Hudson sat on an upholstered armchair next to her. He kept his voice low as he asked, "Has something transpired between you two that I need to be aware of?"

Charlotte's hand stilled as she turned to face him. "My stepmother and I have come to an understanding."

"Meaning?"

"She is not as terrible as I once thought."

"I am relieved to know that, but may I ask how you discovered that?"

Charlotte glanced at the door before she replied in a hushed voice, "My father treated her horribly, as well."

"She told you that?"

Charlotte nodded. "Furthermore, my father hadn't revealed that he had been married before until later on in their marriage. Lydian didn't even know about me until I was ready to attend Miss Bell's Finishing School."

"Why would your father keep that secret from his own wife?"

She shrugged nonchalantly, but he could detect the hurt in her voice as she said, "I don't know."

Hudson moved to sit on the edge of his chair. "Have you read the note from your father yet?"

"No, I haven't," she replied. "I have picked it up a few times, but I haven't found the courage to open it up."

"You will," he assured her.

"I wish I had your confidence."

He gave her a reassuring smile. "Read it or don't read it," he began. "It won't change who you are."

"That is kind of you to say," she responded. "I just can't seem to make sense of who my father was. How could he treat his family so deplorably?"

"Perhaps that answer is in the letter he wrote you."

"Or he could have written it in an attempt to justify his actions. That would cause me to hate him even more."

"Your father can't hurt you anymore," Hudson said with compassion in his voice. "He is gone, leaving you a part of his fortune."

Charlotte glanced down at her hands in her lap. "I wish I could have spoken to my father about my mother, even for just a moment. I know so very little of her."

"Didn't your grandparents talk about her?"

"Hardly," she shared. "Whenever they did speak about her, my grandparents would start crying." She turned her attention towards the portrait above the fireplace. "At Chatsmoor Hall, there is a portrait of my mother before she got married, but a black cloth was draped over it."

"How long were your parents married?"

"A little over a year," she replied.

"Not very long then."

"My grandparents refused to speak about my father," she revealed, "but it was evident that they did not care for him."

"I can only imagine why," Hudson remarked dryly.

"How could a father cast aside his own child?" she asked. "It was as if I meant nothing to him."

Hudson shook his head. "I'm afraid I can't answer that question."

"No one can seem to answer that question," she said in a resigned voice.

Hearing the sadness in her voice caused Hudson to reach out and encompass her gloved hand in her lap. "I cannot speak for your father or his horrific actions, but I want you to know that you have grown into a remarkable young woman."

Charlotte didn't respond as her eyes searched his, as if gauging his sincerity.

"You are perfect exactly as you are, Lottie."

Her lips parted in surprise. "You called me 'Lottie'."

"Is that all right?" he asked, hoping she would agree.

"Yes, I would be honored," she replied with a smile on her lips.

"That pleases me greatly," he said. "And I hope you will call me Hudson."

Keeping hold of his hand, she leaned closer to him, and he could see the vulnerability in her eyes. "Do you truly think I am perfect?"

"I do," he murmured, his eyes darting to her lips.

She opened her mouth to respond, but was interrupted by Lady Huntley exclaiming, "Lord Hudson! What a pleasure it is to see you again."

Hudson and Charlotte jumped apart, not realizing until that moment how close they had been to each other.

He quickly rose and bowed. "Lady Huntley."

Lady Huntley nodded approvingly at him as she walked over to Charlotte and picked up the pile of fabric. "I must admit that I am quite eager to get started on the patchwork quilt."

An adorable blush was on Charlotte's cheeks as she averted her gaze from his. "As am I."

Lady Huntley held up the fabric in her hands. "Shall we start organizing these scraps of fabric?" she asked. "Hopefully, we shall have some sort of design."

"I am hoping to have a bouquet of flowers in the center of the quilt," Charlotte said.

"Wouldn't that be grand?" Lady Huntley replied. "This is much more fun than reading about birds."

Hudson cast Charlotte a baffled look, and she explained.

"My stepmother was looking for a new hobby, and she thought studying birds might have been an interesting pastime. But, ultimately, we decided to make a patchwork quilt, instead."

"I see," he said.

Lady Huntley started looking through the different color scraps of fabric in her hand as she asked, "What are your hobbies, Lord Hudson?"

Charlotte answered for him. "He likes to work as a district judge," she said in an amused tone.

Lady Huntley frowned. "Surely, you have other interests?"

"I am beginning to," he replied, glancing over at Charlotte.

Lady Huntley humphed, drawing back his attention. "That is very disconcerting," she chided. "What brings you by today?"

"I was hoping to speak to Lady Charlotte about an important matter."

"Were you not speaking to her when I walked into the room?" Lady Huntley questioned with a knowing expression.

Hudson cleared his throat, annoyed to find he felt nervous. "I'm afraid we had gotten off topic."

"And do you wish to discuss this matter in private?" Lady Huntley asked directly.

"I would, if you are not opposed."

Lady Huntley pressed her lips together. "I am opposed, Lord Hudson. I believe I gave you ample time for privacy when you first arrived."

Charlotte met his gaze. "You may speak freely around my stepmother," she encouraged.

He lifted his brow. "But I wish to speak to you about a pressing matter."

"Is it in regard to Lady Thornley's masquerade ball tonight?" she questioned.

His eyes darted towards Lady Huntley as he confirmed, "It is."

"Are you and Isabella attending?"

"We had planned on it, assuming you would come along."

Lady Huntley turned to face Charlotte. "Please say you are not actually considering attending this ball."

"I am," Charlotte said, "and I want you to come with me."

"Good heavens, child!" Lady Huntley crossed the room in a few strides and closed the door. "Are you mad? You can't attend a ball when you are in mourning."

"It is a masquerade ball," Charlotte pointed out. "Everyone will be wearing masks, and we will depart before the unveiling."

"And what if someone recognizes you?" Lady Huntley asked as she approached Charlotte. "For once your reputation is tarnished, nothing can bring it back."

"No one will recognize me, or you," she replied confidently, "and we shall wear masks that hide most of our faces."

Lady Huntley crossed her arms over her chest. "You don't know what you are asking of me."

"I do," Charlotte stated. "For one night, we can balk at Society's ridiculous rules behind the safety of a mask. We can have an adventure together."

Lady Huntley's face softened. "I do have a few masks that would work quite well for us."

Charlotte smiled at her stepmother. "You must trust me. We will have such fun tonight."

"How exactly would we travel to the masquerade ball?" Lady Huntley asked, not appearing convinced. "We wouldn't be able to use our coach without alerting the whole household."

Hudson spoke up. "We shall meet you and Charlotte at the back gate tonight around eight with our coach."

Lady Huntley dropped her hands to her sides and glanced over at him. "Why are you going along with this madness?"

He smirked. "My sister was rather insistent on the matter."

With an arched brow, Lady Huntley asked, "And how are we going to exit the townhouse without alerting others to us leaving?"

A mischievous smile came to Charlotte's lips. "We will climb out."

"Oh, no," Lady Huntley said, placing her hand up in front of her. "You cannot possibly be serious!"

"I assure you that I am completely serious." Charlotte turned towards Hudson. "We shall meet you tonight at eight."

He felt elated by the news, but he resisted the urge to smile. "Wonderful," he replied with a slight bow. "I shall be looking forward to it."

As he exited the drawing room, he was mindful to close the door behind him. He had no doubt that Lady Huntley and Charlotte had much to discuss.

"I can't believe Lottie is bringing her evil stepmother along with us," Isabella declared as she sat next to them in the coach.

Hudson sighed as he adjusted his white cravat. "I wish you would stop referring to Lady Huntley as 'evil'," he replied. "There is no evidence to corroborate your theory."

"Do you think she tricked Lottie into bringing her along?"

"No," he said with a shake of his head, "it was Lady Charlotte who seemed to be doing the insisting."

Isabella tugged at the cuff of her long white gloves. "That doesn't make any sense. Lottie can barely stand Lady Huntley."

"They appeared to be getting along quite nicely when I called on her earlier."

"Perhaps Lady Huntley cast a spell over Lottie?"

Ignoring his sister's ridiculous comment, Hudson turned his attention towards the small, open window and saw two figures emerge from the grove of trees. Lady Huntley and Charlotte were wearing capes, but their hoods were down, and they were each holding large, ostentatious masks in their hands.

He put his hand through the window, pulled down on the latch and opened the door. As he stepped out, he heard Lady Huntley grumble, "I can't believe you made me climb down a tree."

To which Charlotte replied, "And you did so splendidly."

He smiled as they approached him. "Ladies, you are looking well."

With a stiff back, Lady Huntley stopped in front of him. "I am here under protest."

"You are?" he asked, glancing between her and Charlotte.

Charlotte placed her hand on Lady Huntley's sleeve. "I promise that you'll have an enjoyable time."

"It is not too late to turn back and have ourselves a nice cup of tea before we retire for the evening," Lady Huntley attempted, turning her head towards the trees. "I always have a cup of tea before bed."

"You are welcome to turn back," Charlotte said, "but I am going to the masquerade ball."

"Then I must go and chaperone you," Lady Huntley replied firmly.

Hudson interjected, "I would be remiss if I did not inform you that rules are less rigid at a masquerade ball."

"I am well aware of that fact, but I dare not let Charlotte out of my sight," Lady Huntley said, extending her hand. "She can be quite the rapscallion."

Hudson assisted Lady Huntley into the coach before giving Charlotte a disapproving look.

"Just trust me," she whispered in response.

Leaning closer, he placed a hand on her sleeve and murmured next to her ear, "I do trust you, but I don't trust your stepmother."

Once Charlotte was situated in the coach, he climbed in across from her and closed the door.

They rode in silence for what felt like hours but was probably only moments. Finally, Lady Huntley broke the silence.

"You are slouching, my dear, and a lady never slouches."

Charlotte straightened her shoulders and responded in a dry voice, "Thank you, stepmother."

Lady Huntley pressed her lips together. "I'm doing it again. Aren't I?"

"Yes, you are," Charlotte replied, smiling.

"I'm sorry. I suppose it is a habit now," Lady Huntley responded, smoothing back her blonde hair. "I will try to be better, I promise."

Isabella spoke up. "I'm glad that you finally said something, Lady Huntley, because I have been telling Lottie for years that she slouches, but she has refused to listen to me."

Charlotte laughed. "Whose side are you on?" she asked jokingly.

The coach came to a stop in front of a three-level white townhouse in the fashionable part of Town. Charlotte held up her mask, which was covered with glossy black flowers. "It is time to don our masks," she advised.

Reaching into his jacket pocket, Hudson pulled out his simple black mask. "Remember, do not take off your mask for any reason. Anonymity is your friend tonight," he advised. "Furthermore, if we get separated this evening, meet back at the coach before the unveiling."

Hudson had just donned his mask when the door was opened

by a footman. He exited first, and then assisted each one of the ladies out of the coach.

Charlotte and Lady Huntley had removed their capes, revealing their gowns underneath. Lady Huntley was wearing a simple maroon colored gown with a matching mask. Whereas Charlotte looked breathtaking in a white gown with pink embroidered flowers along the round neckline. Her features were partially obscured by a black, feathered half mask which covered the upper portion of her face, so only her full lips and chin were visible.

"You look lovely this evening," Hudson said, extending his arm towards her.

"Thank you," she replied, placing her hand into the crook of his arm. "You look rather dapper yourself."

They started following the line of people into Lady Thornley's richly decorated townhouse, and Hudson kept glancing over at Charlotte, feeling immense pride that she was on his arm.

As they stepped into the large, rectangular ballroom, Hudson raised his voice so he could be heard over the large group of people and the orchestra playing in the corner. "Will you save me the waltz tonight?" he asked, holding his breath as he waited for her reply.

Charlotte turned her masked face towards him. "I will."

The masquerade ball was a crush, and hordes of people were standing against the walls, leaving the center of the room open for dancing. They started maneuvering themselves towards the open French doors that led towards the gardens, letting in the cool night air. A table was set up in the corner filled with glasses of champagne.

"Would you care for something to drink?" he asked Charlotte.

She shook her head, causing the black feathers to sway back and forth. "I'd better not. Miss Bell warned us that getting inebriated at a ball can have dire consequences."

Isabella didn't seem to share Charlotte's reservations, and she went to pick up a glass of champagne. She took a sip, and her eyes widened.

"That is quite bubbly," she commented.

Hudson held up one finger. "That is your one and only glass of champagne tonight. Do I make myself clear?" he asked, his tone brooked no argument.

"Yes, brother," Isabella replied.

A familiar man broke through the crowd and approached them. "Am I dreaming, or do I see my good friend, Hudson, here at a ball?"

Hudson arched an eyebrow at his friend, Lord Ewin. "Isn't the point of masks being to keep our identity a secret?"

"My apologies," Ewin replied. "I am just surprised to see you. You haven't attended a ball in years." He turned his attention towards Isabella. "I see you brought your sister along."

Isabella frowned under her white mask. "Good evening, Ewin."

"You are looking as enchanting as ever, Bella," Ewin said with a slight bow. "Will you save me a dance?"

"I'm afraid that is impossible," Isabella declared.

"Is it now?" Ewin asked with a smile on his lips.

Isabella nodded. "I don't dance with dandies."

"I am not a dandy."

"No?" she replied, her eyes left his to scan the crowd. "You could have fooled me, my lord."

Ewin chuckled. "As usual, I have enjoyed our little chat." His eyes drifted towards Charlotte. "And who is this lovely enchantress?"

Hudson answered for her. "Don't answer that," he remarked sternly. "We are attempting to go incognito."

"Ah, a lady of mystery, then," Ewin said. "How intriguing."

The next set was announced, and to Hudson's surprise and horror, Ewin held out his gloved hand towards Charlotte.

"Will you do me the grand honor of dancing with me?" Ewin asked.

Charlotte hesitated only for a moment before she slipped her hand into his. "I suppose so," she murmured, glancing over at Hudson.

He gave her an encouraging nod. "Go on," he said. "I will be waiting here for you when the dance is finished."

Ewin smiled at him. "Do not fret. I shall return her to you after the set."

Hudson watched as Charlotte disappeared into the crowd with Ewin, causing him to clench his jaw so tightly that he could hear the grinding of his teeth.

"Why did you let Charlotte dance with Ewin?" Isabella asked as she came to stand next to him.

"She is free to dance with whomever she chooses to," he admitted reluctantly.

Lady Huntley spoke up from the other side of him. "Is this Ewin a rake?"

"Yes," Isabella replied.

"No," Hudson said at the same time.

"Which one is it?" Lady Huntley asked, turning to face them.

"Ewin is not a rake," Hudson defended.

Isabella huffed. "I respectfully disagree."

Before he could respond to his sister's outlandish comment, Hudson saw another familiar face in the crowd. She was wearing a thin gold mask, but he would recognize her anywhere. It was Hannah. The temptress that he had loved so dearly for many years. A woman that had taken his heart and stomped on it, leaving him hollow inside.

Their eyes met from across the crowded room, and he felt as if time had slowed down. He could hear the beat of his heart as he stared at the woman he had wrongly assumed would be his future. He watched as she slowly approached him, then stopped in front of him. She was dressed in an emerald green gown with her blonde hair piled high on top of her head.

"Hello, Hudson," she said, her eyes remaining fixed on him.

Keeping his voice devoid of any emotion, he replied, "Hello, Hannah."

She gave him a weak smile. "It is good to see you again."

"What do you want?" he asked.

Her eyes drifted towards Lady Huntley and Isabella. "Is there some place that we can talk more privately?"

"No," he replied. "I am not interested in anything that you have to say."

"Please," she breathed. "It is important."

As much as he wanted to decline, he could hear the distress in her voice. "Fine," he said. "We can speak out on the veranda."

Turning towards his sister and Lady Huntley, Hudson ordered, "Stay here. I will be back shortly."

He didn't offer his arm as they walked side by side out the French doors. Once they stepped onto the veranda, Hudson turned to face her and asked, "What is so important that you needed to speak to me alone?"

Hannah continued to stroll towards an iron bench and sat down. She patted the seat next to her. "Will you not sit with me, Hudson?"

"No," he answered, crossing his arms over his chest.

Her lips tightened into a line. "I wanted to speak to you alone because I wanted a chance to apologize to you."

"Save your empty words," he replied. "I don't need, or want, your apology, Hannah."

"But you are going to get it, just the same," she declared.

Hudson remained silent, hoping she would say what she wanted to say and be done with it.

After a long moment, Hannah rose from her seat and walked over to him. "I am sorry for what I did to you. For breaking our engagement, and in the manner that I went about it," she said. "That was wrong of me, I know that now."

Hudson lifted his brow, but still he didn't say anything.

"I was scared, confused," she explained, "and I didn't know what I wanted out of life."

He dropped his arms to his side in frustration. "You knew exactly what you wanted. You wanted to become a duchess."

"I did, but after I married Lord Skeffington, everything changed," she shared. "He would hit me for the slightest infraction, and I never dared complain when he was with his mistress. He even had the nerve to bring her home to live with us. It was awful, Hudson. I became a prisoner in my own home."

Hudson felt a twinge of compassion towards her, but he kept his voice stern. "You made your choice."

Hannah stepped closer and stared up at him, her eyes pleading.

"Please say that it is not over between us," she requested softly.

"There is no 'us', not anymore," he replied.

"Don't say that," she breathed. "Just give me one more chance."

"No."

"But we were good together, you and I," she pressed, placing her hand on his chest.

Hudson stepped back, and her hand dropped to her side. "I'm sorry. You made your bed, and now you have to lie in it." He turned to leave but stopped at her next words.

"You should know that I never stopped loving you," she declared.

He slowly turned back around, choosing his next words carefully. "That changes nothing between us, Hannah. You should know that."

Tears started rolling down Hannah's cheeks. "I made a mistake. I should have chosen you," she murmured.

Reaching into his jacket pocket, he pulled out a handkerchief and extended it towards her. "That is the past now. What's done is done."

Hannah accepted the handkerchief and wiped her cheeks. "Will you not give me a second chance?"

"No, Hannah," he sighed. "I won't."

She took a step closer and tilted her chin to look up at him. "May I ask why?"

"Because I have moved on and so should you," he advised.

Her moist eyes glistened in the moonlight. "There is someone else?" she questioned weakly.

He nodded.

She let out a slight whimper. "I am too late, then?"

Hudson's voice softened as he admitted, "I'm sorry, but my heart hardened to you the moment you eloped with Lord Skeffington. I don't think I could ever trust you again."

"Perhaps this will help," Hannah said before she went up on her tiptoes and pressed her mouth against his.

He reared back, breaking the kiss. "What do you think you are doing?" he demanded.

"I had thought... I just wanted you to remember..." Her voice trailing off as her hands came to her cheeks. "Please don't hate me."

Hearing the sadness in her voice, caused Hudson to reach out and place a hand gently on her shoulder. "I don't hate you, Hannah," he stated. "I truly don't. But you must understand that nothing can happen between us again. It is over."

"I understand," she replied in a shaky breath.

"I'm glad," he said, removing his hand from her shoulder. "In time, you will see that this was for the best."

The music came to an end in the ballroom, drawing his attention towards the French doors. That is when he saw Charlotte standing just outside of the opening, and he could make out the stunned look of disbelief under her mask. She met his gaze, and he could see the questions lingering in her eyes.

He wanted to run to her, to shout to her that she misconstrued the situation, but instead, he remained rooted in his spot. Never in his life had he felt so completely frozen. No words came to his head, no thoughts he could formulate.

Charlotte's eyes filled with tears before she spun around and disappeared back into the ballroom.

"Was that her?" Hannah asked softly.

"It was."

"Then go after her."

As he took a commanding step towards the door, he said, "I have every intention to."

❧ 14 ❧

As she headed into the ballroom, Charlotte knew that she was a fool. She had wrongly assumed that Hudson held her in some regard, but he had just been toying with her emotions. And she had fallen for it like some love deprived female.

She angrily blinked away the unbidden, unwanted tears that had formed in her eyes. She refused to cry over Hudson. Not when he'd treated her so distastefully. She had never imagined that he was capable of such deceit, such underhandedness. Hadn't he been the one who had warned her about how some men were wolves in sheep's clothing? Little had she suspected he was speaking about himself.

"What is wrong?" Isabella asked as she approached them.

"It is nothing," she attempted.

Lady Huntley placed a hand on her sleeve and gently prodded, "Clearly, it is not nothing. You have been crying."

Glancing back at the open French doors, she replied, "I just saw Lord Hudson kissing a woman on the veranda."

Isabella reared back. "You did?"

She bobbed her head as the tears threatened once more.

Groaning, Isabella remarked, "Not Hannah. Not again."

"By Hannah, do you mean his former fiancée?" Charlotte questioned, dreading the answer.

Isabella gave her an apologetic smile. "I do."

"I am such a fool," Charlotte murmured.

"No," Lady Huntley replied firmly. "You are not the fool; Lord Hudson is. No, he is worse than a fool. He is a scoundrel, a rake."

"I would like to return to Wellesley House now," Charlotte stated. "I find that I don't want to be around Hudson anymore."

"Of course," Isabella said with compassion in her voice. "You may use our coach to travel back to your townhouse, and I will inform Hudson that you departed early."

"Please tell him that I developed a headache."

Hudson's deep, baritone voice came from behind her. "Do you truly intend to leave the ball so soon?" he asked, the concern evident in his voice.

Charlotte slowly turned around, hoping that he wouldn't notice that she had been crying. "I'm afraid I must."

"Then, I shall escort you home."

"No," she rushed to say. "I would prefer it if you stayed at the ball. I wouldn't want you to miss out on all the festivities."

"But it wouldn't be fun without your company," he pressed.

"I doubt that," she replied dryly. "I am sure you can find ways to amuse yourself."

Hudson winced at her harsh words. "May I speak to you for a moment in private?"

Isabella's eyes narrowed as she stepped closer to her brother. "I understand you had a tryst on the veranda," she said in a hushed, accusing voice, "with Hannah. Are you mad, brother? Don't you remember what she did to you?"

"I remember all too well, and I did *not* have a tryst with her," he replied, running a hand through his blond hair. "I just need a moment to speak to Charlotte alone and explain what happened. It is…"

Lady Huntley spoke over him. "Perhaps another time," she asserted. "It is time for us to depart."

"Wait! Don't go, Lottie," Hudson cried. "Just hear what I have to say."

"I am not interested in anything you have to say," Charlotte replied, tilting her chin stubbornly at him. "You are not the man I thought you were."

Hudson looked crestfallen, threatening her resolve. "Please don't say that."

The next set was announced, and it was to be the waltz.

"Dance with me?" he asked, holding his gloved hand out towards her.

She glanced down at his proffered hand. "I'm afraid I don't feel like dancing."

His eyes implored hers, pleading with her to change her mind. "Just one dance, and I promise that you will see this has all been a big misunderstanding." He paused before adding, "Please."

Charlotte couldn't seem to find the words to deny his request, and she hesitated only a moment before putting her hand in his.

"Thank you, Lottie," he sighed.

Hudson led her towards the dance floor, held up her left hand, and placed his other hand on her right shoulder. She laid her right hand on his upper arm, and they waited in uncomfortable silence for the music to start.

As the music began, Hudson took long steps and guided her effortlessly around the other couples. His hand held hers with just the right amount of strength, making her work exceptionally hard to remain stiff in his arms.

Charlotte kept her gaze lowered to his chin as they danced, avoiding eye contact with Hudson.

"Will you please look at me, Lottie?" he asked.

She brought her gaze up, and the familiar dark blue depths of his eyes seemed to pull her into the comfortable warmth they offered. She cursed herself for being so weak when it came to Hudson. She was stronger than this.

A slight frown marred his features. "Did Isabella tell you that I was engaged before?"

"She did."

"Then did she tell you why my engagement was called off?"

She nodded. "Your betrothed eloped with another man."

"Ah, but there is so much more to the story than that," he asserted, holding her gaze. "Perhaps I should start at the beginning."

"If you must," she remarked dismissively.

His jaw clenched visibly as he appeared to struggle to rein in his emotions. "The first time I saw Hannah was at a country dance when I came home for a holiday from Oxford, and I was immediately smitten. She was everything I thought I wanted in a bride," he explained, "and I knew it was only a matter of time before we would marry."

"How delightful," she remarked as she attempted to create more distance between them.

"Between the carriage rides and walks through her gardens, I fell in love with Hannah," he shared. "When I turned twenty-one, I approached Hannah's father, the Earl of Rutgers, and I asked for his permission to court her, which he freely granted."

Charlotte didn't think she could take much more of Hudson confessing his love for another woman. It was heart wrenching to her. She glanced towards the corner of the ballroom where she'd left Isabella and her stepmother.

"This is a lovely story," she said, "truly heartwarming, but I fear that Isabella needs me. Perhaps we should go check on her."

Hudson tightened his hold, drawing her closer to him. "But I am not finished with my story yet."

"No?" she asked. "I just assumed…"

He smiled, a devastatingly charming smile that drew her attention to his lips. "You are a horrible liar, Lottie."

"Then please proceed, but I truly hope that Isabella hasn't been absconded by a rake and is traveling to Gretna Green as we speak," she declared. "I wouldn't want that on my conscience. Would you?"

"I am willing to take my chances, especially since I see Isabella standing next to your stepmother by the wall. They are speaking to Ewin and another gentleman," he said. "That is one advantage of being tall. I can see over the heads of most people."

"I suppose it is," she responded, wishing she could think of something clever to say, but she was at a loss.

Hudson held her gaze for a moment before he continued with his story. "You should know that Hannah decided she didn't want to marry me, and she eloped with Lord Skeffington instead."

"How terrible for you," she murmured.

He nodded somberly. "She willingly chose a known rake over me. It was more important for her to become a duchess than to marry for love."

"That is awful."

"I was told later that her father went after them, chased them all the way to Gretna Green, but it was too late. By the time he found them, they were legally wed."

Charlotte could see the pain radiating from his eyes at his admission. "I'm sorry, Hudson."

"I had never felt so betrayed as when I heard the news. I retreated from Society, knowing my heart couldn't stand seeing Hannah again," he said. "I decided then that I would never fall in love again, never trust another woman, and I focused only on my goal to become a High Court Judge."

"You locked away your heart," she breathed.

"It is true."

"That is a sad way to live."

"No, it is much easier than to have your heart shattered time and time again."

Charlotte's heart ached for him, but she still had a question of her own. "If what you are saying is true, then why were you kissing Hannah on the verandah?"

"I wasn't," he replied. "Hannah kissed me after pleading for another chance, but I swear that I did not kiss her back."

"It matters not," she said, her eyes lowering to the lapels of his jacket. "You are free to kiss whomever you want. There is not an understanding between us."

Hudson slowed his steps and waited until she met his gaze.

"There is only one lady that I want to kiss," he said, "and it isn't Hannah."

"Then who?" she asked with bated breath.

"I think you already know the answer to that, Lottie."

A twinkle of amusement banished the harsh looks in his eyes, and she found herself responding with a shy smile.

"Perhaps we could take a walk on the veranda later?" he asked softly.

"I would like that very much."

The music came to a stop, but Hudson didn't release her immediately. She cast him a questioning look.

"I like you in my arms," he said, his eyes holding her transfixed. "You fit perfectly."

She could feel the warmth rising to her cheeks as she replied, "You'd best let me go or it could cause a scandal."

"You seem to have forgotten that we are wearing masks," he pointed out. "No one knows our identity."

"Then I suppose we could be as scandalous as we want to be," she joked.

He smirked. "My thoughts exactly."

Isabella's voice broke through their private interlude. "It was just announced that everyone is to unmask before the next set," she revealed. "We need to go... *now*."

Hudson stepped back and offered his arm. "I think it is time we make a hasty retreat."

"I couldn't agree more," she replied as she accepted his arm.

"I shall call upon you tomorrow," Hudson said, reaching for her gloved hand.

As they stood next to the coach, Charlotte felt no urgency to abandon this moment. A thrill of excitement raced up her arm at his touch.

"I will be waiting."

He brushed his lips over her knuckles. "Until tomorrow, then."

In an exasperated voice, Lydian spoke up from next to them. "I believe we have sufficiently coordinated our schedules for tomorrow. Don't you agree, Charlotte?

"I do," she replied, reluctantly removing her hand from his.

Hudson's lips curled into a brilliant smile. "Would you like me to escort you ladies to your townhouse?"

Lydian put the hood up on her cape as she answered for them both. "That won't be necessary, Lord Hudson. The townhouse is only on the other side of this grove of trees." She started walking towards the trees. "Come along, Charlotte."

"Goodbye, Hudson," she murmured before she hurried to catch up to her stepmother.

The full moon was high in the sky, casting more than enough light for them to navigate through the trees. They walked side by side in silence until they saw Wellesley House looming ahead.

"I must admit that I am not looking forward to climbing that tree outside of your window," Lydian said, glancing over at her. "Frankly, I am rather curious how you became so proficient at climbing trees."

"One of my dear friends at finishing school used to climb trees and always invited us to go along," she revealed.

"Was this the Duchess of Blackbourne?"

"Heavens, no," she replied. "It was Madalene, the Marchioness of Lansdowne."

"Perhaps Miss Bell's Finishing School isn't the right fit for my Rebecca," Lydian remarked. "It would appear you had too much time to get involved with tomfoolery."

Charlotte gave a slight shrug of her shoulders. "We learned the usual accomplishments at our school, but Miss Bell was adamant that we spent time outdoors each day."

"Hopefully, you wore a bonnet."

"I would when I was in public, but I rarely wore one when we climbed trees," she admitted. "It is hard enough to climb in a dress."

Her stepmother frowned disapprovingly. "That is most unfortunate. You must always think of your complexion and avoid unsightly freckles on your face."

"You need not concern yourself," Charlotte replied. "I am well aware of that fact."

"I am relieved to hear that."

They stopped at the bottom of the large tree and stared up at it. Charlotte was pleased to see that her lady's maid had left her window open.

Turning to face Lydian, she asked, "Do you want to go first, or me?"

A haunted look came to her stepmother's face, causing her to ask, "What is wrong?"

Tears welled up in Lydian's eyes. "What am I doing?"

"Whatever do you mean?" She glanced up at the tree. "Are you nervous about climbing up the tree?"

"No, that is not the problem." Removing her hood, her stepmother shared, "My husband died a few weeks ago, but I just attended a masquerade ball with *you*."

"It is all right to enjoy yourself," Charlotte assured her.

The tears rolled down her cheeks, and Lydian reached up to wipe them away. "That is the problem," she replied. "I did enjoy myself, more than I had been expecting."

"I'm afraid I don't understand the problem then."

Lydian's jaw grew tight. "I should be mourning the loss of my husband. But, instead, I am gallivanting around London with my stepdaughter. What kind of cruel, unfeeling monster am I?" she asked, her voice hitching.

"You are not any of those things," Charlotte replied gently. "The ball provided you with only a brief respite from your grief."

"I loved your father, despite him not loving me," Lydian explained. "I don't know why, but I did."

"I know."

Lydian looked up at her with pain-filled eyes. "Why didn't *he* love me?" Her words came out as barely a whisper.

"I'm afraid I can't answer that question," Charlotte replied with an apologetic smile.

"Perhaps the problem wasn't him, but it was with me?" Lydian asked, a sob escaping her lips. "What if I am unlovable?"

Reaching out, Charlotte placed a hand on her stepmother's sleeve. "I didn't know my father at all, because of his utter neglect, so I cannot even presume to understand his complex emotions. But I am beginning to know you, Lydian, and I can assure you that you are a woman of worth."

"You believe so?"

Charlotte smiled, lowering her hand. "I know so. My father was a nincompoop to treat you so distastefully."

Lydian's laugh was light and airy. "I thought the same thing on a few occasions, but I never dared to say it out loud. That would be improper."

"It is all right to occasionally be a little improper," Charlotte quipped.

Keeping her hand next to the side of her mouth, as if sharing a secret, Lydian said, "I did flirt with a few gentlemen this evening."

"You did?"

Her stepmother nodded. "I did. Although, I wasn't bold enough to dance with anyone." She grinned. "I couldn't help but notice you and Hudson seemed rather close after you danced the waltz."

Charlotte covered her mouth with her hand, trying to stifle a smile, but failing miserably. "I suppose we were."

"Did he explain what happened with Hannah?"

"He did," she replied. "Hannah had kissed him after pleading for another chance with him."

"And you believe him?"

"I do."

Lydian nodded. "Just be careful. Your father was many things, but unfaithful was not one of them."

"I understand."

"Good." Her stepmother glanced up at the tree. "I shall go first. It is best to get this over with."

Charlotte waited below as her stepmother started climbing the thick, low hanging branches. Once Lydian reached the window, she began her ascent of the tree, moving quickly and proficiently.

Once they had both entered her bedchamber, Charlotte was startled to see Duncan sitting on the armchair in the corner with a candle burning on the table next to him. He wore no jacket, and his cravat was untied.

Duncan rose from his chair slowly, his eyes narrowed. "May I ask where you ladies have been this evening?"

To her surprise, Lydian stepped in front of her, and announced, "We went to Lady Thornley's masquerade ball."

"And whose ingenious idea was that?" he asked, his knowing gaze focused on Charlotte.

"It was mine," Lydian blurted out.

Duncan's brow lifted as he shifted his gaze towards her. "It was yours?" he asked, surprised. "Not Lady Charlotte's?"

"It was mine, entirely," Lydian replied. "It took some effort on my part, but I managed to convince Charlotte to join me."

"I hope you were clever enough to leave before everyone removed their masks."

"We did."

"That is a relief, but need I remind you both that you are in mourning?" he questioned sharply. "It is wholly inappropriate for either of you to be attending any social function."

Keeping her head held high, Lydian replied, "I am well aware of that fact."

"Yet, you chose to go anyway," Duncan said as he started pacing in front of them. "Why?"

Lydian glanced over her shoulder at her before saying, "I needed a respite from my grief. Even if it was only for a moment."

"And did you succeed?" Duncan asked dryly.

Lydian nodded. "Yes."

"How did you travel to this ball?"

"We took a hackney," Lydian lied.

Duncan stopped pacing and stared at her in disbelief. "You *what*?"

"We took a hackney," Lydian repeated calmly.

His jaw dropped, but he recovered quickly. "You both are mad. Do you have any concept of what could have happened to you, two unescorted ladies on the dangerous streets of London?" he asked, his voice rising.

"We were well aware of the risks," Lydian stated.

Duncan took a commanding step closer to her, and Lydian took a step back. "You are still the Countess of Huntley, and I expect you to behave accordingly. If you do not, then I will have no choice but to cut your monthly allowance. Do I make myself clear?"

Lydian nodded, her eyes turning downcast. "Yes, Lord Huntley."

"As for you, Lady Charlotte," Duncan turned his gaze towards her, "no amount of money can take back a tattered reputation. You need to be mindful in the future to remember that. One slip up can drastically alter your future forever."

"I understand, my lord," she replied.

"Good," he said, crossing his arms over his chest, "especially since we all have a solemn duty to uphold this family's reputation."

Lydian brought her gaze up. "I can assure you that it won't happen again."

"See that it doesn't," Duncan asserted.

They watched in silence as he walked over to the door and placed his hand on the handle. He sighed before he turned to face them. "I would have you know that it does not give me great joy to lecture you about decorum. I had expected better from both of you."

Duncan turned the handle and exited the room, closing the door behind him.

Charlotte stared at her stepmother in amazement. "Why did you take the blame? We both know it was my idea."

Lydian turned around to face her. "Because I could have stopped you, but I didn't. I chose to go along. And I'm glad I did."

"As am I," Charlotte replied.

"But may I propose that we don't make sneaking out a habit?" her stepmother suggested.

Charlotte smiled. "I can agree to that."

"Excellent. Now it is time for me to retire for bed," Lydian said. "I shall request a breakfast tray for both of us tomorrow morning so we can sleep in."

"That sounds wonderful."

Lydian walked over to the door and opened it up. "Thank you for including me on your adventure this evening." She paused. "Now don't forget to put a cap on before you get into bed."

Charlotte laughed at her stepmother's advice. She couldn't seem to help herself. But now, it didn't seem as irksome.

15

CHARLOTTE'S EYES BLINKED OPEN. SHE HAD NO IDEA OF THE time, but she felt remarkably well-rested, more so than she had felt in weeks. She rose from her bed, walked over to the curtains and pulled them open, causing the sun to stream into the bedchamber. She took a moment to listen to the sweet sounds of chirping birds from just outside of her open window.

What a beautiful day, she thought, as she placed her hands on the windowsill. The image of Hudson came to her mind, bringing a smile to her face. She couldn't believe that he had spoken so freely to her last night and confessed that he had wanted to kiss her. Not that she minded. She would have gladly kissed him, given the right circumstances.

Now that she knew he held her in some regard, she felt almost giddy with delight. But she was well aware that nothing could come from this flirtation. Not yet, anyway. She was still in mourning. But for the time being, she could enjoy his company and hope he did not tire of her. For she had developed deep feelings for Hudson, and she was in agony not knowing if there was to be a future between them.

A knock came at the door.

"Enter," she called.

The door opened, revealing Ellen holding a tray in her hands. "Good morning, milady," she said cheerfully. "I see that you are finally awake."

"I must have been more tired than I realized," she commented.

Ellen smiled. "I brought your breakfast."

"Thank you."

Her lady's maid placed the tray down on a side table. "Can I get you some tea?"

"Yes, please," she replied. "That sounds heavenly."

"Do you still intend to go riding this morning?" Ellen asked as she poured the tea.

"I would like to."

"Then I will retrieve your riding habit," Ellen said as she picked up the teacup. She walked it over to her. "There you are, milady."

"Thank you."

Charlotte took a sip of the tea and immediately noticed the bitter taste. She made a face. "This is rather bitter."

"I am not sure why that is," Ellen commented. "Lady Huntley prepared the tea this morning."

"Did she?"

Ellen nodded. "She does so every morning," she revealed. "Would you care for some sugar or honey to make it sweeter?"

"No," she said, glancing down at the contents of the cup. "I am not sure if that would help the taste."

"Would you prefer your chocolate instead?"

"I would, very much," she replied, walking the teacup back over to the tray.

Ellen picked up another cup and extended it towards her.

"Thank you," she murmured before taking a sip of the warm drink. "This is much better."

"I am glad, milady."

Charlotte walked back over to the window and looked out as she enjoyed her chocolate while Ellen tidied up her bedchamber.

"How was the masquerade ball last night?"

A smile came to her face as she turned to face her lady's maid. "It went well."

"Did anyone recognize you?"

She shook her head. "No. We left before the unmasking."

"That is good."

Charlotte leaned back on the windowsill and asked, "How did the visit with your mother go?"

Ellen gave her a sad smile. "Not well. My mother is sicker than I had realized. The doctor has given her some medicine. My sister and I will have to pitch in more to help her."

"I am sorry to hear that," she said. "Do you require additional funds to help pay for the doctor or medicines?"

"You already have been more than generous, milady," Ellen stated, turning away from her. "We shall make do with what we have."

"But I am more than willing to help."

"I know that, and I thank you for it." Ellen stopped in front of the dressing table. "Should we start preparing you for the day?"

"That is a splendid idea," Charlotte said, straightening from the windowsill. She walked over and sat in front of the dressing table. "A simple chignon would do just fine for my morning ride."

"As you wish, milady." Ellen picked up the brush. "I can't help but notice that you are wearing a cap this morning."

Charlotte laughed. "Lady Huntley reminded me to put one on before I went to bed last night."

Ellen removed the cap and placed it onto the dressing table. "I am relieved that I left one out for you then."

"As am I."

"Will Lord Hudson be calling on you today?" her lady's maid asked as she started brushing her brown tresses.

"I hope so."

"You certainly have been spending a lot of time with him, between him coming to call and your little adventures."

Charlotte took the last sip of her chocolate and placed the empty cup onto the dressing table. "I suppose we are."

"Do you have any escapades planned for the near future with Lord Hudson?"

"No," she replied. "I promised Lady Huntley that I would behave for the time being."

Ellen placed the brush down and began to twist her hair into a tight chignon. "Do you still intend to retire with Lady Huntley to her dowager house in Blackpool?"

"I haven't decided yet."

"Isn't she planning to leave soon?"

She nodded. "Yes. I believe she still plans to leave next week."

"But what about Lord Hudson?" Ellen prodded.

"What about him?" Charlotte asked, placing a hand to her stomach. For some reason, she started to feel slightly nauseous. Perhaps she drank her chocolate too quickly, she mused.

Ellen pressed on. "You would leave him behind?"

"I am not sure," she replied. "It is not as if we have an understanding between us."

"And what about Lord Huntley?"

Charlotte met her questioning gaze in the dressing table mirror. "What about him?"

"He is also rather handsome," Ellen said with a smile.

"I can assure you that we are just friends."

Ellen bobbed her head as she placed a pin in her hair. "I was just curious." She stepped back. "Shall we get you dressed now?"

Charlotte rose, and she instantly regretted her swift action. She felt light-headed. She placed her hand on the back of the chair for support and leaned into it.

"Are you all right, milady?" Ellen asked.

She took a moment to reply. "I am, but I'm afraid I'm feeling a little dizzy."

"Would you care to lie down?"

"No, that won't be necessary," she replied, bringing her other hand to her forehead. "I just need a moment, and then I should be feeling up to going riding."

Ellen stepped closer to her and placed a hand on her sleeve. "You don't look well, milady. I think you should lie down."

Charlotte blinked a few times, and she realized that her vision had gone blurry. What was happening to her?

"Yes, I think that might be a good idea," she said as she accepted Ellen's assistance.

Ellen led her over to the bed and helped her lay down. "Would you like for me to call for the doctor?"

As she placed her head on her pillow, she replied, "That won't be necessary. I think I just need to rest."

Her lady's maid covered her with a blanket. "You are looking rather pale," she commented. "I will bring up some wet cloths and place them on your forehead."

Feeling too weak to nod her acknowledgement, she just whispered, "I would appreciate that."

"I'm going to fetch Lady Huntley," Ellen said, stepping back from the bed.

Charlotte attempted to keep her eyes open, but she realized she was fighting a losing battle. She'd never been so tired in her life, and her eyelids were so incredibly heavy.

"Lady Charlotte?" Ellen asked, her voice sounding very far away.

Feeling the darkness creep in around her, Charlotte

succumbed to the desire to close her eyes and drifted off into a peaceful slumber.

Charlotte could hear voices of people she knew and of those she didn't, but she couldn't seem to make herself want to open her eyes. Tired, she thought. *So incredibly tired.*

"Lady Charlotte," an unfamiliar man said from above her, "can you hear me?"

Why wouldn't these people just let her sleep, she wondered.

There was a long moment when she heard nothing, and she hoped that meant they had finally given up, leaving her in peace. Then, the familiar voice of Lord Huntley said, "It is time to wake up, Charlotte."

"No," she muttered. "Sleep."

There was more silence before she heard her stepmother say, "Finally. She is starting to wake up."

Charlotte blinked open her eyes begrudgingly and saw a group of people staring back at her. In a moment, she went from groggy awareness to fully alert in the span of a breath. Gasping, she reached for the covers and pulled them up to her chin.

"What are you all doing in my room?" she demanded in a raspy voice.

Lydian stepped forward. "We all have been extremely worried about you."

"You have?" she asked, confused.

With a nod, her stepmother explained, "You took ill two days ago and have been unconscious ever since."

"But that is impossible. Isn't it?" she asked, turning her gaze towards Duncan.

"I'm afraid it is true," he replied with a solemn expression. "We weren't sure if you were going to live or die."

"I was that sick?" she questioned in disbelief.

Duncan came to stand closer to the bed, the concern evident on his brow. "You were," he answered. "You gave all of us quite a fright."

Ellen appeared next to Lord Huntley with a glass of water in her hand. "Would you care for something to drink, milady?"

"I would," she replied, moving to sit up in her bed.

Once her back was resting against the wall, she reached out and accepted the glass from her lady's maid. She took a small sip, enjoying the soothing trickle of cool water down her throat.

A tall, older man with a thin brown mustache cleared his throat, drawing her attention. "My name is Dr. Wellington." He pointed at a short young man standing near the door. "That is Dr. Lowery. He is my associate."

She gave the doctor a weak smile. "Hello."

He smiled kindly at her, setting her at ease. "How are you feeling?"

"Tired."

"That is to be expected," he said. "Now can you tell me some of your symptoms when you first felt ill?"

Charlotte brought a hand up to her temple. "I started feeling light-headed, nauseated, and I felt very weak."

"Very good," Dr. Wellington remarked. "And what had you been doing before you felt these symptoms coming on?"

"I had been drinking a cup of chocolate, and my lady's maid had been styling my hair," she replied.

"Had you felt sick before these symptoms?"

She shook her head.

His thin mustache drooped as he pursed his lips thoughtfully. "Just as I suspected." He reached for a brown satchel on the ground and placed it on a chair next to him. "Lady Charlotte had a bout with influenza."

"How horrible!" her stepmother exclaimed.

"I believe that she is recovering," Dr. Wellington responded reassuringly. Then, he reached into his bag and pulled out a piece of paper. "I don't believe breathing a vein or leeches will be required in this case. But I do recommend alternating cold and warm baths in the next few days."

"Thank heavens for that," her stepmother murmured. "I don't think I could stand by and watch someone else going through bloodletting."

Dr. Wellington gave her an understanding look. "The sight of blood can make people a bit squeamish, but sometimes it is necessary." He turned back towards Charlotte. "If your strength does not return in three days, then we will use leeches to help cleanse your body of the bad blood."

"That sounds awful," she remarked under her breath.

"I assure you that leeches are highly effective at curing most ailments," Dr. Lowery shared, walking closer to her bed.

Dr. Wellington walked over to her writing table and removed a quill. He dipped the end into the ink, dabbed off the excess, and wrote something on the piece of paper. He blew on the ink before he folded the paper and slipped it into his jacket pocket.

"I would like to examine my patient in private before I depart," Dr. Wellington requested. "Would you mind all stepping out of the room?"

Her stepmother tipped her head. "Of course, doctor. But we shall leave Lady Charlotte's lady's maid in for propriety's sake."

"I would expect nothing less," Dr. Wellington replied with a smile.

Lydian reached out and encompassed her hand. "I am relieved beyond words that you are finally awake."

"Don't crowd the girl," Duncan teased. "We all want to give our well-wishes."

Her stepmother took a step back and said, "I shall bring back a whole pot of tea for you, and some biscuits. Would that please you?"

"It would, very much."

Lydian smiled down at her one last time before she departed from the room.

"I knew you were too stubborn to die," Duncan joked, looking down at her.

"Was that supposed to be a compliment?"

He chuckled. "It was," he confirmed. "Was it too soon?"

"Perhaps," she said, smiling.

Duncan watched her for a moment, and she could see his deep concern evident in the wrinkle of his brow. "I have never been so scared," he admitted softly.

"I will be fine," she assured him.

"You'd better be," he stated. "I will be back shortly to check on you."

Dr. Wellington turned his attention towards Dr. Lowery and ordered, "Why don't you go get something to eat while I examine Lady Charlotte?"

"I can stay and assist," Dr. Lowery remarked hopefully.

"That won't be necessary."

Dr. Lowery tipped his head in response before he followed Lord Huntley out of the room, closing the door behind him.

Once the door was closed, Charlotte saw Ellen move to sit on a chair in the corner and picked up some needlework.

Dr. Wellington came to stand next to the bed. "May I listen to your pulse, Lady Charlotte?"

"You may," she said, holding up her hand.

He pressed his fingers to her wrist, and he had a deep look of concentration on his face. After a moment, he stated, "Good."

"How is your vision?" he asked.

"It is well."

"Did you have any problems with your vision when you felt your other symptoms come on?"

She nodded. "I did. My eyesight became blurry."

"I assumed as much." Reaching into his pocket, he discreetly pulled out a piece of paper and placed it in her hand. He then closed her hand around the paper and gave her a pointed look. In a low, hushed voice, he said, "Your pupils are back to normal, which is a good sign. They were dilated before. I believe that you will make a full recovery."

She nodded her understanding. "Thank you, doctor."

"Everything else appears to be in order," Dr. Wellington declared, his voice returning to normal. "If you are not opposed, I shall come back tomorrow and check in on you."

"That would be wonderful," she replied.

Dr. Wellington held her gaze while saying, "Take care, Lady Charlotte." He turned towards her lady's maid. "Would you mind showing me to the kitchen to where my associate would be?"

Ellen rose and placed her needlework onto her chair. "Yes, Doctor Wellington. Follow me."

Once they departed from the room, Charlotte opened the note and read:

You were poisoned. Trust no one.

Her eyes widened as she lowered the note to her side. She had been poisoned? Who would have done such a thing? Suddenly, the memory of the bitter tea came to her mind. That had to have been it.

Crumbling the paper in her hand, she attempted to formulate a plan. What was she going to do? She couldn't very well stay here when someone was trying to kill her. But where could she go?

Tossing her legs over the bed, she rose and walked over to the armoire. She removed a simple white gown and started the arduous process of attempting to dress herself. Her stays were a little loose, but no one would notice that. Not if she put a spencer on to cover her gown.

After she was dressed, she pulled her hair back into a loose bun and placed a straw bonnet atop her head. She stepped over to the window as she tied the strings under her chin.

There was only one place that she could think of that was safe. She had to escape before anyone discovered her intent.

16

"You need to have them all arrested," Isabella declared, tossing her hands up in the air.

Hudson was attempting to keep himself calm.

"For what, exactly?" he asked.

"For keeping Charlotte imprisoned at Wellesley House." She started pacing in the drawing room. "For the past two days, I have been turned away from seeing her."

"As have I," he pointed out.

Isabella stopped pacing and gave him an exasperated look. "But I am her dearest friend. I know she would want to see me, even if she was sick."

He sighed, frowning. "This hardly constitutes an emergency," he stated. "When I received your missive at my office, I truly thought something was horribly, terribly wrong. That is why I left the Old Bailey and rushed over here as fast as I could."

"Why would you think that?"

With a huff, he pulled the note out of his jacket pocket and unfolded it. "It says, and I quote, 'This is an emergency. I need to speak to you right away'."

"Well, it is an emergency!" she exclaimed, unabashed. "I know that Charlotte is being held against her will."

"Or she is merely sick as we were both informed by the butler at the door," he replied. "Besides, I don't have time for any more of this nonsense. I need to get back to my office. I have cases to review before tomorrow's trials."

"But we both saw her the night before she supposedly was sick," Isabella pressed, "and she gave no indication that she was feeling at all ill."

"That is true," he agreed. "She didn't show any signs of sickness... yet. But that doesn't mean anything."

Isabella crossed her arms over her chest. "What is the point of having a brother as a judge if you aren't going to arrest anyone?"

"In order to have someone arrested, you need to have proof of a crime," he explained, "and your accusations have no merit."

"Fine," Isabella said, her eyes narrowing. "Then I will go and climb the tree outside of her bedchamber window, and I will find the proof required."

"I think that is a foolhardy thing to do."

"Why?"

"Because what if she is truly sick?"

"I don't believe she is."

Hudson gave her a frustrated look. "Let's say for argument's sake that she *was* sick," he said, holding up his hand. "What, then?"

"Then I would know for certain that she was safe, but I don't believe that to be the case," Isabella asserted stubbornly.

"Pray tell, what purpose would Lady Huntley or Lord Huntley have for keeping Lady Charlotte imprisoned?" he asked impatiently.

Isabella snapped her fingers and smiled victoriously. "They want her money."

"So, you truly believe that they are keeping Charlotte locked away so they can have access to her money?"

Isabella nodded.

Hudson brought his fingers up to the bridge of his nose. "You are imagining things."

"Why else would they keep her locked up?"

"They are not…" His voice trailed off as he tried to rein in his anger. "This whole conversation is ridiculous. They are not keeping her locked away."

Isabella's face fell. "You aren't going to help me, are you?" she asked softly.

Hudson's voice softened at her crestfallen look. "What if we go speak to Lady Huntley together about this matter?"

"And demand that we see Lottie?" she asked firmly.

Despite his annoyance, he found himself smiling at his sister's stubborn nature. "Lady Huntley is not an unreasonable woman," he said. "I am sure if we explain that we are worried about Lady Charlotte, then she will grant permission for you to see her."

Isabella nodded, slowly. "Perhaps that might be for the best," she hesitated, "for now."

"It is admirable how much you care for your friend," Hudson commented, "but storming her bedchamber might not be the best course of action."

"I am just worried about Lottie," his sister said. "She hardly ever got sick when we were at school."

Hudson reached for his pocket watch and glanced down at the time. "If we hurry, I believe we have enough time to call on Lady Huntley before I am expected to be back in my office."

Isabella clasped her hands together. "You mean it?" she asked excitedly.

"I do," he replied.

"I must admit that you are my favorite big brother," she declared.

He chuckled. "Don't let Everett or Dudley hear you say that."

With a shrug, Isabella said, "If they want to assume that title, then they will need to work a little harder to win my favor." She started walking towards the door. "Allow me to retrieve my bonnet…"

Her voice trailed off when Charlotte walked through the door, wearing a white gown with a maroon spencer. Her straw bonnet was askew on her head and tendrils of her hair were falling haphazardly around her face. What alarmed him the most was that her green eyes met his with an expression that bordered on panic.

"Lady Charlotte," he started, "are you all—"

"You need to help me," Charlotte exclaimed as she placed her hands on the back of the settee. "Someone has poisoned me."

Hudson reared back, stunned, but he recovered quickly. "Why do you suppose you have been poisoned?"

Charlotte winced, drawing attention to her pale face. "I know I sound rather mad, but it is the truth."

"No one is doubting you," he said reassuringly. "Why don't you take a seat and start from the beginning?" He held his hand out towards the settee. "Can I get you some refreshment?"

"No, thank you," she murmured as she moved to sit on the settee.

Once Charlotte was situated, Isabella came to sit next to her and declared, "I knew something was going on at your townhouse. I hadn't suspected poisoning, though."

"Isabella," Hudson said, lifting his brow, "perhaps we should let Lady Charlotte speak."

His sister nodded. "I agree." She turned her attention back towards Charlotte. "So, who do you think has poisoned you?"

"I haven't the faintest idea," Charlotte replied. "Two days ago, I drank some bitter tea, and shortly thereafter, I started getting light-headed and weak. I woke up just a couple of hours ago to everyone standing around my bed."

"I want you to be more specific about who was standing around your bed," Hudson said. "I need as many details as I can when I report this to the constable."

"Lord Huntley, Lady Huntley, Dr. Wellington, Dr. Lowery, and my lady's maid, Ellen," she listed.

"Then what happened?" Hudson asked.

Charlotte reached up and untied the strings of her bonnet. "The doctor asked me a few questions and announced to the group that I had come down with influenza."

"Influenza?" he repeated.

Charlotte bobbed her head. "Yes, then he asked if he could examine me in private. That is when he slipped me this note," she said as she reached inside of her reticule.

She held up the slip of paper, and Hudson closed the distance between them. As he unfolded the note, he read, 'You have been poisoned. Trust no one'." He lowered the note. "Did he say anything else, possibly about how he came to this conclusion?"

"Yes," Charlotte replied. "He told me that my pupils were back to normal, and that I should make a full recovery."

Hudson clenched his jaw into a hard line. "Dilated pupils can be a sign that someone has been poisoned."

"How do you know?" Isabella asked with a curious glance.

"Trust me," Hudson remarked. "I have tried enough cases in court where the defendant has poisoned their victims, and I have listened to many hours of expert testimony on the subject. I daresay I could recite the symptoms in my sleep."

He held up the note and asked, "May I keep this note?"

"Why?" Charlotte questioned.

"So that I can give it to the constable as evidence."

"In that case, yes, you may," she replied.

Hudson folded it and slipped it into the pocket of his waistcoat. Then, he grabbed a chair and repositioned it in front of Charlotte.

"You said earlier that you drank some bitter tea," Hudson prompted.

"Yes, I did."

He leaned forward in his seat. "Did your lady's maid bring you your tea or was it another maid?"

"My lady's maid," Charlotte confirmed.

"Do you have any reason to suspect that your lady's maid might be trying to poison you?"

She shook her head. "No, Ellen wouldn't do such a thing. She is much too sweet of a girl."

Hudson's eyes turned calculating. "Who else had access to your tea that morning?"

"Only my stepmother who prepared the tea," Charlotte said. "But she does that every morning." She paused, before adding, "And, no, I don't believe my stepmother poisoned me."

"Have you ever noticed the tea being bitter before?"

Again, she shook her head. "No, I haven't."

"How much of the tea did you drink?"

"Just a sip," she replied. "It was much too bitter to drink any more."

"That is good," Hudson replied. "What was everyone's demeanor this morning when you woke up?"

Charlotte removed her bonnet and placed it down on the settee. "They all appeared relieved that I was awake."

"Do you have any reason to believe that a member of the household staff might be trying to hurt you?" Hudson questioned.

"For what purpose?" Charlotte asked. "I only recently moved in, and I have barely interacted with many of them."

"What of the butler?"

"Baxter may be intimidating with his piercing stare, but I don't believe he has any nefarious intentions towards me."

Hudson grew silent, contemplating his next question. "And what of Lord Huntley?" he started. "Do you believe he might be capable of poisoning you?"

Charlotte shook her head. "Lord Huntley had no access to my morning tea, nor do I believe he would try to hurt me."

"Regardless, someone poisoned you at Wellesley House, and it is not safe for you to go back there," he said. "At least until we discover who the culprit is."

"I would agree," Charlotte replied.

Hudson leaned back in his chair. "I will contact the constable about this matter, and I will send a note to Lord Huntley, informing him that you will be residing at our townhouse for the foreseeable future."

Charlotte nodded her understanding. "Thank you, Lord Hudson."

"Furthermore, with your permission, I would like to speak to Dr. Wellington about his diagnosis," Hudson said, rising.

"By all means," Charlotte agreed.

Hudson met her gaze directly, hoping his words conveyed his sincerity. "You are safe now. You need not fear for your safety here."

"I cannot thank you enough for your assistance," Charlotte acknowledged.

"No thanks is required," he said, gently. "It is my privilege to help you."

Charlotte offered him a weak smile. "You are very kind."

The memory of dancing with Charlotte came into his mind, bringing with it the sudden urge to pull her into his arms and never let her go. He quickly banished the thought and cleared his throat. Now was definitely not the time to be thinking about such things. He needed to have his wits about him.

"If you will excuse me, I have a few letters that I need to write," he said with a slight bow.

As he left the drawing room, Hudson discovered that he was

growing increasingly angry at the thought that someone had poisoned Charlotte. His Charlotte. Why would anyone want to hurt her? She was kind-hearted and loving. And perfect in so many ways.

It mattered not. He would do everything in his power to ensure that Charlotte stayed safe, starting with contacting the constable and insisting that he open an investigation.

After a long rest, Charlotte felt refreshed and reinvigorated as she headed towards the drawing room on the main floor. She still couldn't quite fathom that someone had poisoned her tea, but she felt immense relief that whoever it was couldn't hurt her here. She was safe.

She heard a familiar laugh drift out from the room as she crossed the entry hall. As she peered inside, she saw her friend, the Duchess of Blackbourne, and Isabella sitting on the settee, with their backs to her.

"I thought that was you, Penelope," Charlotte declared as she walked further into the room.

"Lottie!" Penelope exclaimed as she placed her teacup on the table in front of her and rose slowly from the settee. "What a delightful surprise."

Charlotte embraced her friend warmly. "It is good to see you."

"Likewise," Penelope replied. "When Isabella informed me that you were napping, I didn't think I would have the opportunity to say hello."

She stepped back. "How are you feeling?"

"Well." Penelope put a hand on her large protruding belly and gushed, "I have a little over a month left."

"Are you nervous?" Isabella asked.

"Frankly, I am more excited than nervous," Penelope revealed. "Nicholas has been pleading with me to rest more, but I have so much I want to accomplish before the baby arrives."

Charlotte sat across from her friends. "I still can't believe that you married your guardian and that you are about to have a baby soon."

Penelope awkwardly lowered herself down onto the settee. "It is all true."

"Was it love at first sight?" she asked.

"Heavens, no," Penelope declared. "At first, Nicholas and I were at such great odds with each other. But, over time, we fell in love."

"I can't wait to meet your husband," Charlotte said. "Is he as intimidating as everyone says he is?"

With a light laugh, Penelope replied, "He can be rather intimidating at times, but he has a good heart."

"May I pour you some tea, Charlotte?" Isabella asked, putting her hand out towards the silver teapot.

Charlotte grimaced slightly. "No, thank you."

Penelope gave her a curious look. "Since when did you turn down a cup of tea?"

"Since I was poisoned," she responded, seeing no reason to hide the truth from her dear friend.

Penelope's eyes widened. "I beg your pardon?"

"Two days ago, my morning tea tasted bitter, but I thought nothing of it," she shared. "That was until I woke up today, and the doctor slipped me a note, informing me that I had been poisoned."

With a stunned expression on her face, Penelope asked, "But who would want to hurt you?"

She shrugged. "I am not sure, but Lord Hudson has contacted the constable on my behalf."

"Good," Penelope replied. "That is a start."

Isabella spoke up. "Poor Lottie has an evil stepmother."

"Is that so?" Penelope questioned.

Charlotte smiled. "At first, I would have agreed with Isabella, but now my stepmother and I get along nicely."

"Could she have been the one who poisoned you?" Penelope pressed.

Charlotte shook her head. "Frankly, there is no reason for my stepmother to poison me. It wouldn't benefit her at all."

"Other than she is evil," Isabella pointed out.

Penelope arched an eyebrow. "Is your stepmother evil?"

"I assure you that she is not," Charlotte replied with an amused huff. "Isabella has been reading far too many fairy tales."

"Isabella does have rather an imaginative mind," Penelope agreed, smiling, "which is one of the reasons I enjoy spending time with her."

Isabella picked up a plate of biscuits from the tray and extended it towards her. "At least have one of the biscuits."

"I would love a biscuit," she said as she accepted one. "I could never turn down a biscuit."

Penelope tucked a piece of brown hair behind her ear as she asked, "Are you not the least bit concerned that someone poisoned you?"

"I am, very much," she replied. "The most logical person who could have poisoned me is my lady's maid, Ellen. But she would never have done that. She is a hard worker, and her dream was to become a lady's maid."

"Then who do you think it was?"

"I have been wracking my brain trying to come up with that answer," Charlotte said, with a shrug of her shoulders, "but I have nothing. I don't believe I have any enemies."

"What about a nemesis?" Isabella asked with mirth in her voice. "Do you have one of those?"

A quick, wry laugh escaped her lips. "Why would I have a nemesis?"

"Maybe your stepmother isn't just evil, but she is also your archenemy?" Isabella question. "Oh, and she has been plotting your demise since you first arrived."

"But for what purpose?" she inquired. "If I die, then what does my stepmother get?"

"The satisfaction of winning," Isabella said matter-of-factly.

Charlotte grinned. "You are way off on this one, but I do appreciate the effort."

"You are welcome," Isabella replied, smiling. "Although, I would be disappointed to hear that Lady Huntley had anything to do with the poisoning, because I did find her to be quite charming at the masquerade ball."

"As did I," she replied.

Penelope gave her a curious look. "Isabella mentioned that your father died, but I see that you are wearing a white gown, and apparently, you attended a ball a few days ago. Are you not mourning your father?"

"That is a ticklish question," she replied. "After I discovered I was poisoned, I put on the white gown because it was the only dress in the armoire that I could put on myself. Furthermore, if I had been wearing a black gown, I would have received unwanted attention as I walked here."

"And the ball?" Penelope asked.

"It was a masquerade ball, and we departed before the unmasking," she shared.

Penelope gave her a disapproving shake of her head. "That was rather a foolhardy thing to do. Your reputation would have been in tatters if anyone discovered you were attending balls while in mourning."

"I am aware of that fact," she replied, somewhat surprised at her friend's chiding tone.

Penelope glanced back at the door before saying in a hushed voice, "I haven't been to a masquerade ball yet. Nicholas says they are too scandalous. Please say that you enjoyed it."

"I did."

"I'm glad," Penelope said, keeping her voice low. "I think the mourning rules are rather ridiculous. Why can't we enjoy ourselves after a loved one has passed away?"

Charlotte nodded. "I would agree with you there. I don't think it is fair that I have to completely withdraw from Society for six months just because my father died."

With a depth of compassion in her voice, Penelope remarked, "I remember you mentioning you and your father weren't close."

"Close?" she huffed. "I hardly knew the man. Sadly, the more I learn about him, the more disdain I have for him."

Penelope gave her a sad smile. "I am truly sorry."

"Don't be," she replied. "Everyone has obstacles in their lives, but how you overcome them is what defines you as a person."

"I agree," Penelope said, reaching for a biscuit. "Obstacles are what make life meaningful. Overcoming them makes us stronger."

"Precisely," Charlotte agreed. "And if I choose to be bitter about my past, then I am no better than my father was."

Penelope brushed her hands together, wiping off the crumbs. "Now, I want to know, when did you arrive in Town, and why didn't you notify me immediately?"

"I arrived in Town over a week ago for the reading of my father's will, and I sent you a letter shortly thereafter, informing you of my arrival," Charlotte said.

"I never received it," Penelope replied.

"But my stepmother said she put it in the post."

Penelope picked up her teacup and took a sip. "If that had been the case, I would have received it by now."

Charlotte frowned. "Do you suppose it could have gotten lost?"

"Anything is possible, I suppose," Penelope commented.

Isabella spoke up. "What if your stepmother intentionally didn't send the note?"

"For what purpose?" Charlotte asked.

"I am not sure," Isabella replied. "I was just wondering out loud."

"I am sure that Lydian posted the letter," Charlotte said, reaching for a biscuit. "It must have gotten lost in the post."

"That is what most likely happened." Penelope lowered the teacup to her lap. "If you ever find yourself needing assistance, please know that Nicholas and I would be happy to help you."

"Thank you, Penelope," Charlotte responded. "I truly appreciate that."

Isabella smoothed out her pink gown. "I hope you don't mind, but I told Penelope that you are an heiress now."

"Not at all," Charlotte said. "I am glad that she knows."

Penelope smiled broadly. "I am so happy for you," she declared. "Being an heiress will give you the freedom to make your own choices, including marrying for love."

The image of Hudson came to her mind, and she found herself smiling. How did the mere thought of him brighten her mood?

"I suppose so," she said after a long moment.

Penelope eyed her suspiciously. "It almost sounds as if you have someone in mind."

"No, I don't," she rushed to say.

Isabella smiled knowingly. " 'The lady doth protest too much, methinks'," she said, quoting Shakespeare.

Before she could respond, Lady Northampton glided into the room and exclaimed, "Penelope, dear, what a pleasant surprise!"

Penelope rose and embraced the dowager countess. "It is good to see you, Mary."

As Charlotte sat back and listened to them converse, her thoughts started drifting towards Hudson. It was evident that he held her in some regard, but were his feelings as deep as hers? She truly hoped so, because she realized that at some point she had unintentionally fallen desperately in love with Hudson Beauchamp.

❧ 17 ❧

THE HACKNEY CAME TO A STOP OUTSIDE OF HIS ANCESTRAL townhouse. Hudson exited the coach with his brown satchel over one shoulder and a large stack of files in his hand. He was pleased when the main door opened, and Howe stood to the side, granting him entry.

"Good afternoon, milord," the butler said. "May I help you?"

Hudson adjusted the files in his hand. "No, thank you," he replied. "I intend to work in the study for the remainder of the day. If anyone comes to call, please alert me at once."

"Yes, milord," Howe responded, tipping his head.

He walked across the entry hall and stopped outside of the drawing room. To his disappointment, it was empty. He had been hoping to catch a glimpse of Charlotte.

Howe spoke up from behind him. "If I may, Lady Isabella and Lady Charlotte have adjourned to the library, and your mother is resting."

"Very good," he said. "Thank you, Howe."

Hudson turned on his heel and headed towards the study tucked in the corner of the townhouse. Everett had granted him permission to use the study whenever the need arose, and he felt an undeniable desire to be close to Charlotte at the moment. He enjoyed knowing that he was under the same roof as her.

He stepped into the square room with two bay windows along the back wall. Dark wood paneling covered the walls, a Persian carpet ran the length of the room, and a mahogany desk sat in front of the windows.

Hudson placed his files and satchel on top of the desk and came around the desk to sit down. He had a lot of case files to review before tomorrow morning. He reached for the first file and opened it up. It was a larceny case. That trial should be simple enough, he thought to himself, as he read the facts about the case.

He had just closed the file when Howe stepped into the room and announced, "Dr. Wellington is here to see you, milord."

"Send him in," he ordered.

Hudson placed the file to the side as he waited for the doctor.

As Dr. Wellington stepped into the room, Hudson rose from his chair and greeted him. "Thank you for coming so soon, doctor." He pointed towards a chair facing the desk. "Please have a seat."

"Thank you," Dr. Wellington murmured as he went to sit down.

Hudson sat back down in his chair. "As I mentioned in my letter, Lady Charlotte is a dear family friend of ours, and she has granted me permission to speak to you on her behalf."

Dr. Wellington nodded. "I must admit I was relieved when you informed me that she was safe and residing with your family."

"It caused us great alarm to learn that she had been poisoned, and we are immensely grateful for your discretion on the matter."

"It was my pleasure."

"If you don't mind, I have a few questions that I would like to ask you," Hudson said in a solemn tone.

"I assumed as much."

Hudson leaned forward in his chair. "May I ask how you discovered that she had been poisoned?"

"There were the usual signs of dilation of the pupils and a slow pulse," he explained. "Furthermore, Lady Charlotte confirmed my suspicions when she awoke and began to list her symptoms, all of which came on rather suddenly."

"Lady Charlotte informed us that her morning tea had tasted bitter, but she had thought nothing of it at the time. Now she believes that is when she was poisoned," he shared.

"I concur," he replied. "Fortunately, the bitter taste kept her from ingesting any more of the poison."

"By chance, were you able to deduce which poison was used on Lady Charlotte?"

Dr. Wellington shook his head. "I'm afraid not. Any number of poisons could have been used, including camphor or hemlock. In fact, both of those have a bitter taste to them," he stated. "At least we can rule out arsenic."

"Because it is tasteless and odorless."

"Yes, and it is deadly in even small doses," the doctor replied.

Hudson let out a sigh. "That is a relief," he said. "Lady Charlotte mentioned you informed Lord Huntley and Lady Huntley that you diagnosed her with influenza."

Dr. Wellington nodded in agreement. "Yes, her symptoms did mimic influenza, and I decided to use that to her advantage. I didn't want to tip off the perpetrator that I suspected poisoning."

"Did you have any reason to suspect Lady Huntley or Lord Huntley could have been the one who administered the poison to Lady Charlotte?"

"I do not have any idea who it could have been," Dr. Wellington said with a shake of his head. "All I know is that Lady Charlotte was poisoned, and I feared for her safety."

Hudson reached for his satchel and placed it on the ground

next to the chair. "You should know that I contacted the constable and requested that he open an investigation."

Dr. Wellington grinned knowingly. "I am sure that he complied, with you being a judge and all."

"He did," Hudson confirmed, "and I have no doubt that he will be in contact with you shortly."

Rising, Dr. Wellington said, "If you are not opposed, I would like to stop by tomorrow to examine Lady Charlotte."

"You are more than welcome, doctor."

Dr. Wellington's brows knitted downward. "Thank you for keeping Lady Charlotte safe. It angers me to know that someone intended to kill her."

"So you believe someone truly intended to kill her?"

"I'm afraid I cannot say for certain at this point," Dr. Wellington replied, "but it most definitely appears that way."

"Thank you for your time," Hudson said, rising.

After the doctor left the room, Hudson sat back down and looked out the window. Why would someone want to see Charlotte dead, he wondered. He needed a motive. A driving force for why someone poisoned her tea.

Could it be jealousy? Perhaps Lady Huntley hated Charlotte to such a degree that she wanted to kill her. Or was it greed? Lord Huntley did stand to gain Charlotte's inheritance if she passed away. But what if the culprit had another motive? What if it was the lady's maid or the butler? Baxter's presence was rather intimidating, but it wouldn't benefit him if Charlotte died.

According to Charlotte, only two people had access to her tea that morning. Her stepmother and her lady's maid. But what if someone else had access? There were lots of people milling around the kitchen in the early mornings. Maybe one of them slipped something into the teapot?

A knock at the door interrupted his musings. "Milord, did you hear me?" Howe asked.

Hudson turned back towards the door and saw his butler

standing there with an expectant look on his face.

"I'm afraid I did not," he replied honestly.

"Lord Huntley is here to see you."

"Send him in."

Howe tipped his head. "Yes, milord."

A few moments later, Lord Huntley strode into the study with a stern look on his face. "I have come to collect Lady Charlotte, and we shall be on our way."

"No."

"No?"

He leaned back in his chair, keeping his expression unreadable. "Lady Charlotte is not going anywhere. She is safe here."

"She is safe back at Wellesley House, as well," Lord Huntley contended.

"I don't believe that to be true."

Lord Huntley scoffed. "And why do you say that, Lord Hudson?" he asked disparagingly.

Hudson leaned forward and intertwined his fingers together. He placed them on the desk and said, "Were you aware that Lady Charlotte was poisoned two days ago?"

Lord Huntley's eyes widened. "I don't believe you."

"It is true," he replied, his alert eyes studying the lord. "The constable will be visiting you shortly to start his investigation."

With a stunned expression, Lord Huntley sat down on a chair that sat across from him. "Are you saying that Lady Charlotte didn't have influenza as the doctor stated?"

"No," he said with a shake of his head. "The doctor only told everyone that to give Lady Charlotte time to get to safety."

Lord Huntley ran a hand through his hair. "Poor Lady Charlotte. She must have been so scared."

"She is stronger than you give her credit for."

"I suppose you are right," Lord Huntley stated, wiping his hand over his mouth. "Does Lady Charlotte have any idea of who poisoned her?"

Hudson shook his head. "Not at this time."

"Then I shall take her home and keep her safe," Lord Huntley declared, rising. "I truly appreciate everything you have done for her up to this point."

"Let me be clear when I say that Lady Charlotte is not going anywhere," he said firmly. "She will remain as a guest in our home."

"But that is completely unnecessary."

"I disagree."

"You would keep her from her family?"

"I would," he paused, "for now."

"Why am I not surprised by that?" Lord Huntley asked curtly.

He reared back slightly. "What do you mean by that?"

Lord Huntley glared down at him. "Don't think for one second that I don't know what you are doing."

"Which is?"

Taking a step closer to the desk, Lord Huntley pointed at the ground. "You are attempting to keep Lady Charlotte for yourself."

"I beg your pardon?" he declared. "That has never been my intention."

"No?" Lord Huntley questioned. "It is just mighty convenient that Lady Charlotte is an heiress, and you are just a lowly district judge."

Not appreciating his tone, Hudson said, "I am also the son of a marquess. Or did you forget that?"

"Oh, no. I am aware of your lineage, Lord Hudson," Lord Huntley remarked. "Regardless, I am more than capable of keeping Lady Charlotte protected—"

He huffed, cutting him off. "If that is the case, you have been doing less than a commendable job since she was poisoned while under your protection," Hudson remarked dryly.

"Now that I know that someone intends to harm Lady Charlotte, I will go to great lengths to keep her safe."

"That won't be necessary," he replied. "As I have been saying, that will be my family's privilege for the foreseeable future."

"Then I shall go to the magistrate."

He smirked. "Make sure you give Judge Beck my regards when you call on him."

Lord Huntley's eyes narrowed. "You think you are so clever," he said. "But Lady Charlotte will see right through you. I am sure of it."

Finished with this futile conversation, Hudson rose from his chair and remarked dismissively, "Thank you for coming by, and I will be sure to give Lady Charlotte your regards."

Lord Huntley stood there, watching him, with contempt in his eyes. "I cannot abide you, but I do care about Lady Charlotte. I want your word that you will treat her with the respect that we both know that she deserves."

"I give you my word as a gentleman," he replied.

"Then I shall hold you to that." Lord Huntley took a step back. "I will call on Lady Charlotte daily to ensure that she is being well taken care of."

"I wouldn't expect anything less."

Lord Huntley pursed his lips. "Make no mistake of it that I will convince Lady Charlotte to come home with me."

"I wish you luck with that endeavor."

With a parting look filled with disdain, Lord Huntley spun on his heel and exited the study, slamming the door behind him.

Hudson dropped down onto his chair and stared at the closed door. He could understand Lord Huntley's anger. After all, he was honor bound to protect Lady Charlotte as the Earl of Huntley, but until they ruled him out as a suspect, he wasn't going to let Charlotte go home.

Home.

Why did it already feel like she was home here with him?

Dressed in a borrowed pale-pink gown, Charlotte sat alone in the library as she attempted to read a book, but her thoughts were continuously turning towards Hudson. The mere thought of him always brought a smile to her face.

She had no doubt that she loved him, but she didn't think it was possible that he would ever return her feelings. He had previously admitted that he willingly chose to lock away his heart after it had been shattered by his former betrothed.

But what if she could change that? What if she convinced him to take a chance on love... a chance on her?

Hudson's voice broke through her musings. "You are wearing a deep, contemplative expression," he said. "I do hope everything is all right."

Charlotte brought her gaze up and saw him standing in the doorway, looking handsome in his blue riding jacket and buff trousers. "Everything is well."

"May I ask what you are reading?" he asked, pointing towards the book in her lap.

She held up the small, worn book. "*Romeo and Juliet.*"

" '*Wisely and slow; they stumble that run fast*'," he said, quoting Shakespeare.

"That is sound advice for all things, including love."

"Especially love," he sighed as he walked further into the room. "I have often wondered how different my life would have been had I not fallen for Hannah so quickly."

She closed the book and placed it in her lap. "I believe everyone that comes into our lives has a purpose."

"You do?"

She nodded. "People may come and go in our lives, but they

all teach us a different lesson, whether it is to love, to laugh, or to let go."

"But what if that one person brings forth heartache and sorrow?" he asked.

With compassion in her tone, she replied, "Then you should be thankful that you were able to experience love, even if it was for only a fleeting moment."

Hudson placed his hands on the back of a chair and leaned in. "I do not consider myself lucky." He paused. "Although, I am relieved that Hannah's true character was revealed before I married her."

"That was rather fortunate."

"I suppose so."

Charlotte noticed that Hudson's eyes looked tired. "You seem tired."

"I must admit that I am," he replied. "The stupidity of criminals never ceases to amaze me."

"Is that so?"

He came around the chair and sat down. "The trials this morning were rather mundane, and I'm afraid I was forced to send many people to Newgate as punishment for their crimes."

"Would you like to talk about it?"

He shook his head. "I wouldn't want to trouble you or weigh you down with my burdens."

"I would be more than happy to listen."

"I know you would, and that pleases me immensely," he said, the briefest smile touching his lips. "But I am much more interested in learning about how your day went."

She ran her fingers over the book's edges. "It went well," she replied. "I met with the constable this morning."

"How did that go?"

Charlotte let out a sigh. "He said he interviewed everyone, but he was unable to determine a motive or even a suspect at this time."

"I assumed that might be the case."

"But what should I do?" she asked. "It is not as if I can live with Isabella indefinitely."

"Why not?"

Charlotte rose and returned the book to its location on the shelf. "I do not wish to become a burden to anyone."

"You could never be a burden, Lottie," he said gently. "I hope you know that."

With her back to him, she murmured, "I want to believe that to be true."

"Then believe it."

She turned back around to face him. "It is not that simple."

"Why not?"

"Your family has been more than kind to me, more than I deserve," she started, "but I cannot remain here forever, hiding away from the world."

"It is only until you are out of mourning, then you can start going out in Society," he said. "If you would like, I could always take you to another fair in the city."

Charlotte turned her gaze towards the window as she reluctantly admitted, "As much as I would enjoy that, I think it might be best if I retire to Chatsmoor Hall until next Season."

Hudson frowned, looking displeased. "That is a terrible idea."

"Why?"

He opened his mouth, closed it again, evidently reconsidering whatever he'd been about to say. Finally, he said, "It is not appropriate for a young lady, such as yourself, to be living alone."

"It is not as if I would be alone," she argued. "I would be surrounded by the household staff."

Hudson rose from his chair. "Regardless, you are an heiress, and you need to be protected from unscrupulous people."

It was her turn to frown. "I can take care of myself."

"Make no mistake about that," he agreed, watching her closely, "but… I… don't want you to go all the way to Scarborough."

"It is only until the next Season starts."

Hudson took a step towards her, his eyes holding an intensity she had not witnessed before. "I would miss you."

"And I you," she found herself boldly admitting.

"Then don't go," he said. "Stay in London, with my family," he hesitated, "with me."

Charlotte felt her heart begin to race as she gazed into his eyes and heard the slight plea in his voice. "What exactly are you saying, Hudson?"

She saw all kinds of emotions appear on Hudson's face, and she wondered what he was thinking. Then, a pained look came to his face as he took a step back. "I… uh… believe that Isabella would miss you dearly."

"Isabella?" she questioned, wondering what had just transpired. Why was he talking about Isabella?

He nodded. "Yes," he replied, clearing his throat. "I don't believe my sister is prepared to let you go."

"I see," she said slowly, hoping he was speaking about himself. "I also would miss Isabella."

"Then you will stay?" he asked hopefully.

Charlotte took a step towards him. "Is that what Isabella would want? For me to stay?"

"It is," he responded, his voice hoarse.

Something undefinable mingled in the depths of his blue eyes, holding her captive for a few moments. Finally, she murmured, "Then perhaps it would be best if I stayed, for Isabella's sake."

A look of relief flashed across his face. "I think that would be wise."

Howe stepped inside of the room and announced, "I apologize for intruding, milord, but Lady Huntley is here to call upon

Lady Charlotte." He met her gaze. "Are you available for callers, milady?"

She nodded. "I am."

"Then I shall direct her to the drawing room."

When the butler left the room, Hudson asked, "Would you like me to accompany you to visit with your stepmother?"

"That won't be necessary," she replied. "Even if she wanted to, my stepmother couldn't hurt me here."

Hudson bobbed his head. "Would you care to go riding tomorrow morning?"

"I would."

"Very good," he said, maintaining her gaze. "If you need me, I will be in the study."

She started walking towards the door but stopped and spun back around. "Will you be joining us for dinner?"

"Yes."

She gave him a timid smile. "I shall see you then."

"I will be looking forward to it," he remarked with a slight bow.

As she exited the library, Charlotte let out a little sigh. She couldn't seem to make sense of Hudson. She had mistakenly thought that he was going to declare his feelings, but, instead, he spoke of how much Isabella would miss her, which was odd. One thing was certain, though, it was evident that Hudson did have feelings for her, but he refused to act on them.

What would it take for him to open up his heart and let her in?

Charlotte stepped into the drawing room and saw her step-mother was standing next to the window, staring out towards the gardens. She was fingering the long, black necklace around her neck.

"Good afternoon," she greeted, walking further into the drawing room.

Lydian turned towards her with a smile on her face. "Charlotte. I am relieved to see you looking so well."

"Likewise." She pointed towards the settee across from her. "Would you care to sit down?"

"I would."

After they both were seated, Lydian spoke up. "The constable spoke to me last night about how someone poisoned your tea. Is that true?"

She nodded. "It is."

"How awful," her stepmother murmured. "I understand now why you chose to run away. Although, a letter would have been most helpful. The entire household was in a panic when Ellen discovered you missing."

"I do apologize about leaving so quickly, but I was frightened when the doctor informed me that I had been poisoned."

"That is understandable, and I do not fault you for that."

"Thank you."

With her hands clasped in her lap, Lydian asked, "Do you have any idea who could have done such a thing?"

She shook her head. "I do not."

"Then we shall depart immediately for Blackpool," her stepmother announced. "You will be safe there."

"I don't think that is such a good idea," she replied.

"Why not?"

"The constable thinks it would be best if I remained here until he concludes his investigation," she shared.

"Why?"

"Because he hasn't identified the person who poisoned me yet."

It took Lydian a few minutes to realize what she was saying, and she saw the moment realization dawned. Her face fell and she shook her head, too rapidly. "You don't think I had anything to do with you being poisoned. Do you?"

She hesitated, diverting her gaze. "Frankly, I don't know what to believe."

"Oh, I see," Lydian murmured, the hurt evident in her tone. She rose swiftly. "I thought we had gotten past the mistrust, but apparently I was wrong."

"Lydian…"

Her stepmother held up her hand. "Don't. Please. I will be residing at Wellesley House until the constable has concluded his investigation, and I pray that *you* will come to your senses before then and return home. After all, think of the scandal that would ensue if the *ton* ever learned that your family was being investigated for attempted murder."

"I am sorry…"

Lydian cut her off. "You have nothing to apologize for," she remarked. "I am just glad that you are somewhere safe and with people that you can trust."

Her stepmother spoke politely, but the underlying curtness of her tone didn't escape her notice.

"Thank you for your understanding," Charlotte replied.

With a terse smile on her lips, Lydian said, "I will have your trunks packed and sent over so you can wear proper mourning attire." Her eyes perused the length of her. "Unless you have decided to forego mourning?"

"I have not."

"That is a relief."

With a stiff back, her stepmother stood there, watching her with an array of emotions flashing across her face. Finally, she spoke. "I shall see myself out, then."

"Oh, before you go," Charlotte began, "did you ever post that letter to the Duchess of Blackbourne?"

Lydian blinked. "I did."

Liar.

Charlotte tipped her head. "Thank you."

As she watched her stepmother leave, she found that she had more questions than answers. If Lydian had been lying about posting the letter, what else had she been lying about?

❧ 18 ❧

HUDSON SAT AT HIS DESK IN HIS OFFICE AT THE OLD BAILEY with files opened in front of him. The room was bright with the light of the afternoon sun streaming through the windows. He was attempting to review his upcoming cases, but his mind kept turning towards Charlotte.

He had made a fool of himself yesterday when he talked to her in the library. He'd started to express his feelings, but then he had stopped himself. He couldn't seem to bring himself to admit the truth to her. That he had fallen in love with her.

But hadn't he already learned his lesson? Hannah had taken his heart and stomped on it. He didn't dare make that mistake again. It would be best if he continued on his current path and avoid the dreaded love noose.

An image of Charlotte came to his mind, and he found himself smiling. Would he be able to live with himself if he allowed her to walk away from him? He had no doubt that she would be the belle of the ball next Season, if she lasted that long. Gentlemen would be lining up to court her, and not just because she was an heiress, but because she was beautiful, on the inside and out.

Hudson slammed a file closed, attempting to banish his thoughts. He couldn't do it. He refused to be vulnerable again. Weak. If Charlotte rejected him, then he didn't think he would have the strength to endure it.

"Is everything all right, Judge Beauchamp?"

Hudson glanced up and saw Judge Bancroft standing in the doorway with a concerned look on his face.

"Yes," Hudson replied dismissively.

The older judge with a full head of white hair stepped into the room and closed the door behind him. "Is this about a case?"

He shook his head.

"Ah, I assumed as much," Judge Bancroft said as he sat down in a chair facing his desk. "Who is the girl?"

"Pardon?"

Judge Bancroft smirked. "Only a woman could warrant such a reaction from you."

He frowned. "Her name is Lady Charlotte."

"I see," Judge Bancroft said. "Are you courting her?"

"Heavens, no," he stated forcefully.

Judge Bancroft eyed him suspiciously. "May I ask why not?"

"Because she is mourning the death of her father."

"And if she wasn't mourning her father's death, would you be courting her?" Judge Bancroft prodded.

He pressed his lips together, hoping to delay his response. "Most likely not," he replied honestly.

Judge Bancroft turned his attention towards the files on his desk. "I couldn't help but notice the odd hours that you have been keeping these past couple of weeks."

"Do you take umbrage with that?"

"No," Judge Bancroft said with a shake of his head. "I am merely commenting on the fact that you have been taking more time for yourself."

"That is because I…."

Judge Bancroft put his hand up, indicating he should stop speaking. "I am glad, and frankly, relieved."

"You are?"

Shifting in his chair, Judge Bancroft replied, "You work much too hard, putting the other district judges to shame. You try more cases than any other judge here, and your reputation is beyond reproach."

"That is good to hear."

Judge Bancroft pointed towards the files on his desk. "But there is more to life than work," he stated.

"With all due respect, you know my dream is to become a High Court Judge."

Judge Bancroft bobbed his head. "I do, and I think you have a real chance at getting there. But at what cost?"

"Pardon?"

"While you are pursuing your dreams, I worry that you are overlooking what is right in front of you."

"Meaning?"

"A chance at true happiness."

Hudson gave him a baffled look. "But I will be happy when I fulfill my dream."

With a knowing look, Judge Bancroft asked, "Is there someone that you would want to share your dreams with?"

An image of Charlotte came to his mind, but he quickly banished the thought.

"You thought about Lady Charlotte, didn't you?" Judge Bancroft inquired.

He shook his head. "It matters not."

Judge Bancroft leaned back in his chair. "I met Diana at a soirée, and we got along splendidly. It wasn't long after that we posted the banns." His eyes grew reflective. "But we both discovered, rather quickly, that we did not suit. We started to bicker incessantly, and it wasn't long before we were living in different residences."

"I had not realized."

"Nor would you," Judge Bancroft said. "I do not speak candidly about the state of my marriage to anyone. But I feel it is best if I give you a bit of advice."

"Your advice is always appreciated."

"Diana and I may have gotten along at the beginning, but we lacked the one thing necessary for a happy, long-lasting marriage," he shared.

"Which is?"

Judge Bancroft's eyes grew mournful. "Love," he murmured.

"Why are you telling me this, sir?"

"Because it is evident that you care for this Lady Charlotte. Maybe even love her."

Hudson sighed as he admitted, "Did you know I was engaged before?"

"I did not."

"Well, it ended rather poorly when she ran off to marry Lord Skeffington," he remarked in a disgusted tone.

"That scoundrel?"

Hudson nodded. "You must see my hesitation now when it comes to courting."

"I don't," Judge Bancroft said. "So, you had one bad experience. Are you willing to write off love completely?"

He ran his hand along the back of his neck. "It is not that simple."

"It is," the older judge contended. "There is not a day that goes by that I wish my life could be different, to have chosen another path. In my old age, I have discovered a simple but profound truth."

"Which is?"

Judge Bancroft gave him a sad smile. "Life is worth living when you have the right woman by your side."

"But what if you are wrong?" he asked. "What if Lady Charlotte shatters my heart even more."

"Then you pick up the pieces, one by one, and try again," Judge Bancroft said. "Just don't give up. Don't settle for anything less than love."

Hudson reached for a file on his desk and held it up. "What if I don't bother, and I focus on work instead?"

"Then you, my son, will have regrets, just like I do," Judge Bancroft asserted, rising. "And regrets are a terrible thing. They remind us of what could have been."

Leaning back in his chair, Hudson found himself saying, "I must admit that I'm afraid of her rejection."

"Good," Judge Bancroft responded. "That means you recognize how much is at stake."

Hudson watched as Judge Bancroft walked towards the door and placed his hand on the handle.

"Thank you for your counsel," Hudson said. "I shall consider your words carefully."

Judge Bancroft's expression became thoughtful. "I sincerely hope you do, Judge Beauchamp." He turned the handle and opened the door.

Once he was left alone, Hudson rose and walked over to the window. He stared out at the courtyard of the Old Bailey and watched the people milling about as he considered the older judge's words.

Was he strong enough to confess his feelings to Charlotte? Would she even welcome his advances? He knew she cared for him, but he wasn't arrogant enough to assume that she loved him. What if she just considered him a friend?

Hudson placed his hands on the windowsill. He had always worked hard to accomplish his goals, but love was an anomaly. No matter how hard he worked, it wouldn't guarantee that he would earn Charlotte's favor.

He could still fail, and that thought terrified him.

But what if he succeeded, he wondered. What if Charlotte agreed to his courtship? Then, she would be his. Forever.

And that was worth the risk.

Without waiting for another moment to go by, Hudson exited his office and walked swiftly out of the Old Bailey.

He had a young lady he needed to woo.

"You climbed up the side of a moving coach?" Penelope asked in disbelief.

Charlotte nodded. "I did."

With a grin on her face, Penelope replied, "Who would have thought you would have been brazen enough to shoot a highwayman and drive a coach?"

"I had no choice in the matter," Charlotte contended. "If I hadn't, then we could have been killed on the side of the road."

"Or you could have been killed falling off the moving coach," Isabella pointed out as she picked up a biscuit from the tray.

Charlotte shrugged. "I daresay that it was easier than climbing a tree."

"I highly doubt that," Madalene said before taking a sip of her tea.

"It is true," she replied. "You should try it."

Madalene laughed. "I am confident that Everett will never let me try something so foolish now that I am increasing."

"Then you are missing out," Charlotte joked.

Penelope leaned forward and placed her empty teacup on the table in front of her. "When Isabella informed us of your escapades, I must admit that I didn't believe her at first."

"It is true," Isabella remarked. "They thought I was exaggerating."

"It did sound rather farfetched," Madalene reasoned. "Although, you were always the more adventurous one of us."

Charlotte sipped her tea, then said, "I think we all enjoy a good adventure."

"That we do," Penelope agreed.

Howe walked into the drawing room and met her gaze. "Lord Huntley is here to call upon you, milady," he informed her. "Are you taking callers?"

"I am," she confirmed. "Please send him in."

Howe tipped his head. "Yes, milady."

After the butler stepped out of the room, Madalene lifted her brow and asked, "Who exactly is Lord Huntley?"

"He inherited my father's title," she explained.

Madalene huffed. "That part was rather obvious," she said. "I am more curious to why he is calling upon you?"

"To ensure that I am being well-looked after."

"Is that so?" Penelope asked with amusement in her eyes. "And a letter wouldn't suffice?"

Charlotte placed her cup and saucer onto the tray. "Lord Huntley and I are just friends."

"Does Lord Huntley know that?" Madalene asked innocently.

"He does."

Isabella leaned forward in her seat and whispered, "I don't think he does, especially since he visited her yesterday, as well."

Before she could reply, Duncan stepped into the room wearing a dark green riding jacket, an ivory waistcoat with matching cravat, and dark trousers. A black band encircled his arm. His gaze scanned the room until it landed on her. He smiled.

"Lady Charlotte. Thank you for agreeing to see me."

Charlotte rose and smoothed out her black gown. "Lord Huntley. Please do come in."

"I hope I am not intruding," Duncan said as he approached her.

"Not at all." She pointed towards her friends. "Lord Huntley, allow me the privilege of introducing you to Her Grace, the Duchess of Blackbourne, and Lady Northampton."

Duncan bowed. "It is a pleasure to meet such beautiful ladies." He turned his gaze towards Isabella. "It is good to see you again, Lady Isabella."

"Likewise, Lord Huntley."

He turned his gaze back towards her, and he almost appeared nervous. "I noticed what a fine-looking day it was, and I was hoping to take a turn around the gardens with you."

She smiled. "What a lovely idea."

Duncan held his hand out towards the door. "After you, milady."

Charlotte made the mistake of looking at her friends, and they were all hiding knowing smiles under their gloves. She almost let out a sigh. Good heavens, she thought, going on a walk through the gardens did not mean that Lord Huntley had feelings for her.

As they approached the rear doors, a liveried footman opened the door, and she noticed that he discreetly followed them outside.

They had just stepped onto the footpath that led through the well-manicured garden when Duncan asked, "How are you faring?"

"I am well," she replied.

Duncan clasped his hands behind his back. "I spoke with the constable this morning."

"Oh?"

"He still is unsure of who was behind the poisoning."

Charlotte pressed her lips together, attempting to hide her disappointment. "I see."

"He did interview the kitchen staff and your lady's maid again," he explained. "But he said he has no credible leads at this time."

She stopped on the path and turned to face him. "So whoever poisoned me is going to get away with it?"

"I never said that," Duncan reassured her. "Investigations take time. You must be patient."

She grinned. "I'm afraid that patience is not one of my virtues."

"I can tell," he said, returning her smile.

Charlotte turned to resume walking down the footpath. "How is my stepmother?"

"I'm afraid I haven't seen very much of her," he replied. "She has been taking her meals in her room."

"And Lady Rebecca?"

Duncan glanced over at her with mirth in his eyes. "I caught her this morning sneaking into the dining room for some bacon."

"She does love bacon."

He chuckled. "Yes, she does."

They continued to walk in comfortable silence as Charlotte watched as the willow trees swayed in the wind.

Duncan cleared his throat, drawing her attention. "I do have another solution which will get you home sooner."

"Which is?"

He reached out and gently grasped her arm to turn her to face him. "I have done some considerable thinking about this, and I feel that it is in our best interest to marry."

Fearing that she misheard him, she asked, "Pardon?"

"If we were married, no one would dare try to poison you, the Countess of Huntley," he explained. "Furthermore, I would be by your side to protect you, day and night."

"You want to marry me so you can protect me?" she questioned.

He dropped his hand from her arm and ran it through his hair. "That is not the only reason," he admitted. "I have grown to care for you… immensely, in fact."

"You have?" Charlotte turned her head towards the drawing

room window, hoping her friends were not watching her at this very moment.

"I have," he said, "and I am hoping that you might feel the same way."

Clasping her gloved hands in front of her, she replied, "I'm afraid I do not return your feelings."

Duncan reared back slightly. "You don't?" he asked, his lips parted.

"I consider you a dear friend."

He stared at her with a crestfallen expression. "But I love you," he murmured, his eyes holding vulnerability.

She offered him a sad smile. "I'm sorry, I truly am, but I am not interested in marrying you," she stated with compassion in her voice.

"Is it because of Lord Hudson?"

Charlotte's eyes turned downcast at his direct question.

"I'm sorry," he said. "I'm embarrassing you, aren't I?"

Bringing her gaze back up, she replied, "No, it is quite all right. It is only fair of me to be honest with you since you are being forthright with me." She nibbled her lower lip. "I do care for Lord Hudson, but I cannot say for certain that he returns my affections."

Duncan frowned. "I would be remiss if I did not warn you that Lord Hudson is a fortune hunter."

She stared at him in surprise. "Lord Hudson? A fortune hunter?"

He nodded solemnly. "It is true," he replied. "A Bow Street Runner confirmed that Lord Hudson's former betrothed was also an heiress."

"That is just a coincidence."

"Is it?" he asked. "Or are you the answer to all of Lord Hudson's problems?"

"What problems?"

"Come now," he said. "You can't possibly be that naïve. He

is the second son of a marquess and works as a district judge. He has no fortune, no property, and no prospects."

"I don't believe it."

"You don't believe it, or you choose *not* to believe it?" he asked knowingly.

Charlotte took a step back. "I need some time to think."

"Come back home to Wellesley House," he urged, "where I can protect you from Lord Hudson and all the other fortune hunters."

"I don't need your protection."

Duncan looked at her with an expression on his face that looked like pity. "I think you do," he pressed. "Lord Hudson has managed to convince you that he is something that he is not."

"Which is?"

"A gentleman."

Charlotte brought her hand up to her forehead. "No, that can't be true," she insisted. "Lord Hudson is a good, honorable man."

"I contend that he is not," Duncan said, taking a step closer. "You have been deceived."

Charlotte's mind started reeling with the possibilities that she had been wrong about Hudson. But her mind always came back to the same conclusion: she knew Hudson had a good heart, and nothing that Duncan was telling her made sense.

Lowering her hand, she met Duncan's gaze steadfastly. "You are wrong. Hudson is none of those things."

Confusion appeared across his brow as he asked, "You would believe him over me?"

"Please don't look at it that way. It is just…"

He spoke over her. "How am I supposed to look at it?" he snapped.

Surprised by his sharp tone, she took a step back. "I'm sorry. I didn't mean to offend you."

He mumbled something under his breath as he turned away

and took a few steps towards the back gate. He glanced over the shrubbery before turning back to face her, his expression stern.

"I had hoped that you would have come willingly."

Unsure of his meaning, she asked, "Pardon?"

He closed the distance between them in a few strides and grabbed her arm. "Come on now," he said as he attempted to lead her towards the back fence. "I am going to protect you whether you like it or not."

"No!" she exclaimed, digging the heels of her kid boots into the ground. "I'm not going anywhere with you."

In one swift motion, he leaned down and tossed her over his shoulder. "Yes, you are, my dear," he said dryly. "We are going to Gretna Green."

She started hitting and kicking him, but he seemed unphased by her efforts.

"If you don't stop this unseemly behavior, then you will regret it," he warned as he opened the back gate.

To her horror, a black coach was waiting next to the pavement, and a footman was holding the door open.

"Someone help me!" Charlotte screamed, hoping to alert someone that she was being abducted.

In the next moment, Charlotte was being tossed onto the floor of the coach, and then everything went black.

❧ 19 ❧

WITH A RENEWED SENSE OF PURPOSE, HUDSON EXITED THE hackney and approached his ancestral townhouse.

The door opened, and Howe greeted him with his usual stoic expression. "Good afternoon, milord."

As he removed his hat, Hudson asked, "Where is Lady Charlotte?"

The butler held his hands out to accept Hudson's hat. "She is taking a stroll in the gardens with Lord Huntley."

Hudson frowned at that unwelcome news. "Is she properly chaperoned?"

"A footman is standing watch at the back door."

Stifling a groan, Hudson asked, "How long have they been outside?"

"Only for a few moments," the butler revealed. "It might please you to know that his grace, the Duke of Blackbourne, is visiting with Lord Northampton in his study."

Hudson nodded. "I want to be notified the moment Lady Charlotte returns to the townhouse."

"As you wish, milord."

Hudson strode towards the study, finding himself growing

increasingly agitated by Lord Huntley's presence. Why did it bother him so much that Lord Huntley came to call on Charlotte? For some reason, he didn't entirely trust Lord Huntley's motives, and he wasn't sure why that was. It was just a feeling in his gut that something was off with him.

Perhaps he should go into the garden and interrupt their stroll. No. That would be madness. He didn't want to upset Charlotte by forcing himself upon her. He wanted to win her favor, not lose her by acting like a jealous suitor.

He stopped by a window that faced the gardens, and his eyes scanned the pristine landscape. He could see Charlotte and Lord Huntley conversing by the back fence.

"Spying on the competition?" his brother, Everett, asked from behind him.

Hudson huffed. "It is not much competition."

"No?"

Hudson turned around to face his brother. "If you must know, I was ensuring that Lady Charlotte was properly chaperoned."

"I see," Everett responded. "So, it has nothing to do with you being jealous?"

With an expressionless face, Hudson replied, "Not at all."

Everett chuckled. "I can see why you were such a good barrister," he commented. "You are quite believable, but I can see right through you." He waved his hand. "Come. Nicholas is in my study."

Hudson followed his brother into the study. The duke was sitting on a chair holding a drink in his hand.

"You found him, I see," Nicholas observed unnecessarily.

Everett nodded. "I did. I caught him spying on Lady Charlotte and Lord Huntley as they strolled in the gardens."

"I was not spying," Hudson argued. "I was just—"

His brother cut him off. "Ensuring they were chaperoned," he said, finishing his objection. "No one believes that."

"I certainly don't," Nicholas remarked before he took a sip of his drink.

Everett walked over to the drink cart. "Would you care for something to drink?"

"No, thank you," Hudson replied as he sat down across from Nicholas. "I have work I must see to after I speak to Lady Charlotte."

Everett took the stopper off the decanter and poured himself a drink. "What is so urgent that you must speak to Lady Charlotte in the middle of the day?"

Hudson adjusted his cravat before sharing, "If you must know, I am going to speak to her about my intentions."

Everett turned towards him with the decanter in his hands, and a bright smile was on his face. "It is about time, brother."

"Are you going to offer for her?" Nicholas asked.

Hudson shook his head. "No. Since Lady Charlotte is in mourning, I don't dare offer for her yet. If I did, it could cause a scandal, and I wouldn't do that to her."

Nicholas gave him a smug smile. "That wouldn't matter if Penelope and I endorse your courtship."

"Would you?"

"Of course. How could you even ask that question?" Nicholas asked. "If it would help, Penelope would even throw a ball to celebrate the occasion."

Everett interjected, "I daresay that Mother would be upset if she didn't get to plan your engagement ball."

"Yes, but if we hosted the ball then the *ton* would have no choice but to accept the courtship," Nicholas explained.

"That is true," Hudson observed. "But this is all assuming that Lady Charlotte returns my affections."

"Have you told her about Hannah?" Everett asked as he sat on a settee.

"I did."

Nicholas lifted his brow. "How did that go?"

"Well, I think," he replied.

"I, for one, am relieved that you are finally moving past Hannah," Everett said, holding up his glass. "You deserve to be happy."

"I am finally starting to believe that," Hudson responded. "After Hannah broke our engagement, she'd left me hollow inside, and I no longer believed in love."

"And now?" Everett prodded.

Hudson smiled. "Charlotte has restored my faith in love. She is the reason that I wake up with a smile on my face every morning."

"Then you must fight for her," Nicholas said.

"I plan to."

"Good," Everett stated. "I have grown rather fond of Charlotte, and I know Madalene would love to have her in the family."

"I suppose I could…"

His voice trailed off when Penelope, Madalene, and Isabella ran into the room with panicked expressions.

"Lord Huntley just abducted Charlotte!" Penelope exclaimed.

"What?" Hudson shouted.

Madalene bobbed her head. "We may have been watching them through the window when we saw Lord Huntley throw Lottie over his shoulder and exit through the back gate."

"When was this?" Hudson asked.

Isabella spoke up. "We rushed over here the moment we saw it."

Without saying another word, Hudson brushed past them and ran out the rear door of the townhouse. He didn't stop until he arrived at the back gate. He opened the iron gate leading to the street and watched the coaches ride by.

His heart dropped.

There was no sign of Charlotte.

From behind him, Everett asked between breaths, "Do you see anything?"

"No!" he shouted. "I am going to kill Lord Huntley."

Nicholas came to a halting stop next to him. "Do you have any idea where he would take Lady Charlotte?"

"No. I don't," Hudson replied, jabbing his fingers through his hair.

A liveried footman came running down the pavement and skidded to a stop in front of him. "Lady Charlotte has been abducted," he announced, his breathing labored.

"We are well aware of that fact," Hudson replied dryly.

The footman took a deep breath. "When I saw Lady Charlotte was growing increasingly irritated, I crept closer to them. However, I wasn't able to stop Lord Huntley from tossing her over his shoulder," he shared. "I raced after them, and I heard Lord Huntley say they were going to Gretna Green."

The footman pointed down the street. "I followed the black coach and saw that it was heading north."

Hudson furrowed his brows. "Are you positive that you heard Lord Huntley say they were going to Gretna Greens?"

"Yes, milord," the footman confirmed.

Everett spoke up from behind him in a commanding voice. "I want you to go to the Bow Street Magistrate and hire every available Bow Street Runner," he ordered. "Inform them that Lady Charlotte has been abducted, and Lord Huntley is taking her to Gretna Greens. I want her found and returned safely home."

The footman tipped his head. "Yes, milord," he said before he started running towards the estate.

Hudson turned back towards Everett. "Do you have any spare pistols on hand?"

"What do you intend to do with one?" Everett asked, eyeing him with concern.

"I am going to get Charlotte back, one way or another," he answered firmly.

Everett nodded. "All right, but Nicholas and I are going with you."

"It might be dangerous," he warned.

Nicholas chuckled. "I hoped you would say that," he remarked. "I thrive in the face of danger."

Hudson glanced back towards the street. "Which road do you think they took?"

"My guess is they would take the most reliable mail coach route and remain on the Great North Road," Everett surmised. "Furthermore, they would need to stop at a coaching inn for the evening. It isn't safe to travel on the roads at night."

"Then, let's go saddle our horses," Hudson stated. "We have a long night ahead of us."

Charlotte groaned as she brought her hand up to her head. It was throbbing and her whole body felt battered and bruised. Without opening her eyes, she knew she was in a coach because she could hear the steady beat of the horses' hooves.

"I'm glad that you are finally starting to stir," Duncan said, his voice sounding anything but relieved. "I was worried I might have hit you too hard."

She blinked her eyes open and saw that it was now dark outside. Only the light of the moon provided any source of light in the coach.

"How long have I been unconscious?" she asked.

"About three hours."

She straightened herself on the plush velvet bench and

lowered her hand to her lap. "Can you explain to me why you felt the need to abduct me?"

He gave her a dashing smile, no doubt in hopes of disarming her. However, it just made her more irritated at him.

"Because I love you, my dear," he practically purred.

"You don't love me."

"No?"

She shook her head and immediately regretted that action. "If you love someone, you don't hit them over the head and force them to travel to Gretna Greens to be wed."

"I thought I was being romantic."

"There is nothing romantic going on here, Lord Huntley."

Lord Huntley shifted on the bench. "I see we are back to using our titles again," he said in an amused tone. "That will change once we are married."

Charlotte crossed her arms over her chest. "I won't marry you."

"I'm afraid you have no choice in the matter."

"Why would you say that?"

"I have already secured a blacksmith who will marry us with no questions asked," he revealed.

She tilted her chin defiantly. "Then I will run away."

"I wouldn't recommend you doing something so foolhardy, my dear," he responded, smirking. "I would have no choice but to punish you for your disobedience."

"I will never stop fighting you until my last dying breath," Charlotte declared, leaning forward.

"So be it," he stated with a shrug. "I shall look forward to taming you then."

Charlotte shifted her gaze towards the closed window, wondering how she was going to get herself out of this mess.

"The windows are locked, if you are curious," he said, following her gaze. "We can't have you escaping through them."

"I will find a way to get away from you."

Duncan reached behind him and retrieved a pistol. He placed it on the bench next to him. "I don't think you will."

"Why don't you kill me now and be done with it?"

He tsked. "I have discovered that you don't die very easily."

"Pardon?"

"I have tried on two separate occasions to kill you, but you always seem to escape death. Why is that?"

"You have tried to kill me twice?" she questioned in disbelief.

He nodded smugly.

"Well then, I must assume it was you that poisoned me."

"It was, but I can't take all the credit," he responded. "Your lady's maid did help me along the way."

Charlotte's mouth dropped. "Ellen helped *you*?"

"Is that her name?" he asked, uninterested. "I found her crying in the hallway about her mother's health, and I offered to pay for the medicine she required, assuming she would help me. At first, she refused, but I was quite persuasive, especially when I threatened termination."

"You are a horrible, vile man!" Charlotte exclaimed.

"Your lady's maid came in useful, though," he said. "Besides dumping some oleander powder in your tea, she also informed me of your coming and goings with Lord Hudson."

She pressed her lips together. "That is how you discovered we went to the masquerade ball."

"It was," he confirmed. "Unfortunately, she didn't administer enough poison and you survived."

"The doctor knew I had been poisoned," she asserted. "He would have discovered the truth."

Duncan looked amused. "I would never have been suspected. After all, it was well known that you and your stepmother had a complicated past, and she was the one that prepared the tea that morning. Even your lady's maid was willing to testify against her."

"You would have had my stepmother take the blame?"

"Gladly." He chuckled dryly. "Ellen was also the one who informed me you were falling in love with Lord Hudson. Although, I must admit, it would have been so much simpler if you had fallen in love with *me*."

She was still curious about one thing. "You mentioned another attempt on my life?"

His lips twisted into a wry grin. "I had hoped to kill you before you even arrived in London, but you somehow managed to stop the attack."

Charlotte's eyes widened as realization dawned. "You sent the highwaymen after me?"

"Not exactly," he replied. "I wanted to have the pleasure of killing you myself, so I tagged along. Unfortunately, the highwayman was incompetent, and I ended up getting shot in the shoulder."

"Good. I'm glad I shot you," she declared. "I hope it was excruciatingly painful."

The lines around his mouth tightened, and he remarked gruffly, "You are just as irksome as your father was. I was ecstatic to discover that he was dying from consumption. But I grew tired of waiting by his bedside, pretending I cared whether he lived or died." He pointed to himself. "I knew once he died, then everything he had would belong to me. It was my turn to be rich."

Duncan's eyes narrowed as he continued. "But I had not anticipated that he would leave most of his fortune to you; a worthless daughter." He scoffed. "I discovered that most unfortunate detail only after I went to the church to read his will, and by then, it was too late."

"So, you tried to kill me?"

"Highwaymen attacks are common on the road you were traveling on. It would have just been considered a terrible tragedy," he explained. "However, I did not anticipate you would fight back."

"I'm glad I did."

Duncan frowned. "Then, my plan was to woo you, but you never quite gave me a chance. Did you?"

She smirked. "It would appear that I'm an excellent judge of character."

"You are an impertinent chit," he growled. "I'm growing tired of your shrewish comments. If you do not cooperate, then I will have no choice but to kill you."

"But how will you explain my death?" she questioned.

"It hardly matters," he replied arrogantly. "I am an earl. Getting away with murder is an inconsequential thing."

The coach came to a jerking stop, and Duncan reached for his pistol.

"If you scream, then I will kill you," he warned in a stern voice, tucking the pistol into the waistband of his trousers. "Do you understand?"

She nodded.

The door opened, and Duncan exited first. He turned back around and extended his hand towards her. "Come, my dear."

"I don't require your assistance," she replied.

Duncan stepped closer to the coach and lowered his voice. "We can do this the easy way or a truly painful way. It is entirely up to you."

Hesitantly, she slipped her hand into his and started to exit the coach.

"Good choice," he muttered as he took her hand and placed it in the crook of his arm.

Duncan led her into the coaching inn, and Charlotte brought her gloved hand up to her nose to try to cover the stench of the hall. Long tables were set up, and dirty looking men sat around drinking out of tankards. One man caught her eye, and he winked lewdly at her before spitting on the ground.

Before she could react, they were approached by a tall, lean man with a large forehead.

"Welcome," he greeted, his hands extended wide. "My name is Mr. Barkley, and I am the innkeeper of this here fine establishment. What can I get for yer?"

Duncan patted her hand. "My wife is tired from the long journey. We require a room and our supper to be brought up."

"That can most definitely be arranged, sir," the innkeeper said. "Do you require a porter this evening?"

"No, we do not. We are traveling light."

"I understand." He stepped closer and lowered his voice. "This inn caters to the most discreet traveler, if you know what I mean."

Reaching into his jacket pocket, Duncan removed a few coins and extended them towards Mr. Barkley. "This should cover our room and expenses."

The innkeeper clasped the money in his hand. "It is more than generous, sir." He turned and directed over his shoulder, "If you will follow me to your room."

They trailed behind the innkeeper as he led them up a narrow flight of stairs and down a darkened hall.

Mr. Barkley stopped in front of a closed door and reached into his pocket. He removed a key and unlocked the door. After he opened it, he gestured that they should enter first.

Duncan pushed her into the room before saying, "This will suit nicely."

Charlotte's eyes scanned the small room, looking for anything that could aid in her escape. A bed was pushed up against the wall, a writing desk sat by the window and a pitcher and basin sat atop a table.

Mr. Barkley spoke from the doorway. "I will send someone to light your fireplace and your supper will be up shortly."

"Thank you," Duncan said as he stepped away from her.

Mr. Barkley nodded in approval before he closed the door. Duncan walked over to the door and latched it.

"We can't have you trying to escape, now can we?" he asked, leaning back against the door.

Charlotte stepped over to the writing desk, attempting to create more distance between her and Duncan. To her surprise, a rusty letter opener was tucked in the corner.

She leaned back against the writing desk and surreptitiously reached behind her for the letter opener. Once she grasped the cracked wood handle, she ran her finger along the edge of the dull blade. It was less than ideal, but it was still something that she could use to defend herself.

Duncan pushed off the wall. "We can still salvage this marriage."

"There is nothing to salvage, because we aren't going to marry," she said firmly.

A look of disappointment came to his face. "You aren't going to make this easy for yourself, are you?"

"I fought you off once," she stated, "and I can do it again."

Duncan closed the distance between them in a few strides, and he stopped in front of her. She tensed as he brought his hand up and started to run his fingers along her cheek.

"You are so beautiful," he murmured.

Charlotte tried to turn her head away from him, but he clasped her chin, forcing her to look at him.

He leaned closer, and she could feel his foul breath on her cheek.

"You will learn respect, my dear. For once we are wed, I will have little use for you anymore. You would be mindful to remember that."

Charlotte gripped the letter opener tighter in her hand as she slowly, cautiously, brought it in front of her. She knew she had one chance at saving herself, and she prayed that her plan would work.

As Duncan's lips moved closer to hers, she reared her hand back and jabbed the letter opener into the side of his leg.

Duncan stepped back as he roared in pain. "You stupid chit," he hissed as his hand grasped the letter opener's handle.

Without wasting another moment, Charlotte ran towards the door, and unlatched it. She flung the door open and nearly cried in relief when she saw Hudson standing there with a pistol in his hand.

彩 20 彩

THE MOMENT HUDSON SAW CHARLOTTE WAS ALIVE, RELIEF washed over him, and he had a sudden desire to pull her into his arms. But this wasn't over yet. They still needed to contend with Lord Huntley.

In one swift motion, Hudson positioned Charlotte behind him as he continued to level his pistol at Lord Huntley, who was holding a bloody letter opener in his hand.

"Put down your weapon," Hudson ordered in a steely tone as he stepped further into the room.

As Lord Huntley stared at him with contempt, Nicholas and Everett came around him and cocked their pistols.

With a menacing glare, Lord Huntley dropped the letter opener to the ground, his hand covered in his own blood.

"And the pistol," Nicholas directed.

Reaching for the pistol tucked into the waistband of his trousers, Lord Huntley leaned over and placed it on the ground.

"You have lost," Hudson declared. "It is over."

"You can have her," Lord Huntley stated, wincing in pain.

He glanced over his shoulder at Charlotte and said, "I intend to."

Lord Huntley placed his hand over his wound and grunted. "I have never known such a troublesome woman before."

"Then why did you abduct her in the first place?"

"It was never about her," Lord Huntley admitted. "It was always about the money."

"But I was at the reading of the will," Hudson contended. "Your predecessor left you more than enough to live on for the remainder of your days."

"That matters not," Lord Huntley declared, "the money he left her rightfully belonged to me."

Charlotte spoke up. "No. That money belongs to me, and Lord Huntley tried to kill me for it." She came to stand next to him and revealed, "Twice."

"Twice?" Hudson repeated with a lifted brow.

"Lord Huntley was one of the highwaymen who attacked us," she shared.

A low growl came from Nicholas. "Is this true, Lord Huntley?" he asked slowly.

With a smirk on his face, Lord Huntley said, "No. Lady Charlotte's mind is just befuddled from eloping with me."

Charlotte's mouth dropped. "I did not try to elope with you!" she shouted. "You *abducted* me!"

"That is not how I recall it," Lord Huntley remarked dismissively.

Nicholas lowered his pistol to his side. "From here on out, I don't want to see you socializing with the *ton*, for any reason. I am ostracizing you from Society."

Lord Huntley scoffed. "You can't do that, your grace," he mocked. "Even you, the mighty navy sea captain, are not that powerful."

"I assure you that I am," Nicholas stated.

"Everyone else may be afraid of you," Lord Huntley scoffed, "but I'm not!"

"That is your mistake, Lord Huntley," Nicholas asserted,

stepping closer to him. "I will ensure that the *ton* will give you the cut direct."

"As will I," Everett announced.

Fear flickered in Lord Huntley's eyes as he swallowed slowly. "You wouldn't dare."

"Furthermore, I am going to request that the magistrate open an investigation into the murder attempts on Lady Charlotte," Nicholas stated.

"It is Lady Charlotte's word against mine," Lord Huntley huffed. "No one will believe a lowly woman over an earl."

"Perhaps, but I am willing to take my chances," Nicholas replied.

"No jury of my peers will ever convict me," Lord Huntley remarked arrogantly.

Hudson met Lord Huntley's gaze. "We shall see, won't we?"

"Regardless, your reputation will be in shambles by the time I am finished with you," Nicholas informed him.

Lord Huntley turned his fiery gaze towards Charlotte. "This is all your fault," he spat out, pointing at her. "Your father had a sudden change of heart, and he left you with *my* money."

"You are imagining things, Lord Huntley," Charlotte said.

"No, I am starting to see things clearly for the first time," Lord Huntley argued as he reached behind him and retrieved an overcoat pistol.

"Lord Huntley," Nicholas growled, bringing his pistol back up. "Put the pistol down."

Lord Huntley turned towards Nicholas. "Don't you see," he declared. "Lady Charlotte won't be happy until she has taken everything away from me. Just like her father was attempting to do."

"If you point that pistol towards Lady Charlotte, I will have no choice but to kill you," Nicholas warned. "It is three against one. You can still walk away from here with your life."

"And let her live?" Lord Huntley questioned. "I hated her father, and I hate her."

"Why did you hate my father?" Charlotte asked weakly.

Lord Huntley waved the pistol loosely in front of him. "Your father didn't think I should be his heir presumptive," he revealed. "He didn't think I was good enough, and he was going to petition Parliament to disinherit me. That is why I felt great relief that he died."

"Did he give a reason?" Hudson asked, keeping his pistol aimed at Lord Huntley's chest.

Lord Huntley huffed. "He thought I was unscrupulous and accused me of being foolish enough to waste all his money at the gambling halls. He even accused me of having something to do with my brother's death."

"Did you?" Hudson asked.

"My brother's death was an unfortunate accident," Lord Huntley stated. "He was the one who chose to ride his horse in the rain, not me!"

"But did you goad him into it?" Hudson pressed.

Lord Huntley grunted. "My brother was weak, easily manipulated. He didn't deserve to be an earl."

"But you do?" Everett asked.

With narrowed eyes, Lord Huntley replied, "More so than my brother."

Nicholas held out his hand. "Give me the pistol, Lord Huntley."

"No!" Lord Huntley shouted. "Charlotte has ruined my life. Because of her, I will never be accepted by the *ton*."

"You brought this upon yourself when you attempted to kill her," Hudson said.

"She left me no choice! That chit refuses to die!" Lord Huntley exclaimed as he brought up his pistol to point it at Lady Charlotte.

Without any hesitation, Hudson fired his pistol at Lord Huntley, just as the sound of multiple gunshots echoed in the small room.

Lord Huntley dropped to his knees and stared up at them in surprise. "I've been shot," he muttered in disbelief. "But I'm an earl."

Nicholas pointed at the door and ordered, "Get Lady Charlotte out of here."

Hudson slipped his arm over her shoulder and led her out the door. "You don't need to watch someone die," he said. "It is something that will haunt you forever."

He escorted her down the stairs and out the main door. When they reached Lord Huntley's coach, he opened the door and assisted her in.

"I believe this will be much more comfortable than waiting in that coaching inn," he said, coming to sit across from her.

"I agree." Her words soft.

"Did Lord Huntley... uh... hurt you?" he asked, fearful of the answer.

Charlotte shook her head. "No. Not in the way that you are implying."

"That is a relief."

Tears came to Charlotte's eyes as she admitted, "I have never been so afraid in my life. I knew you would come after me, but I didn't think you would reach me in time."

Hudson moved to sit next to her on the bench and reached for her hands in her lap. "I'm sorry that it took us so long," he said, "but we stopped at multiple coaching inns along the route searching for you."

"How did you know I was at this coaching inn?"

Hudson's lips twitched. "Never underestimate the power of a bribe."

She met his gaze, her eyes filled with warmth, gratitude. "Thank you for coming after me."

"Always," he murmured. "I would never have stopped searching for you. I hope you know that."

"I do."

A tear slid down her cheek, and he reached up to wipe it away, his fingers lingering. "I have been a fool when it has come to you, Lottie," he said.

"You have?" she asked, a line appearing between her brows.

Growing serious, he replied, "I have been so afraid of losing my heart again that I have kept it tucked away, hidden from the world. But you changed that. You took my broken heart, piece by piece, and put it back together again. You have made it whole again."

"I'm glad to hear that."

"My heart beats only for you, Lottie." He hesitated, before saying, "I love you."

Her lips parted, and a small sound of delighted surprise escaped her lips. "You love me?"

"I do, with all my heart."

Charlotte smiled through her unshed tears. "Oh, Hudson, I love you, too."

Hudson brought both of his hands up to cup her cheeks. "I was hoping you would say that."

"What are we going to do now?" she asked, relaxing into his hands.

A smile came to his lips. "For starters, I am going to kiss you."

"I am not opposed to that," she replied with a coy smile.

He leaned close, moving slowly, until his lips brushed across hers. He pulled back a little, pleased to see Charlotte's eyes were still closed. Then, he kissed her again. But this time, he gathered her closer, deepening the kiss, showing her how much he truly loved her without the use of words. Lottie… his Lottie… kissed him back with equal ardor, and he found himself quickly becoming undone.

He leaned back, breaking the kiss.

"Marry me, Lottie," he begged breathlessly. "You are the only woman I want to kiss for the rest of my days.

A broad smile came to her lips. "Yes, I will marry you."

"Good," he replied. "I will post the banns tomorrow."

Her face fell. "But I am in mourning."

"Not only will Nicholas and Penelope endorse our marriage, but my family and friends will as well, and I am confident that the *ton* will follow suit," he shared.

"Do you truly believe so?"

"Do not fret, my love," he said. "It will all work out."

Her smile returned. "I believe you."

"I'm glad, my dear, because you make me so blasted happy."

She laughed. "I should scold you for your language."

Hearing her laugh caused his heart to soar, for it was the sound of genuine happiness. Unable to resist, he kissed her forehead, her cheek, her chin, and then her mouth.

A knock came at the coach door before it was wrenched opened, and Everett stuck his head in. "I think it would be for the best if we departed from this coaching inn and travel home."

"Do you think that is wise?" Hudson asked.

Nicholas spoke up from behind Everett. "Everett and I will ride alongside the coach to protect it from highwaymen." He paused. "Unless you would rather have us ride inside the coach with you and Lady Charlotte?"

"Not at all," he replied quickly.

Nicholas chuckled. "We assumed as much."

Everett shifted his gaze towards Charlotte. "I am relieved to have you back safely with us, Lady Charlotte."

"Thank you. And, please, you must call me Charlotte," she insisted. "After all, we are going to be family soon."

Everett smiled. "That pleases me immensely," he remarked. "We should depart shortly. Fortunately, we retrieved the driver before he was too deep in his cups."

"That is good to hear," Hudson stated.

With a brief nod, Everett said, "I will tie your horse to the back of the coach."

After Everett departed, closing the coach door behind him, Hudson turned towards her and noticed that she was shivering.

"Are you cold?" he asked. "I can retrieve a blanket for you."

With a flirtatious smile on her lips, she said, "I can think of another way to keep me warm."

"I am happy to oblige, my love," he murmured right before he pressed his lips against hers.

———————

"I can't believe you fought off Lord Huntley!"

Charlotte reluctantly opened her eyes and met her friend's gaze. "May I ask why you are sitting on my bed?"

Isabella gave her an unrepentant shrug. "It is noon," she replied. "You have nearly slept the day away."

A yawn escaped her lips as she sat up in her bed. "It is not as if I am being lazy," she explained. "We didn't arrive at your townhouse until rather late last night."

"I know," Isabella said. "Everett told me everything over breakfast."

"Then why are you in my bedchamber?"

"Because I want to hear it from you."

Smoothing back her brown hair, she asked, "What exactly do you want to know?"

"Are you truly engaged to my brother?"

Charlotte smiled. "I am."

Isabella let out a squeal. "We are going to be sisters!"

"Yes, we are."

In an animated voice, Isabella shared, "My mother is downstairs, and she is already planning your wedding luncheon. But Nicholas and Penelope will be hosting your engagement ball, and I have no doubt that it will be the event of the Season."

"How wonderful," she murmured.

Isabella gave her an expectant look. "How did you fight off Lord Huntley?"

"With a letter opener."

Her friend lowered her voice and asked, "Is it true that you saw him being shot?"

She nodded.

"How awful," Isabella said. "And he admitted to poisoning you and was behind the highwaymen attack?"

She nodded, again.

"Who would have thought such a handsome man would have done something so vile and distasteful," Isabella remarked. "I should have seen it coming."

Charlotte laughed. "Why was that?"

"I had suspected your stepmother was evil, and I'm afraid that it clouded my judgement," Isabella surmised. "She was much too obvious a choice for the villain."

"I would agree with you," she said. "Although, I did have my doubts about Lydian as well."

Isabella rose from the bed. "Would you like me to request a tray be sent up to your bedchamber?"

"Yes, please," she replied. "I am rather famished. I never had supper last night."

Isabella started to walk over to the door. "You better hurry and get ready for the day. Hudson is downstairs waiting for you."

"He is?"

Isabella smiled as she placed her hand on the handle. "I have seen more of my brother these past two weeks than I have my whole life. I wonder why that is?"

After Isabella had departed from the room, Charlotte rose and walked over to her dressing table. She picked up a brush, and her fingers skimmed against her father's letter. It had arrived in the trunks that her stepmother had sent over.

Did she dare read it now?

She picked the envelope up and ran her finger over the waxed seal. Perhaps it was time. After all, now that she had secured Hudson's affections, she felt stronger somehow. As if she could take on the world, with him by her side.

Charlotte lowered herself down onto the chair and opened the envelope. She pulled the piece of paper out and unfolded it, immediately noticing the shaky handwriting. She read:

My dearest daughter, Charlotte,

My time on this earth is coming to an end, and I would be remiss if I did not write to you to say my final goodbyes.

Oh, that I could turn back time, erase my terrible mistakes, and do everything differently with you. I have failed you, my child. I have failed your mother. But at the time, I did what I thought was right by you.

Your mother was the love of my life, my everything, but Catherine did not come from an impressive enough lineage for my parents. They rejected her; they rejected us. We were forced to elope and live at our Scottish cottage.

For a year, everything was perfect. But then tragedy struck, and Catherine died during childbirth, taking with her my heart. Distraught and overcome with grief, I returned home with you, but my parents refused to recognize you as their grandchild. I had no choice but to take you to be raised by your maternal grandparents. I knew you would be happy there, for your mother spoke of her childhood with great fondness.

Shortly thereafter, I discovered that my father had squandered the family fortune, leaving our futures in peril, and had arranged a marriage with me to a tradesman's daughter, Lydian. I consented to the marriage, knowing this was the only way to save our future from ruination.

Years went by, but I could never find the strength to have you come live with me, nor did I dare. You have been blessed with the uncanny appearance of your mother, and my heart couldn't abide being near you for too long. It is not your fault, but mine alone, entirely.

Finally, my sweet Lydian convinced me to host a Season for you, and I became overjoyed at the prospect. But, again, I have failed you. My health is deteriorating, and I am dying, taking with me any chance at a reconciliation with you.

Miss Bell has informed me that you have grown into a woman of incredible worth. She also noted how cleverly resourceful you are, which pleases me immensely. Your mother would be proud of the woman that you have become. And, for what it is worth, I am proud of you, too.

I implore you to be kind to Lydian. She is a good woman and is kindhearted. I regret that I could not give her the one thing that she so desperately wanted from me - love. For my heart died alongside your mother.

The reason I left behind such a large inheritance for you is because I wanted you to know that you have always been loved. Truly, deeply, and without restraint. But I was weak and pitiful. That is my curse, and I will have to live with it forever, and I hope that you will not hate me for my misdeeds.

My time is running short, but, even as I am writing this, my heart is soaring at the thought of seeing Catherine again. And, one day, we will be together as a family.

Please excuse the ramblings of an old man, and I hope you will have a lifetime full of joy and laughter; a life that you wholly deserve.

With much love,

Your Father

Charlotte lowered the paper to her lap as she continued to stare at the words of her father in disbelief. He had loved her! And he had loved her mother, desperately. There was no denying that.

She felt a huge burden lifted off her chest, and she found herself feeling compassion towards her father. Something she never thought would be possible.

Her thoughts turned toward Lydian, and she only felt sadness for her stepmother. She had tried to secure her husband's love, but it had all been in vain. He never loved her, couldn't love her. Her father had been in love with his first wife, her mother, and that never changed.

Charlotte gently folded the paper and slipped it back into the envelope. She opened a drawer and placed it with her other keepsakes.

It was evident what she needed to do. She needed to make amends with her stepmother. After all, Lydian and Rebecca were the only family she had left.

21

"WHY EXACTLY ARE WE TRAVELING TO WELLESLEY HOUSE?"
Hudson asked as he encompassed her gloved hand.

Charlotte turned her attention away from the window and
met Hudson's gaze. "I already told you that I needed to speak to
my stepmother."

"Wouldn't a note have been sufficient?"

"No," she replied with a shake of her head. "Not in this
case."

"May I ask why?"

"Because I realized that I was wrong about her, and I want to
make amends," she shared.

Hudson looked curiously at her. "What exactly were you
wrong about?"

"Mostly everything," she said, "especially when I accused
her of being the one who poisoned me."

"Ah," Hudson stated. "I see the problem now."

Charlotte glanced down at their intertwined hands as she
admitted, "I read my father's note."

"You did?" Hudson asked, lifting his brow. "What did it
say?"

"He told me that I was loved and that he desperately loved my mother."

"But hadn't he married Lydian only a month after your mother passed away?"

She nodded. "He did because he was trying to save his family from ruination. He confessed to me that his heart had died, alongside my mother."

"I see," Hudson murmured. "How does that make you feel?"

She smiled. "It brings me great joy and peace to know that my parents loved each other so passionately."

"Have you forgiven your father for how he treated you?" he asked, his eyes searching hers.

Her smile dimmed a little. "Not yet, but I am not as angry anymore, and I'm starting to see things from a different perspective."

"That is a good start," he replied.

"I'm glad that my father wrote the letter," she said. "It gives me a sense of why he did what he did."

"I don't think I will ever understand how a father could abandon his own child," Hudson remarked.

"When someone is grieving a loss of a loved one so deeply, I believe they don't always make the most rational choices," she reasoned. "It was evident from my father's letter, that he never fully came to terms with my mother's passing."

Hudson brought her hand up to his lips. "I'm blessed to be marrying such a wise and forgiving woman."

The coach came to a stop outside of Wellesley House, and a footman came around to open the door. Hudson exited first, then he assisted her out of the coach.

The main door opened, and the butler greeted them.

"Welcome home, Lady Charlotte," Baxter said with a slight bow. "I'm relieved to see that you are in good health."

"Thank you, Baxter," Charlotte replied. "Is my stepmother available for callers?"

He tipped his head. "I shall inquire, milady."

As they watched the butler start to walk up the stairs, Lady Rebecca's voice echoed throughout the entry hall.

"Charlotte!" Rebecca exclaimed as she practically skipped across the tiled entry. "You came back."

"I did."

Rebecca came to stop in front of her. "Mother said you weren't going to ever come back."

"Is that so?"

Placing a hand next to her mouth, Rebecca lowered her voice. "She also said that you weren't traveling with us to Blackpool. Is that true?"

"I'm afraid it is."

A frown puckered Rebecca's lip. "Why?"

Putting her hand out towards Hudson, she replied, "I am going to stay in London and marry Lord Hudson."

"Can I stay for the wedding?"

Charlotte went to reply when her stepmother spoke up. "Rebecca, you should be in the nursery," she chided lightly as she gracefully descended the stairs. "It is well past the time for your lessons to begin."

"Yes, Mother," Rebecca said, turning towards the stairs.

Lydian nodded approvingly. "Go on now." She came to a stop in front of Charlotte. "I understand that congratulations are in order."

She gave her a baffled look. "How did you hear so quickly?"

"Word travels fast amongst the servants, my dear," Lydian explained. "You would be wise to remember that." She held her hand out towards the drawing room. "Would you and Lord Hudson care to join me in the drawing room?"

"We would," she replied.

Her stepmother gave them a terse smile and headed towards the drawing room.

As they stepped into the room, Lydian pointed towards the

settee. "Please have a seat. I have requested some refreshment to be sent up."

"Thank you," Charlotte said.

After they were situated, Lydian shared, "The constable came by this morning. He informed us that Lord Huntley had been killed, and he arrested your lady's maid, Ellen."

"He did?" she asked, surprised. "I had hoped that termination would have been enough punishment for Ellen."

"She did poison you," Hudson pointed out.

"But only because Lord Huntley coerced her to."

Hudson gave her an understanding nod. "I would be happy to speak to the judge over her case, and I will let your feelings be known on the matter."

"I would appreciate that," she replied.

Charlotte turned her gaze back towards Lydian. "I am sorry I ever implied that you had something to do with me being poisoned."

Her stepmother waved her hand dismissively in front of her. "I know why you did, and I do not fault you for that. You were in an impossible position."

"It was still wrong of me."

Lydian clasped her hands in her lap. "Is it true that Lord Huntley abducted you and was going to force you to be his wife?"

She nodded.

"I knew there was something off about him, but I only had my suspicions," Lydian said. "That is why I encouraged you to spend less time with him."

"How did you know?"

Lydian pressed her lips together. "I saw it in his eyes. I'm afraid I had seen that look before... in my father's eyes. It was the look of greed."

"I wish I had been as astute as you were," she replied. "It would have saved me a considerable amount of trouble."

"Do not blame yourself," Lydian said. "Lord Huntley was rather convincing at being charming."

Charlotte hesitated a moment, and then she asked, "May I ask you a question?"

"You may," Lydian responded, her voice reserved.

"Why did you lie about posting the note to Penelope?"

Lydian lowered her gaze to her lap. "How did you know I was lying?"

"Because Penelope never received the note."

Her stepmother sighed. "I thought I was protecting you," she admitted. "I had underestimated your friendship with the duchess, and I thought I was sparing you from undue embarrassment."

"In what way?"

"The duchess is an important person, and it is rumored that she rarely makes house calls, to anyone," Lydian explained. "I was afraid she would find it rather presumptuous of you to request a visit from her, especially while you were in mourning."

"I see," Charlotte said.

Lydian met her gaze. "I was wrong, and I am sorry."

"I understand your reasonings," she replied. "Thank you for attempting to look out for me."

"I know you think rather poorly of me…"

Charlotte spoke over her. "I don't," she asserted. "I must admit that my admiration for you has grown immensely over these past few days."

"That is kind of you to say."

Moving to sit on the edge of her seat, she said, "I finally read my father's note."

"Oh?" Lydian asked. "What did he say?"

"He spoke of his love for my mother, and of his regrets, including how he wasn't able to give you the love that you deserved."

Lydian's eyes grew wide. "Your father said that?"

"He did."

"Did he say why?"

She nodded. "He said that his heart died with my mother."

"I assumed as much," Lydian murmured as tears came to her eyes. "Thank you for letting me know."

"He also said it was you that convinced him to give me a Season, but you had informed me that it was his idea," she said. "Why was that?"

Lydian gave her a sad smile. "I suppose I wanted you to have at least one good memory of your father."

Charlotte glanced over at Hudson, then back at her stepmother.

"I was hoping you would delay your departure to Blackpool and stay for our wedding," she said sincerely. "It will be an intimate affair with only family and close friends attending the ceremony."

Lydian shook her head. "I wouldn't dare intrude."

"I want you to," Charlotte insisted. "After all, you are my family."

"That is kind of you to say, but I…"

Charlotte spoke over her. "I want you to be a part of my life," she reached for Hudson's gloved hand, "of our lives."

"Do you truly mean it?" Lydian asked, glancing between them.

With a smile on her lips, Charlotte replied, "I never knew my mother, but I have come to realize that I have been blessed to have a stepmother that emulates the qualities I hope my mother had. You are kind, loving, and you do not hesitate to chide me about my irreverent behavior."

"Sometimes to a fault," Lydian joked.

"And I appreciate you even more for that."

Lydian laughed. "I daresay that cannot be true, but I will try to be better."

"Does this mean you will stay for our wedding?" she asked hopefully.

Her stepmother smiled through her tears. "I would be honored to."

"That makes me truly happy."

A tear slipped down Lydian's cheek, and she quickly wiped it away with her hand. "Thank you for letting me be a part of your lives. It means more to me than you will ever know."

Charlotte smiled over at Hudson with a full heart. Not only was she going to marry a man she admired, but she had established a loving relationship with her stepmother. Something that had seemed like an impossibility only a short time ago.

Though her journey was far from perfect, she realized that she had ended up exactly where she wanted to be. For along the way, her heart had been mended by a man who loved and accepted her for who she was. She never wished to be parted from Hudson from this day on.

She'd finally found where she belonged.

EPILOGUE

"SHE IS PERFECT," HUDSON SAID AS HE STARED IN AWE AT THE bundled baby that the midwife had just placed in Charlotte's arms.

"I agree," Charlotte breathed.

He sat down on the bed and kissed her forehead. "You were so brave."

"It was worth it," she replied, her eyes lingering on the sleeping baby.

Hudson leaned forward, moved the blanket aside, and touched his daughter's tiny hands. "I have never seen anything so precious."

Charlotte tilted her face towards him. "Thank you for remaining with me during the birth. I know it couldn't have been easy for you."

"There is no place I would have rather been," he replied honestly.

She smiled. "It pleases me to hear you say that."

"Although, I could have done with a little less screaming," Hudson joked.

Charlotte laughed as he hoped she would. "Childbirth was much more intense than I imagined it to be," she admitted. "I daresay that Penelope and Madalene lied to me about their experiences."

"Well, you managed it splendidly, my love," he praised as he bent to kiss her on the cheek.

"I can't believe we have a daughter," Charlotte murmured. "She even has your eyes."

Running his hand along the tufts of brown hair on his daughter's head, he said, "But she has your hair color." His hand stilled on her little ears. "I hope she has more of your traits than mine."

"Why do you say that?"

He grinned. "Because, my dear wife, you are absolutely perfect."

"You flatter me, husband."

"That was my intention," he remarked, smiling. "You continuously amaze me."

Charlotte shifted the baby in her arms and asked, "Would you like to hold your daughter?"

Hudson hesitated. "What if I hurt her?"

"By holding her?" she asked in an amused tone.

Glancing down at the bundled baby, he pointed out, "But she is so small."

"It will be all right," she encouraged. "Trust me."

Hudson extended his arms and nervously accepted the baby. "She hardly weighs anything," he said as he drew her close.

As he gazed at his baby daughter, he felt a surge of protectiveness wash over him, knowing he was now responsible for this beautiful girl. Tears of happiness welled up in his eyes as he realized how truly blessed he was. Not only had his wife survived childbirth, but she had given him a daughter, making him a father.

He brought his gaze back up to meet Charlotte's. "Thank you," he said, his voice hitching with raw emotion.

Charlotte smiled. "You are welcome."

"I love you more every single day," he shared. "Because of you, I am happy, truly unequivocally happy."

Reaching out, she cupped his right cheek, and her thumb started caressing his cheekbone. "Our daughter is lucky to have a man like you as her father. You are kind and loving, and you make me feel special, allowing me to believe that I am capable of anything."

"As you should," he replied. "You are far more clever than I."

"And you," she started slowly, her eyes searching his, "are my match, in every sense of the word."

He smiled. "Are you only saying that because I now enjoy watching pig running with you?"

"Perhaps," she teased, lowering her hand.

A knock came at the door before it was pushed opened, and Lydian walked into the room with a bright smile on her face. "How are you feeling, my dear?"

"I am well," Charlotte replied. "Thank you for seeing Dr. Wellington and Dr. Lowery to the door."

Lydian ran her hand down her lavender gown with black trim. "It was my pleasure," she said. "I am relieved that their services were not required during the birth."

Charlotte smiled lovingly at him. "Having two doctors present was rather excessive," she commented. "Perhaps next time we should just use the midwife."

Hudson shook his head. "I disagree. I would do anything to keep you safe, including hiring every doctor in Town to assist with the birth. I refuse to lose you. I can't lose you."

"Spoken like a man in love." Lydian walked closer to the bed and peered down at the baby in his arms. "She is perfect."

"She is," Hudson confirmed.

Glancing between them, Lydian asked, "Have you chosen a name for her?"

Charlotte met his gaze before saying, "We have."

Lydian looked at them expectedly.

"For her given name, we are going to call her Catherine," Charlotte shared.

Lydian nodded approvingly. "That is a fine name, and it is a way to keep the memory of your mother alive."

"That is what we thought as well," Charlotte agreed. "And her second name will be Lydian."

Tears quickly formed in Lydian's eyes as she stared back at them. "Truly?" she whispered.

Charlotte nodded. "I would never have been able to get through this pregnancy without your help," she replied.

"It has been my pleasure," Lydian said, swiping at the tears flowing down her cheeks.

Reaching out, Charlotte encompassed her stepmother's hand. "My daughter is named after the two women that I admire the most."

Lydian gave her a look filled with love. "Thank you for allowing me to be a part of your lives. I have never felt so loved."

"I'm glad that you were not an evil stepmother," Charlotte teased.

Lydian laughed. "As am I."

His daughter let out a tiny cry, drawing Hudson's attention back. He smiled, his heart full of joy. He was glad that he had taken a chance on love, because he was happier than he ever thought was possible. And, he knew, without a doubt, that life was truly worth living with Charlotte by his side.

The End

ABOUT THE AUTHOR

Laura Beers is an award-winning author. She attended Brigham Young University, earning a Bachelor of Science degree in Construction Management. She can't sing, doesn't dance and loves naps.

Besides being a full-time homemaker to her three kids, she loves waterskiing, hiking, and drinking Dr. Pepper. She was born and raised in Southern California, but she now resides in South Carolina.